Dear Mike,
Thanks for always being on
and most respectful guy friends a girl
could hope to have! Much love and
wishes of success!

Rebecca Rose

Love, Politics, and Survival

A Whitfield Family Narrative Book One

By Rebecca Rose

Solstice Publishing - http://www.solsticeempire.com/

Prologue

There are worse things than picking the losing side of an attempted coup. George Whitfield, formerly Director of the Department of Ethics, had learned that the hard way. He had been on nobody's side, ready with open arms to begin a process of healing no matter which side of party politics turned out to be the victor. Or so he thought, for there had been no such thing as nobody's side.

The coup had not only failed but was dealt with swiftly and harshly. Its lead instigators were jailed and many were later killed. Technically, the nation still had to abide by the continent-wide ban on the death penalty, so these deaths were ruled suicides or accidents. Many who were not killed by the State still ended up dead by their own hand. All of them lost their positions, title, wealth and status.

George may as well have been one of the lead supporters of the coup. He was not only removed from his position, his department was completely disbanded. George, however, was not sent away to be put to death, as he had feared, as he had even contemplated preparing his family for. Instead, he was given a position in the Department of Security and Action—as the Deputy Director, no less. Such a position, which George never wanted and which his friend Harry Maier hoped to have, was not meant to be a promotion, although it was seen as such. George was reminded of this every single day.

The coup had been planned against and ultimately quashed by Director Edward Roth, who was serving as the head of Security and Action.

Edward did not fail to notice that George did not act in any way to support an uprising against Roth, who had presidential aspirations of his own. That was not enough, however. Edward had expected George to lend his support and loyalty to him; the two men had even met to discuss what to do about the coup. George had denied knowledge of any such plans, as he preferred and strongly advised all in the cabinet to work instead on party unification. It mattered not that George was telling the truth.

The coup was led by Senator David Wells, who, like many, was disgusted by Roth's behavior and influence and was tired of doing nothing more than whispering about it. Senator Wells brought the matter to the Senate to vote to censure and remove Edward as Director of Security and Action and have the department disbanded. Several of his supporters went to department headquarters to confront Edward, whose lack of appearance was taken as a form of cowardice. In reality, Edward had been planning their arrests before they even arrived.

George was not the only one to take such a position in choosing nobody's side. That included his close friend, Karl Bradford, who, as the Director of the Treasury, was in charge of one of the few departments, perhaps the only other department unaffected by the attempted coup.

No matter how he would have liked to forget those days of the attempt and the aftermath, it was as if the memory had been branded into George's brain.

***

The first few hours of that day had been quiet. George even wondered if he would be able to hold onto that glimmer of hope that it wouldn't involve him. Deep down it had been a foolish hope, though, as George realized all too well when Edward came personally to tell him what was to happen next.

President Travers was to remain in power, though that was never the issue. Had he been a problem, Edward would have dealt with him quickly. After all, Edward had killed a previous vice-president, his own younger brother, when he got in the way of Edward's ambitions. The president, who would in all likelihood serve out his term, was only mentioned to make it clear to George that he could not look forward to immediately succeeding Travers. Not in three years, perhaps not ever.

There were far more important matters to discuss. Edward felt George could be most useful by being made into an example. It wasn't *entirely* personal, although Edward couldn't help feeling somewhat slighted with how in choosing nobody's side, it meant George wasn't choosing Edward's side. That's just how he saw it.

To truly get to George, though, Edward knew he could use others to get the message across. Harry was George's long-time best friend. He had been a thorn in Edward's side as an employee of the department who was always looking for a promotion, undeserved as Edward saw it.

Edward, along with a staffer, marched George to the next wing over from Ethics to Security and Action. It was a quick walk, one George had made many times before. This time, however, it was the most silent and tedious it had ever been.

The silence ended once they got closer to the department headquarters. George couldn't say he preferred that, however.

George could recognize that hysterical yelling all too well. It seemed Harry had had a drink—or perhaps several.

"Hey, get your hands off of me! What the fuck do I have to talk to Director Roth for? I had *nothing* to do with this! Do you hear me? Not a goddamn thing. I—"

Harry cut himself off just as he noticed Edward and George walking in. George was ashamed to admit he could barely even hold eye contact with his friend. Edward dismissed his nephew Scott and his friend Howard, staffers of the department, who had been speaking to Harry.

"I… I'm terribly sorry, Director Roth… but what is going on, sir?" His looks to George for any kind of indication, even the slightest, were ignored.

"I take it that you have been informed that we need to discuss today's events, Harry?"

"Yes, sir, I have. But why? I had nothing to do with this. I thought I was supposed to be up for the promotion? I was expecting us to talk about that. Instead I'm being treated like some criminal organizer."

The lingering hesitation was so painful, George wanted to scream. He couldn't blame Harry for drinking then; he wanted to have a few himself. This was especially the case once Edward turned to George.

"Well, Harry, you were being *considered* for a promotion. Let's not forget that distinction." Edward's tone was dripping with condescension, making the experience all the more painful. George had gotten his position and so had Karl. Why couldn't Harry have his? "It's a promotion you did not make. Due to these foolish attempts—if we can even call them that—today, we are going to be doing some re-organizing of the department."

The nudge that Edward gave George may have been light, but the power of suggestion which came with it was a heavy one.

"Harry, you won't be the Deputy Director." George wished, prayed silently even, that he didn't have to tell Harry the reason. *He was going to find out eventually, but it would be better to break the news in a less volatile environment, wouldn't it?* Edward didn't give a damn, though, and when he was deciding all of their fates, what he thought was what mattered.

"I'm going to take the position, Harry. It's going to be me."

Harry's face tensed up, but only slightly, because he knew that George couldn't have been doing this from his own desire. He had never wanted the Deputy Director position, not when he was heading Ethics.

"Well, at least I can't think of a better person to be working under than you, George."

It was the wrong thing to say, perhaps the worst thing Harry could have said. Edward would find a way to use it against him, as he had a penchant for doing.

***

The dramatic aftermath of the day did not end there for George. If he thought he was being treated as a condemned man, he needed only to think of those who had been arrested. George's family had been trying to reach him. They had not been able to, as only Edward had commanded his attention.

"Don't worry, they'll find out soon enough you're safe," Edward told George in what was to become his new office. It just was not to be through a phone call or a text. They would find out the same way everyone else would.

Compulsory airing of such news in places of school, work, common shopping areas and on television screens in the city streets meant that if Edward was going to make an announcement, people were going to hear it.

Edward had an address set up to announce details. George would stand beside him, as the loyal deputy he had already been approved by the president to be.

"Fellow citizens, I'm sure you have no doubt heard many different things about the day's events," Edward began. He was not blind to the way many felt about him and the influence his department had, but Edward was going to speak as if he had the nation's full support. "This morning a group of rebellious men, those who should have used their time wisely as public servants instead of doing otherwise, tried to ruin and dispose of the Department of Security and Action. I was not present. Neither I nor any of my staff members were harmed. The authorities were brought in to arrest the perpetrators before they could do any real damage beyond their pathetic and cowardly attempts of sowing discord and chaos in our political system. Without further ado, here is a list of the perpetrators…"

The names were read in no particular order, in part so that all who were listening would pay full attention.

George Whitfield was not on that list, though he would get his own mention.

"One name which I'm sure many are eager to hear about is Director George Whitfield, or should I say Former Director George Whitfield." It was as if the nation was collectively holding its breath. "After today, the Department of Ethics is to be disbanded." *Had George Whitfield been part of the attempted coup then? Had he tried to stop it?* Such questions were never satisfactorily addressed.

"It has been decided that George Whitfield's talent and skill sets will be better used with him serving as the Deputy Director of the Department of Security and Action." It was then that George stepped forward to make his appearance beside Edward, too afraid to show any sign of any emotion, as the nation, his family included, learned of his fate.

George remained in a daze for the rest of the day, a condition which did not end with the announcement. He was part of a meeting with the president, vice-president, Edward, and the Director of the Department of the Rule of Law. All of them would be responsible for a task force to seek out how the attempted coup had gotten as far as it did in the first place and what was to be done to ensure it didn't happen again, especially to someone so integral as Edward.

This would extend to looking into, and investigating if necessary, anyone who might have had the slightest amount of involvement, from politicians and other public officials, to their aides as well as citizen leaders of vocal grassroots organizations. Nothing was to be overlooked, no piece of potential evidence considered insignificant. George was to use his influence, especially since he was so trusted and beloved, to find out whatever he could.

After the meeting, George excused himself to be sick, though nothing came up. With the expectation of casting such a wide net, nobody was safe. George figured that just about every grassroots organization was considered vocal, whether they had registered with the government or not. That included George's brother-in-law, his brother and his son. George didn't even want to ask if they would be considered, for he already knew the answer. Nobody was safe meant that nobody was safe. That was yet another price to pay for being on nobody's side.

Once Edward acknowledged it was indeed very late, he deemed it acceptable to send George home. He was provided with a driver, not merely to spare George from having to drive himself home but to ensure he went straight there. Being watched, whether at home, in the office or anywhere else, was something George was going to have to get used to.

By the time George arrived home, there was less than an hour left in that day. All three children and his wife Maria were awake and waiting for him at the kitchen table.

Maria had tried to get the children to go to sleep. George knew as much, and after seeing the tired but eager look on his wife's face, he knew he could not blame her or them for such anticipation.

It was initially silent when George walked in, as they waited for their husband and father to speak first. Sitting down at the table, his head in his hands, without saying anything, was all too much. Each of the three children tried their best to be the one to be heard, to be the first to be answered.

"Danny, Cassandra, you should especially know better about giving your father a moment," Maria pointed out to the older two. George was already waving away to his wife that it was useless as he welcomed their youngest daughter, Amelia, into his lap.

"I'm fine. It's just been… a long day." George had left the house nearly eighteen hours prior. He welcomed their older daughter, Cassandra—known to be his favorite child—into his arms as well.

"You're really all right, dad?"

"Yes, Danny. I'll be fine." Had he not been so distracted, George would have been suspicious about his son's sudden interest.

"Good. Because then I can ask what the hell you were thinking today!"

Amelia threw her arms tightly around her father's neck. Cassandra and Maria, each of them fiercely protective of George in their own way, refused to join in with Danny just because he was passionate about the day's events.

While George appreciated the sentiment, the continued yelling and attempts to outshout each other was too much for him.

"Enough. Enough, please!" George yelled.

"How could you do this?" Danny passionately declared. "To Harry, your best friend? You had to know that was the position that he always wanted. He could have made something out of it. That we all could have benefited from having a neutral party in that position! We were all worried sick about you, having heard nothing, thinking you were involved in this and taken away somewhere, shot in the street." Maria covered her face at the last part. "That's what I first thought as I tried to figure out how I was going to be there for mom, Cassandra, and Amelia. But then I realized if that was the case, I could make it as the man of the house and take care of them. I would be proud of you dying for something like that. Just the opposite, though, you took a position to work right alongside that man who has caused so much shit!"

George didn't know how he was going to explain things to his son. He hadn't been ready to tell Danny that night. George supposed he owed the young man something, though he preferred not to say anything in front of the others.

"Danny, I'm sorry. I really am. I'm just not sure you understand…" George tried feebly, well aware he was getting nowhere.

With George's worst fears confirmed, his son marched off his to his room; the slamming of a door could be heard throughout the whole house. Their twenty-one year old son was still slamming that door. George merely shrugged. He couldn't blame him, not tonight at least.

Although he would have liked nothing more than to crawl into bed and pretend the past eighteen hours had not happened, George had a duty to take care of his family. It was a duty he was honored to carry out, even in painfully difficult moments as this. By accepting his fate and such a position, he *was* taking care of his family, but that didn't mean he had to do so while dismissing the pain others were in.

Fortunately, Danny had let George in quickly enough. He was too tired to play games, even if he doubted his father's ability.

Perhaps George ought to have been more honest with Danny. Of course he didn't want this position. It wasn't merely that, but also how Harry had wanted it. Harry wanted to make something of the position as well as a deserved name for himself after all this time, while George and Karl had made names for themselves already. George was too afraid though to confide in his son at such a level on such a night. There was always an excuse why George decided not to get too close.

There were too many reasons why turning down the position had not been an option. Not merely because George's life could have been on the line, though Danny could get over that, seeing it as martyrdom. It was as much whether they wanted to remain living together as a family, if they wanted to have three meals a day, healthcare when they needed it, to be able to go out in public, even.

Everything they held dear, everything they might have ever once taken for granted was reason enough for George to do exactly as he was told. Whether Danny liked it or not, that included him working directly beside Edward Roth.

Be that as it may, that such reasons were a true and sobering reality, George did not end up getting very far with Danny. That was the day George's life changed.

As George left the bedroom, the clock switched from 11:59 over to the new day.

***

The girls had understood that the best thing they could do for their father was to let him speak with Danny. Cassandra would offer whatever comfort she could once her father had a chance to get what sleep he could.

Maria was up waiting for George once he shuffled into their bedroom, feeling exhausted, beaten down and ashamed. Part of him wondered if he could have felt any worse. That answer was clear—he could and would. For all that had happened that day, George had walked away with his life and his freedom, his home and still holding a job. It was more than what so many others could say.

As his wife searched for the right words to say, George spoke first. "Maria, please know that no matter what happens, that I did not want to take this position. I never wanted anything to do with it, just as I never wanted anything to do with either side of this coup. But, more importantly, Maria, I am forever determined to do whatever it takes to protect you and the children. I promise you that this family will always be my motivation."

"George," Maria said his name softly and comfortingly. "I already know that." The man had been through enough for the day, at the office and then at home with their son. If only for these next few hours, he would not have to worry about being so strong, not when lying beside her. He already *was* strong; he always was to her, and she truly believed he would remain so, especially as she held him in her arms, cradling him tightly against her chest.

***

It was fair to say that things were not going to get better for George. Then again, that was not what he was striving for. He left even earlier the next morning, not only to avoid further confrontation with Danny but because he hoped to savor the last few hours that he could with his department and staff. It was to be dismantled immediately. Edward moved quickly and deliberately, after all, which he felt necessary for sending out the clearest message possible.

The transition was to happen so quickly that George barely had any time to advise and direct his staff. As the newest department, the Department of Ethics was the smallest, at a few hundred people. Those who were willing to move on would be going to Security and Action and the Rule of Law. George was able to assure himself he had done that much at least. He hoped that finding an immediate job would be freshest in their minds, rather than the confusion which was to come from the loss of their department and their boss. It was as if the department and the positions with it had never even existed at all.

No matter how much of a punishment the position was to George, it was to be regarded as a promotion. That right there was part of the punishment. Because George had foolishly believed he could be on nobody's side, that had let Edward publicly place George on the side Edward had chosen. The public was to see George as celebrating the reorganization of the Department of Security and Action, considering it was he who was supposed to be benefiting the most. There was to be a department gala in a few weeks' time, billed as a sort of cabinet and department update. Edward informed George that it would be more than enough time for him to invite his brother and brother-in-law. Edward knew about the activities of Gregory Whitfield and Thomas Campbell, and he wanted an eye kept on them as much as possible.

George had put off the headache of dealing with these two men, best friends who were thick as thieves and who had chosen common goals over blood ties. Thomas did not keep it a secret that Maria married the wrong Whitfield, as far as he was concerned. George saw no reason to make it a habit of having his name insulted by his brother-in-law. Considering his new position thrust upon him working for Edward Roth, he wanted even less to do with Thomas. George admitted that when Maria asked what she should tell her brother about George's new position, he sharply replied that he didn't care so long as he didn't have to deal with it. He hadn't even bothered returning his own brother's phone calls, at home, at his office or on his cell.

It wasn't that George had to reach out directly to invite them to the gala. If Edward insisted they show up, he could have officers arrive at their homes to drag them there if need be. There were still the options of sending notice through the mail or having Maria reach out. If George was looking for a reason to ensure that he could not ignore Gregory and Thomas any longer, he had found it.

George would make sure they were present at the gala for Edward to use him as a way to engage in another display of his power trips. He would play that game because he had to, but he was also determined to make sure that such an occasion was not the first or only time he saw them.

Even under different circumstances, George dreaded the idea of meeting with the two men. He and his brother never agreed on much, though their differences had become much more pronounced once Gregory met Thomas. George taking on the role as Director of Ethics, which he happily announced at a family barbecue, was seen as an act of betrayal. Gregory and George lost almost all contact then once their father died, the last connection the brothers had.

Fortunately, however, Harry and Karl were committed to being there for their friend. In public, both men had their hands tied. Karl's Department of Treasury had even less to do with the attempted coup than the others, and George assured him it was crucial that it remained that way. Harry's role was further complicated as a subordinate who had been demoted. With the three men as fiercely loyal to each other as they were, the least George's friends felt they could do was to be there when George sought to explain the circumstances to Gregory and Thomas.

George and Harry often left work together, and so it caused no suspicion that they did so on the night they found themselves at Karl's office. The Department of Treasury was far away from Security and Action, and required a nighttime stroll through the now mostly quiet city. It had a kind of charm to it. For the first time in a long time, genuine smiles could be seen on all three of the men's faces.

The good cheer of being together like old times and sharing a drink from Karl's liquor cabinet did not last long. This was not like those old times. Karl and George had not had much time together between the two of them for as long as either could remember, but in the moments they had, they both agreed they needed to talk to Harry about his drinking.

The moment felt quite similar to when George had prepared to tell his family at a summer barbecue about his position as the Director of Ethics. He had to laugh thinking about it, and it rang with bitterness. His father, Philip Whitfield, was no longer with them, having left this life for the next one. It was not merely sad for George and Gregory to be without their father. To say he had been a peace-keeper was in many ways an understatement; there had been instances when he was the only one who could get his sons to be in the same room together. The situation had been tense enough for George to announce he would be the director of a new, non-controversial and sorely needed department, which he was heading up of his own free will. Those seven summers ago George had felt cocky and confident enough to stand by his decision when it came to the harshest critics in his own family. Now he was desperate and despondent. Gregory and Thomas both loved Maria, in their own way, as well as their nieces and nephew. This was what George had to do to protect them, even if others were unhappy as a result. For all the perks he had as Deputy Director, namely his life, George doubted there could be a soul more unhappy with his holding the position than himself.

There was little or nothing Karl or Harry could do to convince Gregory or Thomas that George truly wanted no part of the department. This wasn't about political ambition for George; it wasn't like one could have argued when it came to heading the Department of Ethics. This was about survival.

They all agreed they had to act quickly. Gregory and Thomas were eager to know what the hell George was doing parading around as Edward Roth's deputy. There wasn't much to discuss or plan other than getting all of them at the same place at the same time. It was unlikely that Karl or Harry would be able to get through to Gregory and Thomas, but they were determined to try.

Gregory had not been to his older brother's house since their father's funeral. The time before that had involved his unceremonious departure from what was supposed to be a pleasant summer barbecue, until George just happened to confirm to all of them that he would be the Director of Ethics. It had been over seven years ago, though Gregory still kept in touch with Danny, perhaps in ways he should not have with his nephew when it went behind George's back. If Gregory was to be honest, however, he had a feeling he would be speaking with Danny a lot more.

While Gregory could be more stoic and reflective of such memories, Thomas could not be counted on to do the same. This included a situation where discretion was paramount. Gregory had only pulled into the elder Whitfield brother's long driveway a moment before Thomas when his thoughts were interrupted by his best friend waving around a gala invitation, wanting to know if Gregory had received it as well and if it was some kind of cruel and elaborate prank. Gregory saw the invitation before he even saw Thomas was fully out of the car.

"Let's talk about this inside," was all Gregory would say. He remained silent despite Thomas' indignation, making the long walk up the driveway and to the porch all the more unpleasant.

Maria met the men at the porch to quickly usher them in. "Thomas, hush! Your complaining really couldn't wait? We could hear you the moment you pulled up."

George had been correct in lamenting the headache his brother-in-law was bound to give him.

Thomas' ranting became only louder once indoors. "Well, Maria, this is a major problem affecting you, my sister, because of the actions of your husband and a madman. Hell, I don't know, maybe George has become mad as well. It would actually be a charitable explanation as to why he's put himself, his wife and his children, my nieces and nephew, at such risk."

As Maria brought the two men into the dining room to join the others, they were greeted by tired, nonplussed expressions. Thomas knew they had heard him, and quite frankly, he didn't care.

"Why don't you announce your presence a little bit louder, Thomas? I don't think that the neighbors down the street heard you." While George shushed Harry, he himself had to stifle a chuckle.

"Should you be the one to defend him, Harry? After all, George has the position we all know that *you* wanted."

"Why don't you go fuck yourself, Thomas, because you understand nothing, not a goddamn thing, you arrogant prick!" Harry exclaimed, his voice reaching a fever pitch before Karl stepped in.

"Gentlemen, let's remember that George is going to explain everything if we'll only let him. Now why don't we make peace and listen up?"

"Well, I'll only apologize if I woke the girls, but not for speaking my mind and the truth."

Maria informed her brother that they slept through anything, thankfully. While Cassandra was old enough to stay awake, she remained in her bedroom as a favor to her parents. Danny was in the dining room and had been since before Harry and Karl arrived; George knew better than to try to stop him.

Already flustered and with a shaky breath, George confirmed he had called this gathering of sorts to explain his new position and the invitation Thomas and Gregory had received. That is, if Thomas would let him do so. If his mind had already been made up about the situation, then Thomas was free to leave. Gregory, Maria and Danny were able to convince Thomas to stay and even to keep his mouth shut and his ears open, at least for a few minutes.

"I am sure that you were shocked and disappointed to see me introduced as Edward's Deputy Director," George said as he addressed his brother and Thomas. While Gregory was not exactly surprised, he dared not step in. As much as Thomas was his good friend, he had made worse a situation which was already tense and unpleasant. "I was just as shocked, if not more so, than any of you. Please know I never wanted this. I never wanted to take it from Harry. I had no intention of leaving my department where I was happy and thriving and had plans and ambitions in mind to implement. The truth is… I think Edward made me his deputy as punishment."

"Don't tell me you were involved in the coup, George," Gregory said, his accidental interruption understood and forgiven.

"No, I was not. Just as I told you, Harry, Karl, my wife and my son, Edward and anyone else who asked or will ask. The answer was always the same, which is the truth. I only want peace and productivity and am willing to work with anyone to achieve it. Thus I had no intention to seek it out or quell it either, especially since I didn't believe the attempt would even be carried out as far as it was. I was on nobody's side. That was not good enough for Edward. I may as well have been against him."

Gregory thought to himself how in some ways he wished George *had* acted or spoken out against Edward, though he did not dare voice it aloud.

"I believe that Edward gave me the position also to punish Harry and sow discord between us." Harry initially was hesitant to make eye contact with anyone in the room, but within a moment had gotten it together to show he would be strong and brave through this. "In using me to punish my friend, I assure you he is punishing me as well."

Any lamenting or comforting by Harry was interrupted by Gregory. "What's the other part? You said 'in part,' didn't you, George?"

"Yes, I did," his brother sighed. "I'm not sure if any of you are going to be too happy about it." Thomas cursed under his breath that they were all already not happy about this, but fortunately George was able to continue uninterrupted. "I believe Edward may be seeking to put me in a position of power to do his bidding in conducting investigations on this coup while also leaving my hands tied."

"What are you going to do then, dad?" Danny, to his credit, had remained quiet until now.

"I don't know, son. I'm afraid I just don't know yet. I wish I could give you more answers tonight, but I'm not quite there yet. Any help would be most welcomed. I don't even care who it comes from."

"The answer is simple, George. You must do the right thing and disband such investigations before they even begin. Or better yet, investigate the department yourself. Surely in your position of power you'll be able to do that? Isn't this what you wanted, anyway, to have control over such a department? Well, why not use your prestige for good, then?" Thomas, once again, proved he was better at speaking than he was listening.

"Christ, man! Have you listened to nothing he's said, Thomas? I've tried to be patient with you, to keep the peace, but I don't know how George puts up with you."

"Karl, please." George, experiencing a migraine by this point, closed his eyes and pinched the bridge of his nose tightly before continuing. His friend was of course right, but George would strongly prefer to end this meeting without getting any closer to a shouting match. "If I do that, Thomas, I'll have overplayed my hand, and then we may as well all be good as dead. If you care for your sister, your nieces and nephew, then I ask you, beg you, *plead* with you, not to make this any more difficult on me. I am going to conduct investigations on these attempted coups. I have no choice. I will do my best, though, to make sure that we're all protected."

"What were you even doing with Ethics then, George? I thought that—"

"Clearly he was not doing his job," Thomas interrupted before Gregory could finish. "He was just doing whatever he pleased! This position wasn't about anyone or making anything better. It was just to stroke his ego while someone, probably a secretary, stroked his—"

"That's enough, Thomas." He truly had gone too far, and not even so much because of such a suggestion. "I know what you think of me. We all know what you think of me, Thomas! That I was never good enough for your sister, that she married the wrong brother, that I was too ambitious to head up the Department of Ethics, which now doesn't even exist! I had you over tonight in hopes that you would listen, that you, for once in the time you have known me, would try to understand my perspective. Because it is quite possible our lives, including yours, depend on us all having a united front on my being forced into a position I never wanted!"

The dining room was awkwardly quiet for some time, save for George's deep breaths as he stared down at his hands. Although it did require effort on his part, Gregory did try to open his mouth to say something helpful, or at least something which would not make the situation worse.

It was already too late. George had let Gregory and Thomas know that he had said his piece and that there likely wasn't anything productive left for any of them to say.

Maria saw Gregory and Thomas out. George remained at the kitchen table, motionless, almost as if he were dead to the world. "Please," she pleaded with the two men as they reached the front door. "Try to see it from George's perspective, for me." They nodded that they would, though all three of them knew how unlikely that was.

As Thomas walked over to his car, quietly this time, he left his sister with an apology and said that they would talk soon if arrangements had to be made. She knew what he meant.

Gregory, however, lingered. Just as he had done inside, also to no avail, he searched for something helpful to say. "I'm deeply sorry, Maria, I didn't mean to..." Gregory didn't finish. He was sorry, yes, but he couldn't quite put his finger on what it was he did or didn't mean while still being true to how he felt.

"I know, Gregory." In reality, neither of them knew, but at least they could share that. He thought of reaching out to touch her, in a simple way, of course—whether it was to reach for her hand or hold her in an embrace. Yet Gregory also wisely feared creating further awkwardness with a touch that lingered for too long.

"You take care, Maria." Gregory said as he walked away, not looking back.

Meanwhile, inside, Harry and Karl remained with George to try to offer what assistance and support they could. Karl kept the three of them sober—for the amount of time he was there, at least. It was not the first time and would not be the last that Karl felt pressured to be the one to keep it together for the three of them.

George stayed outside even after Karl and Harry's car had pulled out of the long driveway and had been gone from sight down the road for quite some time. It was not quite yet summer. The pool would not be open again for a few more weeks, if they opened it at all. Among many other things which came to be seven years ago, that was when George had the pool put in. Heading a department meant they would have the money for a swimming pool their three children could all enjoy. Amelia had learned to swim in that pool. The backyard of the house where they had lived for the past eight years was the sight of many, now almost too many, memories. Once pleasant, George worried they would become tainted just as everything else was about to.

Though he had no alcohol outside with him, George would have given anything to be able to drink until he forgot. Instead, all he had were those memories which refused to be forgotten.

It was hours before he went back inside. Though it was past two in the morning, Maria was still awake. Danny had gone to bed in a sour mood. Though her son concerned her, Maria remained at the table, dutifully waiting for her husband to return.

"Hello, George." Though one could say there were very few, if any things to be happy about, Maria had to try. It was a sad smile on her face, though a smile nonetheless. They had each other, and if they had nothing else, they at least had that.

"I'm sorry."

"Sorry for what, George?" she asked.

In his state he did not hear the sympathy and compassion in her voice. He didn't know where to begin. *Was he sorry for agreeing to head the Ethics department? For getting involved in politics in the first place? Was he sorry for claiming he didn't have a choice but to accept this current role thrust upon him? Thomas and Gregory were difficult, but should he have tried harder to be the stronger, better man?*

As he searched for the words, Maria coaxed her husband over. He slumped into the chair and not for the first time that evening, buried his face in his hands.

"All of this. I'm sorry for all of this and what it is doing to our family, including your brother and mine. I just... I truly want to do what is best for our family and right now that means going along with Edward, loath as I am to admit it."

Gently, Maria took hold of George's hands. "Please always be assured, no matter what, that I know that. I know you put our family first, that you always will. It's not something to forgive you for, it's something to thank you for." She took a deep breath then, lest her voice be shaken or affected by tears. "I know you and I have had our fair share of troubles, especially with Danny, but I want to be there for you and support you, to be proud of you. I don't say that enough, especially now. But I *am* proud of you. I really am, George."

"You're proud of me, Maria?"

At such a question her voice did waiver. "Of course I am. I'm still your wife, George." She clutched his hand tighter then, in a firm but loving way.

They had each other then, in that moment, and for many moments to come. If he didn't have his wife, George feared he would have truly lost everything.

***

It did not take long for Edward to find out about the late-night gathering. Though they never found out exactly how he knew, Harry and George figured at least one, if not both of them, were being monitored. No matter how George tried to convince him otherwise, Harry never stopped feeling guilty.

As a result, George was informed with a week's notice that he and his family were to move. While the department would cover the expense and labor of placing the Whitfield family into a larger, grander residence, there was no mistaking that George was to be under tighter scrutiny. *It was quite a pity*, Edward mused more than once, *that the Chinese had beaten them to implementing such a tactic*.

Maria had a conversation with her brother the same day George was told such news. As much as George and he did not see eye to eye, Thomas still felt like an irrational fool for the way he reacted and begged her to believe him, that he had not been the one to reveal their meeting. Maria already knew that, though her brother wanted to be sure. He was leaving to go to the United States almost immediately after the gala. The change in social credit score had meant even more uncertainty for all of them. He would send her money every chance he got then, making her promise she would stash the American dollars as if her life depended on it.

***

The gala came the evening after George had a dream that he was going to his inaugural ball. The reality of the event, already tainted by so much, seemed that much more cruel then.

The Whitfield family got themselves ready and departed in silence. During a moment the two of them had alone, Maria had George help her with the zipper of her dress. She asked if there was anything more she could do for him. She was fine with Danny sitting next to both of his uncles; George had already agreed with her that it was best for them to have each other during the event. Nobody knew when Danny—or any of them—would be seeing Thomas again. Maria had also gone ahead with one more plea to her son, her brother and her husband's brother, as a man whom she once loved as she now loved her husband, that they not say or do anything to make it worse. Maria wanted to know what she could do for him, though, for George, the man she loved and whom she so desperately wanted to be there for as he had been there for her.

Before tucking her hair back in place, George kissed her neck and asked that she simply remain as she was for him, as beautiful, loving and hopeful as she was at that moment. He would think of her that way when, not if, the night became difficult.

George had told himself he would not betray a hint of emotion. With his wife by his side, he changed his tune to not be so hard on himself.

No kind of emotion came though. Not when his name was called by the president himself up at the podium in discussing staff updates. Not when he read the speech prepared for him. As he looked out at the faces before him, including those feeling so hurt or betrayed, he felt nothing. Not even on the way home. No matter how much he wanted the release, it would not come for George.

***

Harry, on the other hand, had plenty of emotions, just as he had plenty to drink. With all of her insisting, his wife Leah was able to convince Harry to let her drive them home. Not only had he refused George's offer of letting them ride in the limousine, Harry had instead thought he was able to drive, putting himself and his family and countless others at risk. He still drank. What he chalked up to a drunken paranoid fear rather than a premonition, all too unfortunately came to be.

Ultimately, Harry met his demise with a self-inflicted gunshot wound to the head following a tragic incident in which alcohol had ultimately gotten the best of the man. George was able to get over his political aspirations and his feeling trapped in his work. He never did stop feeling guilty about Harry, though, or that his son, Adam, was left behind.

The punishment hadn't ended with George taking on such a role. As Edward's Deputy Director, George held hiring and firing power. Harry and George were working far too closely for Edward's liking, even with it being made abundantly clear that Harry was not George's personal assistant. He was an employee of the department whose work productivity and devotion to the cause had been faltering, according to Edward.

George was ordered to carry out the deed of firing Harry. No matter how he wanted to make Edward see that Harry would be a worthwhile employee if only George would just be allowed to speak further with him, George's hands were tied. Edward assured George that there were two ways the firing could go. George could dismiss the man and send him on his way nicely, or Edward could do it, likely sparking a fight between the two of them, after which Harry would be publicly escorted out with potential future consequences to come.

There had been none of the excitement or hysteria such as what there had been the day of the attempted coup. The situation was almost worse, though, with how personal it was. When George had thought there were few things he would dread more than having to tell his friend about the status of the Deputy Director position, he had been wrong.

While George assured Edward that there would be no reason to employ the more involved method of firing Harry, Edward still insisted on being there to see it was done properly. George couldn't offer suggestions or referrals for other employment nor any comfort.

With shaking fingers, George picked up the phone and called Harry into his office. His voice was steady, though. He had been forbidden from giving anything away until the exact moment.

That Harry made his way in without any sort of suspicion, at least not until he noticed Edward Roth standing beside George, made it all the more worse.

"Harry…" George initially trailed off, but his voice remained calm. How he wished he could have shown emotion. This was a man who was his dear friend, who was like a brother to him, whose son was his godson. Yet now George had to tell him he was no longer employed. Without that emotion, his apology meant nothing. George had wondered at times if the circumstances could become worse. They could.

Though he had been heartbroken, Harry took it in stride, at least while he was still at the office. He understood that if it were up to George, he would never have been fired. It still stung, though. There was so much hurt. Even though George told him that he didn't need to drink, that George would get him help in whatever way Harry needed, Harry still indulged the habit. In those dark moments, no matter how much he ended up regretting it, alcohol was Harry's most consistent friend. It wasn't George's fault or doing, but Harry didn't even have George anymore. The bottle was the last one left.

It was made clear to George in no uncertain terms that Harry was going to go regardless of who fired him. It had just been a matter of when. Edward was more than happy to do so if it came to that, because of George's inability to assert his role as a deputy director. If that was the case, though, George was also told he could not be sure his brother-in-law would not be extradited from the United States, or that his son and brother wouldn't find their way onto a list somewhere.

They would no longer be working together, but George was certain he could still look out for his friend. It was naive of him to think so. Edward would stop at nothing to punish both men. No matter how George looked into openings for Harry at other departments, there was nothing to be accessed. It was as if the position or Harry Maier himself did not even exist.

Harry continued to drink more and sink deeper. The gambling, another habit of his, never turned out the way Harry so desperately needed it to. He kept going until there was nothing left to gamble away and nothing to show for it. Bills went unpaid. The house was nearly foreclosed on. Harry still, being proud and irrational, refused to let George help him.

Harry felt so helpless that he needed to make someone else feel that way, even if it was his own son.

Harry had had so much pain, carried for so long and recently it came to a head because of Edward, his boss—no, former boss. It was all placed upon Adam, all those marks of pain.

Perhaps the most remarkable part of that night forever burned into George's memory was that it was otherwise nothing out of the ordinary. Adam had the misfortune of being in the same room as Harry when he was drowning in his current predicament. What started as a screaming match among the Maier family ended with Adam being beaten within an inch of his life and fading in and out of consciousness as Harry shot and killed Leah before shooting himself in the head.

After that, Adam took time off from school and almost didn't finish college at all. He did so only after receiving support from the Whitfield family, whom he had lived with for some time. Upon graduating, Adam worked beside George in the department. George believed that Harry had not planned on injuring his son to the point where his hearing would always be spotty in his left ear or killing his beloved wife or himself, no matter how deep the self-loathing. George took solace, then, that he had done right by his friend in having his son work for him in such a capacity. If he didn't find that sort of comfort there, George wasn't sure where he would.

***

In a matter of hellish days, George had gone from a respected family man and the director of an up-and-coming, sorely-needed Department of Ethics to Deputy Director for Security and Action, working for a man as corrupt and evil as the department.

Two years after being forced to take on the deputy role, George still regarded himself as a shell of a man. Despite this, George knew he had a duty to protect his family. It was a duty he would follow, at all costs.

His family remained protected, including Thomas, who was still in the United States. Gregory remained largely under the radar in his own way. George was still planning and leading investigations and committee hearings. He worked alongside those who were once considered friends. *So much had already changed, why not the status of these work relationships?*

Danny dropped out of college and refused to go back. George prayed every day that he would not end up having to investigate his own son, though the possibilities looked greater every day because of activities he suspected the young man was involved in. Cassandra was nearly eighteen and wise beyond her years. She was her father's biggest fan and he was hers.

George couldn't help but worry for Amelia. She remained fine, and that was what made him worry. *Would she ever know a different political climate than the one they were embroiled in at the time?* He wondered. Lately, though, he didn't want to think about the answer.

George and Karl remained friends, though they both felt a hole with Harry gone. The economy remained booming, much to Karl's credit. His home life was another story. While Edward would otherwise have no reason to get to him, Karl had handed him the perfect chance.

It was an open secret that Karl, who was otherwise a good and capable man, had had many affairs. He loved his wife, Sarah, and adored his children, Jack and Emma. For whatever reason, though, Karl just couldn't seem to shake that habit. It didn't help that it was difficult not to like his latest, who was his current secretary, Miss Tara Wilson.

George and Karl didn't only need to hold on for each other and for the memory of Harry. As Karl and Gregory, even Thomas on occasion, had been reminding George, he still had clout amongst those who could do good for their country and the world. George was determined to use that clout wisely and for good, once he figured out how. If he did, it could possibly mean once more that George Whitfield felt as if he could rule the world.

The Birthday Party

There wasn't much reason to feel different when it came to turning eighteen, at least not in Cassandra's mind. It was true that the Whitfield family had been through a lot in the past few years, but Cassandra thought it was her father who had changed, not herself.

Regardless of what might be affecting their family, Cassandra was still determined to make it a pleasant day. She woke up to a message from Adam wishing her a happy birthday and declaring his excitement over seeing her that night. Her father had received clearance to hold a birthday party that evening at the house.

As much as she loved her older brother, Cassandra sensed she could count on Danny to make things complicated, or at least more eventful than necessary.

It began that morning when, seeing his sister come downstairs, Danny picked Cassandra up and swung her around in his arms as if she were turning eight, not eighteen. "Hey, you! Happy birthday!"

From a young age Cassandra had sensed that she was her father's favorite, and while she adored the man, she did not want any hint of special treatment, even if deserved.

"You know how your sister hates to make a big deal of anything, such an important birthday included," Maria pointed out. She could not help laughing, however, as she put breakfast out for Cassandra.

"Mom, please," Cassandra pleaded self-consciously. Maria just responded with a smile as Danny asked what the matter was. Ultimately, Cassandra was able to concede that there was no harm in having this special day for her acknowledged, celebrated even, especially when she would have to get used to it later that evening. Soon enough then, they were all wishing and singing a happy birthday to the young woman, who, while in so many ways was wise beyond her years, still was innocent.

Within a few hours, the atmosphere had changed. Initially it was merely due to the bustling for the party. When Cassandra finally had a chance to stop and think, she realized that her brother was no longer home. Pleasant though he might have been that morning, he had become more distant and more secretive lately, if one could count two and a half years as being 'lately.' Had it been any other day, nobody would have been surprised to find Danny not at home, or even that he had not let anyone know where he was going.

Cassandra was more aware of these disappearances than she let on, even staying up late into the night to see when he came back. She hadn't made it to staying awake for some nights of the past weeks. Everyone seemed to be pretending nothing was wrong. Their mother was either too afraid to show it or too strong to let Cassandra see her own worry. George was so busy with work, Cassandra wondered if he even noticed.

Such pretending was not new for the family. It had been their way for a better part of two years now. Cassandra could not blame them, especially when it came to the particularly painful events, which included Adam losing both of his parents. There were, though, those subtle moments which stayed with Cassandra, too, such as the face of desperately masked pain she saw on her father's face at that department banquet.

It could not be underscored that it was not like any other day. Just as Cassandra had become used to the attention of such a special day, her brother had to confuse and conflict her further. This wasn't like him—at least Cassandra thought it wasn't.

The caterers had already been there for hours. The cake had been brought in and the decorations were hung up. It wasn't long before the party was to begin, when Cassandra wished to take pictures with her brother and sister, that she even noticed Danny had left. The irony, that when she finally wished to commemorate the day, her brother wasn't there, was not lost on her.

The pictures were the least of her problems. If Danny was not there before the party or when it started, even he could face a long line to get inside. Cassandra knew that her brother would not react kindly to having security checking anyone going inside. It had not been her father's decision but that of Director Edward Roth; cabinet members and department heads had been included in the approved guest list, which was a trade-off for George being allowed to host anything these days. It was yet another reminder as to how much control Edward had over their lives.

Cassandra quickly regretted asking her mother about Danny's whereabouts. He hadn't said much and he was adamant that he didn't have time to say goodbye to his sisters or explain where he was going to anyone. His father did not even know yet, and Maria thought it best not to involve George until the last possible minute. She still hoped that Danny would return in time so that his father wouldn't have to find out at all. As they watched the minutes go by, however, she feared that George would figure it out, and at an evening event buzzing with eyes and ears they weren't sure they could trust. The Whitfield family, even Maria, had been gripped by paranoia for the past couple of years, though she tried her hardest not to show it around her children.

With less than an hour before the party was to begin, Danny had still not arrived. Cassandra's heart sank every time someone showed up to the door only to have it be about party business.

Those remaining minutes flew by, forcing Cassandra to begin her party without her brother. It was billed as a birthday celebration and that's how Cassandra would have to behave, regardless of who was not there.

Once her father arrived, though, all other concerns and worries ceased to exist for Cassandra. If just for that moment when they were locked in each other's embrace, George and his daughter were the only ones at the party. Danny's absence could be put aside for the moment.

George would have to spend much of the party socializing with those guests suggested by Edward. Director Roth decided it would not be necessary for him or his family to attend and told George to consider it a gift that he was being given such freedom. George would not argue. That they had their own responsibilities towards their guests that evening made the moment between father and daughter all the more special.

Cassandra decided she would be able to relax more once she found Adam. Until then, she had a feeling her brother would not be able to escape her mind. He should have been there by now, both of them should have, yet as late as it was, Adam had still not found his way over to her. Cassandra frowned at that thought.

Outside, the scene in question was occurring as Adam arrived far later than he had planned. He had thought, and ardently hoped, that checking in on Danny was a worthwhile excuse for being a few moments late. He arrived over an hour after the party had begun, with barely any update on his friend other than that something was going on and it wasn't good. Adam had wanted to stay to find out more once he saw Danny at department headquarters, of all places, but in the end the two decided it would be best if at least one of them made it to Cassandra's birthday party.

That parking was not the issue generated a brief false sense of security for Adam. Most of the adult guests had been chauffeured to the party. Many of Cassandra's friends had been dropped off by their parents. The driveway was vast to begin with, and Adam was pleasantly surprised as well as completely grateful to find ample space to park.

His cheerful mood at the hope of seeing Cassandra was dashed upon finding two armed unfriendly-looking men standing at the doorway.

Adam was an employee of the department, but he was much more often seen as George Whitfield's pet project to atone for how things had gone with Harry. Through no fault of his own but rather by accident of birth, then, Adam was often seen as a marked young man.

This was one of those times, when all Adam wished to do was to be allowed inside a party he had every right to be at and see his Cassandra on her birthday.

He approached the guarded doorway with bated breath. "Good evening, I'm here for Cassandra Whitfield's birthday party."

"You're an hour late, you know," one of the guards said, not returning the greeting or Adam's nervous smile.

"Yes, about that. I do apologize. I got caught up at work." Adam nervously fumbled out the last part, as he was not being entirely truthful. "I will be going on my way, then, into the party?"

"We need to see your identification card," said the first man.

The second guard had more personality to him. "If you're already an hour late, what's the rush now?"

Adam said nothing then as he just handed over his identification card. He suffered in silence as subsequent guests were greeted warmly and showed inside ahead of him. They were later than Adam and likely less important, at least to Cassandra.

The men, each of them, studied Adam's identification card for longer than necessary. Lest there be any doubt as to if Adam was being sincerely wished well, the second man tossed Adam's identification onto the ground as he told Adam to enjoy himself. Adam said nothing as he bent down to pick up the card, even when he had his hand stepped on in the process. The two men roared with laughter.

It was at that moment, however, that George Whitfield walked outside. "What on earth is going on here?" The men stopped laughing right away. Adam almost smiled at the reversal of fortune. "I'm waiting for an answer, gentlemen. You may have been hired by Edward Roth, but this is *my* home and I will not have you toying with my guests, particularly when that guest is a member of my staff."

"We're sorry, Deputy Whitfield, sir. We didn't realize. It won't happen again."

"Really," George asked, his tone completely deadpan. "You didn't know, even after checking his identification card, that Adam Maier was an employee of the Department of Security and Action? I was not born yesterday, and I don't think you were either."

"Sir, please accept our apologies and our word that this will not happen again."

"Save your apologies for Adam. And know that it had better not happen again, or you *will* be having a discussion with Director Roth, who I'm sure would not like having to waste his time with a matter as this."

After a mumbled set of apologies and without another word, George led Adam inside.

"I'm sorry, sir."

"Think nothing of it," George said, slightly distracted. He had not caused a further scene outside in part because it was nothing any of them wished to waste their time with. He also knew, though, that while it was his home and Edward would likely acknowledge that, these were still security hired by Edward, at a party which was going on thanks to Edward's good graces. "I'm glad you made it, Adam. It'll help Cassandra tremendously for you to be here."

"I'll do what I can, sir."

George was kept from responding further as they reached Cassandra in the crowded living room. She had her back to Adam and had not yet seen him. George was delighted that Cassandra turned not only to see her father, but Adam as well.

The embrace she gave him was different from a usual greeting, as she held onto him so very tightly. Cassandra wondered if he knew how much his presence meant to her then, especially when her brother had still not arrived. Danny hadn't even called.

Cassandra was distraught about her brother. When she was in Adam's arms, though, resting her head upon his chest, it was as if it were only the two of them without a care in the world. There was no Director Roth, armed security, or whatever it was that was keeping Danny from being with his family.

That scenario, however, was sadly not reality. Adam eventually released Cassandra. While in some ways he hated to have to do so for fear of disappointing her, Adam couldn't help seeing it as a reward to be able to gaze upon her lovely and gracious face.

"Well, Cassandra, I'm delighted to see you too!"

They both laughed, and for the same reason. Cassandra had already given quite the greeting, and none of it through words.

"I missed you, though…" She missed not only his presence or seeing his face, but the feel of his arms around her, his lips on her cheek, his scent.

Cassandra had heard from Adam that very afternoon and seen him just a few days prior. He knew how she meant it, though. "I know. I'm sorry I let myself get so caught up."

Adam almost wished it had been work that kept him from arriving on time. He had even less control over what had actually been the case. Despite his father's position, Danny did not keep his dislike for the Department of Security and Action a secret. He often spoke out against it, calling on someone to investigate the investigators—even if his own father was one of those investigators.

Never until now, though, as far as Adam knew, had Danny done something to result in being brought in. It made no difference that Adam was a member of the department as well as his friend, that perhaps he could have helped Danny in some way. Danny still told Adam nothing about why he was there. Adam couldn't say for certain if it was more Danny's stubbornness that kept him from opening up to Adam, or because, just like Danny said, he himself didn't even know why he was there. What Adam did know, however, was that even for his lateness, he had very little helpful information to provide to Cassandra. Adam would tell her what he knew at the appropriate time.

The three of them were privileged enough to have those few minutes together. Time was a luxury they would not have for much longer, though. Even Adam had to pay his respects, and Cassandra knew this. Her mother would surely like to welcome Adam in a proper manner. Other than maintaining such appearances, however, Cassandra had Adam's word she did not have to worry about him leaving her. While it did not erase the anxiety over her brother, Adam's presence did significantly brighten Cassandra's mood, at least.

George was not so lucky. The guest list was not only approved by Edward but had been partially compiled by him. There were more than a couple of guests whom George would have to socialize with and impress.

While he wished he could spend more time with them, George was happy that Adam and Cassandra had one another. This was especially true when George himself had no such luxury as time with his daughter. He, too, could sense how Cassandra worried about Danny, even if Cassandra assured him and Adam, perhaps the two people alive who knew her most, that she would be all right. "I'm sorry about your brother, Cassandra. I fear it may be some time before he decides to grace us with his presence," George mentioned.

Before he knew what he was doing, George found himself concocting a story that he and Danny had important matters to discuss. Danny took something the wrong way and was sulking elsewhere. George wasn't entirely sure if it would work on Cassandra or if it would have the desired effect of having her worry less, even if she was angry. He had to try, though. If and when Cassandra found out that this was not the entire story, that George knew just as much as Adam did, which wasn't much, he would gladly take the fall.

"We're not waiting for him, are we?" Cassandra could only appreciate her father's efforts so much. In order to do so, she had to know what to expect. Dinner was to begin in a matter of minutes.

"No, I'm afraid not. Do try to enjoy your birthday party, my dear." With a soft kiss on her cheek and a nod at Adam, George said not another word as he went to direct the caterers to begin serving. Then it was another potential donor to impress and to mingle with. If only Cassandra knew how much it broke her father's heart to have to leave them like this with no other word of comfort.

Adam did have some idea and assured Cassandra that her father meant well, his best, even. Before everyone sat down to eat, George took advantage of the moment to thank everyone for their presence at the event and more importantly, to offer a blessing over dinner and a toast to his daughter, Cassandra.

"I wish to thank you all for gracing us with your presence as we celebrate my dear daughter's eighteenth birthday. Cassandra, our oldest daughter, has made her mother and me beyond proud." George had been struggling as to whether or not to mention Danny, and nearly faltered as he continued. As he spoke from the heart though, rather than worry, as he found himself doing nearly every moment nowadays, George found more confidence. "Since the day she was born, my Cassandra has been the light of my life. I have watched her grow and mature into the beautiful young woman she is today. When I give thanks each day, especially over these past few years, it is for Cassandra, her siblings and their doting mother, my wife, Maria. Happy birthday, my darling Cassandra. You make a proud father all the more lucky to have you for his daughter."

While others applauded and toasted to her, Cassandra found herself gingerly wiping tears away from her eyes. Adam tightly clutched and caressed her hand under the table. They initially sat in silence, though Adam felt the need to assure her once more as he noticed Cassandra distressed again. It just wasn't the same without her brother.

Adam realized he still had not told her why he hadn't showed up sooner. George was far too distracted, and it wasn't likely that he knew anything to begin with, especially considering he had probably made up information to tell Cassandra to shift her anger and blame.

"Cassandra," he asked her. "Do you know why I was late?"

"No, you never told me," she reminded him.

Adam sighed. He would have to tell her. If Cassandra didn't find out from him she would likely find out from her brother when he arrived, and everyone was already likely going to be tense with Danny as it was.

"I was… at the office when he… I was at the office when your brother arrived at headquarters." As he watched Cassandra's expression shift, it pained Adam to just continue on rather than concentrate solely on comforting her. He could do both at the same time, however, and he was determined to do so. Perhaps, Adam reasoned, Cassandra would become more calm as his own confidence grew. "Now, he didn't tell me what he was there for." With such uncertainty regarding Danny, Adam would need to be a comforting presence of security and assurances. "I tried to get him to tell me, which is what delayed me. I'm sorry I don't have anything more for my efforts. I can at least tell you he was safe, though, Cassandra."

There was so much, almost too much, to process.

She had been unsure whether to believe her father, though she didn't have the time or the heart to push him further on what he said about Danny. Cassandra knew that regardless of whether he was truly honest and whether he should have told her the story he did, her father did it for the right reasons.

Hearing all of this now from Adam, Cassandra truly did not know what to make of it. She had been preoccupied planning things in her head to say to her brother about her dissatisfaction with him being gone, out of nowhere, on tonight, of all nights—until this new information came in. Now all of a sudden she had to consider if she felt assured that her brother was safe. It was not who the information came from; she'd always trust and believe Adam. That was not the issue, though. It was whether Adam himself even knew. *What if Danny was no longer safe?*

Cassandra had still not said anything. She pulled herself out of her thoughts to do so. She owed Adam at least that. "It's all right. I'm just grateful you tried." Without a care for who else was at their table or in her home, Cassandra took his hand and placed it on her cheek, determined to hold it there for as long as she pleased.

The two of them could share in their frustration, Cassandra in not having her brother there and Adam whose efforts were for naught. He did not dare tell her that he was further delayed by the exchange outside. He was here in the moment, and that was what mattered.

Adam's presence did have an effect on Cassandra. She was able to come out of her shell, to interact and enjoy herself around others. Danny's lack of presence was still felt, but at least it was not felt so strongly.

Despite the party being in her honor, Cassandra was able to take advantage of her time alone with Adam as the two sat at the top of the staircase and talked. Talking was truly what they did. Naturally, Cassandra found her way to settling nicely onto his lap, and Adam found his hand stroking her hair. His fingers laced their way through hers. The two of them fit so well together, such movements were entirely natural on their part.

Being the daughter of a deputy director thrust into the public eye, even as the favorite child, was not an easy or quiet life. That George was tasked with investigating many men and women, including seemingly ordinary citizens, did not go unnoticed. Cassandra would never dream of complaining, and she didn't need to; Adam could sense it was challenging for her as she was preparing to attend university. It was in this time that she was blossoming from a young woman into an adult.

Their bodies fit well together in such a way, but so did their souls, their minds, their hearts. Though he was almost four years older than her, Adam knew and admired how Cassandra was wise beyond her years. It was part of what made her beautiful to him on the inside, as well as on the outside. Where not everyone could understand her maturity and her intelligence, Adam revered her. Cassandra often thought that he understood her better than anyone alive, perhaps better than her own self.

While Harry's downfall came quickly at the end, the roots of it had been developing for years. No matter how deep the friendship was between him and George or how much George wished to help him, Harry was not

George's equal in society. He lacked the position, the social credit, the salary. Their children were likely to face the same barriers in being together, yet Danny considered Adam his best friend and Cassandra swore she would never love another as she loved Adam.

Adam loved Cassandra's smile. He could get lost in it for hours, much as he could be entranced by her green eyes or the way her chestnut brown hair curled. Just as he was about to tell Cassandra how lovely her smile looked, Adam saw George making his way from the dining room to the parlor. He was clutching his jacket tightly around him, as the nights were still particularly chilly as of late. George was not making eye contact with anyone; in fact, he seemed to be specifically avoiding it. From what Adam could tell, George seemed to be experiencing a wide range of emotions, from frustrated to worried to stressed.

"What is going on with my father…?" Cassandra trailed off at the end so quietly that had Adam not already assumed what she was asking, he might have not heard her.

"I don't know," Adam said as he started walking downstairs over to the older man. He looked ahead at his boss as he signaled for Cassandra to remain where she was. "But I'll try to find out," he said, mostly to himself by this point.

It was in that moment, as she was speaking to Karl, that Maria noticed her husband trying to flee without anyone realizing. If anyone was going to get answers from George, it would be his wife. Adam's place was to comfort and keep Cassandra calm, and so he returned to the stairway where they had been sitting.

"Good evening, Adam, I do apologize," Karl said as he looked up at the young couple. You surely did not intend to be interrupted this way." Karl could often be counted on for his wry humor, even in such circumstances.

Adam implored Cassandra not to try too hard to listen. It would do no good to strain to hear what they were not meant to hear. He himself, however, was doing his best to read lips. Cassandra could hear, just as Adam could read that Danny's name was being evoked. Of course it was. He was bound to come up.

Just as the conversation seemed to turn particularly tense, Maria shook and then hung her head, lightly patting her husband on the shoulder as he took his leave. Their patience paid off, in a way, perhaps for Cassandra most of all, as her father said goodbye to her.

"Goodbye, my darling, I will be right back. I hope not to be too long, and then we may enjoy cake."

She had had her brother and her father leave her, on the same night. At least her father told her beforehand and promised he would return. Cassandra did find herself wishing she could feel better than she presently felt, however.

What a birthday party this is turning out to be, Cassandra thought as she sighed and slouched. If only she could keep herself hidden that way and disappear from everyone but Adam.

She regretted such thoughts almost immediately. Her poor mother was in an even worse position than she. Cassandra wondered why her mother had not said anything. It was not because she was silently despairing, as Cassandra feared, as Cassandra herself was doing in a way. Karl was communicating an idea of his to her.

It was feasible, likely even, that people would become suspicious if George was gone from the party for very long. Even if that could not be helped, there was no reason for the party to not be able to flow properly. Cassandra could help ensure that it did.

It was time to collect herself, she knew. That Adam was beside her helped.

As she sat down in the parlor, full of lavish gifts, Cassandra had a moment before the guests filled the room to join her. She was able to thank Karl for his idea to save the evening then, and she had Adam's hand to hold in comfort.

The presents Cassandra was piled with amounted to mostly money, jewelry, and perfume—exactly what Cassandra expected to receive. She had thus already planned the gracious attitude of gratefulness to exude.

Then, in the midst of Cassandra's acting on duty and expectation, Adam pressed a jewelry box into her hand. She had not anticipated receiving such a gift from him, at least not at that very moment. It was obviously a piece of jewelry, as Cassandra had figured he would give her, though that did not make it any less special. In fact, Cassandra did not know if she had yet to be gifted with something so important and lovely.

Cassandra seemed to be nearly in a trance as she opened the box to discover the most beautiful locket she had ever seen. While it did not appear to be new, that endeared it to Cassandra the most.

It had belonged to Adam's mother.

Had it just been the two of them, no words would need to be spoken. Adam would have taken the locket out of its box and kissed this last reminder of his mother. It was time for it to be passed onto Cassandra now. She would have barely been able to wait for Adam to finish putting it around her neck before kissing him.

Alas, it was not to be. The moments Cassandra took to silently admire the locket may have already been too much. Cassandra thanked Adam, gave him a kiss on the cheek and looked forward to thanking him more fully once the party ended. Adam understood.

It was a touch on the shoulder which pulled Adam out of his thoughts. Seeing Danny standing behind him, Adam nearly forgot where he was as he went to embrace his friend.

Cassandra was just finishing up with presents when she saw her brother for the first time in hours. Their father was with him. She didn't know what to say; she wouldn't have known what she would have said if it was just them celebrating as a family for her birthday. She held onto her father for as long as possible and the same with her brother. Fortunately for Cassandra, Danny assured her that he realized he owed her an explanation, which would come later.

Next came the cake. As she blew out the candles, with all of her immediate family and the young man who she loved present, the smile on Cassandra's face was completely genuine.

George had assured Cassandra that they need not spare expense. She didn't believe him until George told her in a conversation between the two of them that it was his Christmas bonus to pay for the birthday party, just several months early. While the family had not had financial troubles despite George's social credit status hit, it was all for appearance's sake. If possible, there was a worse stress than having no money, and that was the knowledge that money could be taken away at a moment's notice, but having no idea when that moment was.

Adam offered Cassandra some advice to the effect that she heed her father's promise. Ultimately, she relented by asking for a chocolate fountain.

Cassandra had asked for a modest one, but, Edward, seeing the opportunity to show guests what a generous man he could be, had one which was anything but sent over to the house.

It took up the entire front room of the house once it was set up. Maria thought it excessive, but she dared not mention it to Cassandra, who only needed the slightest amount of influence to feel guilty. It was their oldest daughter's eighteenth birthday, after all, and she could do with some fun. If anyone deserved it, it was Cassandra, the kind soul who dealt with her family's situation without any selfishness or complaint.

Still, seeing the chocolate fountain in their home, Maria murmured to herself that it was good her brother was not there to see it. Even the thought of Thomas, whom she had not spoken to in months, other than the birthday card with a more than substantial amount of money he had sent for Cassandra, brought sadness and stress. At least Gregory would have smiled at how the children, especially his younger niece, enjoyed it. Maria was more disappointed about him not coming, though she should not have been surprised. Her husband told her it was best if Gregory were not there around so many department employees.

Danny wolfed down a dinner before enjoying himself beside Cassandra, Adam and Amelia at the fountain. Maria made sure her son ate some real food, a pointed look being all that was needed.

It was nearly midnight by then, and the first of the party goers to leave departed soon after getting their fill at the chocolate fountain. Such a tasty and creative idea had been a hit.

It was one in the morning by the time the last of the guests had talked George's ear off enough. Amelia had been asleep for an hour and Cassandra felt herself nodding off as well, which did not go unnoticed by Adam.

"You know, it's late, Cassandra. I'm sure nobody would be the wiser if you went upstairs to bed."

"I am *not* going to bed." Cassandra supposed she sounded like a petulant child. "And the hell with appearances. It's not about that, Adam, I know you know it." The last part came out in a much harsher tone than she intended, and sighing, she laid her head against Adam's chest where they were standing beside the chocolate fountain, having just finished another chocolate covered pineapple, her favorite.

Perhaps sleep was not a bad idea after all. Resting her eyes where she was now, where she felt safest, was not the worst thing. Cassandra had to stay up, though, if she truly wanted to get answers from Danny, and she did.

Karl had spent a long time talking with her father. It partly had to do with his avoiding Sarah at home. Sarah had come as had Jack and Emma, but she and the children left without Karl. The dynamics of it all were slightly beyond Cassandra's understanding. He and her father did seem to have much to discuss. Karl was her father's last living friend, after all. Cassandra was happy they had that time together then.

The Bradford family had given Cassandra a lovely pearl bracelet. Emma, a few years younger than Cassandra, had been excited to share that she particularly liked the various shades the pearls came in. When Cassandra went outside with Adam as he walked to his car, Karl placed a significant sum of money into the young woman's hand. It was, he pointed out, her eighteenth birthday after all. Cassandra had to smile. Of all the teasing she got for acting mature and wise beyond her years, she appreciated it the most from Karl.

Soon it was just Cassandra and Adam left outside, and as they made it over to Adam's car, it was clear neither of them were in a rush for him to leave. Had this been a more ordinary night, Cassandra would have daydreamed about asking her parents to let Adam spend the night. This was not such a night, considering she still had to speak with her brother. Adam was also far too proper.

That did not, however, mean they would not cherish the moments they had to linger outside in blissful privacy. As Cassandra leaned up against the hood of his car, Adam reminded her that he still had the locket, which he had been holding onto for safekeeping, and that he could still be the one to put it on her.

The weather had been chilly when the sun was not out, though that was not why Adam's fingers trembled as Cassandra turned away from him and held her hair to the side. The tremors were because there was such emotion, such passion in transferring over from the mother who loved him to the young woman he was in love with.

"It has a picture of me as a baby my mom had put in. I hope that's all right. You can change it if not. I don't mind."

Cassandra opened up the locket to see. She was overcome by a loss for words for a moment. "No. I could never change it, Adam," she finally said. "It's perfect. Just like your love for me."

"So you don't mind me regifting then, in a way?" Though he nervously laughed, Adam was serious. He only wanted the best for her. Though Cassandra had been a child at the time of Leah and Harry's deaths, Leah had been talking about passing the locket on to her someday, especially if Cassandra and Adam were to be married, as many thought they would be.

"I don't mind in the slightest. I love it. I love…" Adam did not wish to wait a moment longer to be able to kiss those lips of hers. It was late, and he did not wish for Cassandra to be cold with only her thin shawl on.

In those few tender moments that they shared that passionate kiss, it was as if nothing else in the world existed but the two of them. They could believe their love was all that they needed.

Reality soon set in as Adam felt the need to break the moment up. "I love you, my Cassandra. I hope that you had a truly very happy birthday."

"You know that I did with you, Adam." She fingered the locket as she said so, still hesitating to step back so he could pull away now. Eventually Cassandra knew it was time. With a blow of a kiss and a reminder of how much she dearly loved him, and the locket, she watched as Adam pulled away.

Cassandra stood outside for a few more moments as she watched his car leave her sight. She knew that Adam would not want her to remain outside, not when it was late and chilly, and she still had to talk to Danny. With a breeze shaking her out of her thoughts, Cassandra trekked back into the house.

If Cassandra had at all forgotten the predicament of that evening for the few moments she had outside, the scene she walked in on was sure to change that. Maria, with shaking hands and puffy red eyes, was cleaning up and preparing herself another cup of tea. Edward had wanted to have his own people clean up after the party but ended up relenting.

This was one of the few instances in which Maria had revealed her true self in front of any of the children.

"I'm sorry, my dear, that you have to see me like this."

"It's okay. Are you okay, mom?"

"Oh, yes!" She even laughed to herself slightly. "I'm just tired. And feeling overwhelmed. Not because of your party though. I… it's just been a long night."

It was in this moment that Danny came downstairs. His mother almost began crying all over again on seeing her son.

"I just wanted to come downstairs to apologize. I, um, I'm sorry I made you cry, mom." Cassandra didn't know who to look at—her brother for making their mother cry, or her mother for lying about the reason why. Danny turned to his sister. "And I'm sorry this all had to happen on your birthday. I really am, Cassandra."

What was she supposed to say? Cassandra wanted to let her brother have it, certainly. He did deserve it, at least in her mind. She didn't want to engage in something further with her mother there and in a rare but fragile state. "It's fine," was all Cassandra said then. She would, with any hope, speak to him upstairs.

Cassandra would not have to wait long before the time came for her and Danny to take their leave. George, looking even more disheveled than his wife, was announcing he was going. It was just a matter of finding his keys.

"And where are *you* going, George, at such an hour?"

"Out. I don't think I need to say more about what it regards, Maria."

Danny and Cassandra looked pointedly at each other. Their parents were speaking to each other as if it were just the two of them. Years ago this would have been unthinkable. It was happening all too often as of recently.

"Well, when are you coming home?"

"I don't know, Maria," George sighed.

"Of course you don't," she lamented. A pause, and then, she dared to ask her next question. "Do you even know if you're coming home at all?"

"No. Please don't wait up for me."

It had been the answer she was expecting. It was no less distressing. She had to blink back tears. "Fine. Goodbye then." Maria would say no more.

Danny and Cassandra quietly muttered their goodbyes. It nearly broke Cassandra's heart for her father to embrace her. She could tell even in that quick moment how exhausted he was.

"I love you, my dear. I hope you enjoyed your birthday party. I look forward to giving you your gift in the morning."

By the time Cassandra thought to tell him she loved him in return, he was already out of the kitchen.

Cassandra watched the door long after her father left. The physical and emotional fatigue from the evening's events was weighing further on her. There was no other reason to stay downstairs. She should have been in bed hours ago, but if she did not seek out answers now, Cassandra feared she would never hear the truth. Danny might still refuse her, but she at least had to try.

With the state their mother was in, Cassandra didn't wish to preoccupy her for much longer. Cassandra could not leave her mother without saying goodnight first. It was with her embrace and well wishes that Cassandra imparted her sincere hope for relief. Her poor mother deserved it.

Cassandra gave Danny his time to say goodnight. She had a feeling he had things of his own to tell their mother.

It was more than just a whisper. She let her son have it. The brief but tense exchange with George was enough to set her off. "I need you to let us know where you are if you're going to continue living under your father and my roof, especially when it occurs on your sister's birthday. Of all days, Danny! Promise me this doesn't have to happen again," she demanded of him.

Cassandra would not hear his response. Maria barely even heard it. Danny promised though, despite not knowing if he could even keep his word.

Then they climbed the staircase, all the more of a trip at such an hour, up to his bedroom.

"We're going to talk about this now, then." Danny didn't have to phrase it as a question. He already knew he owed Cassandra. Never mind that it was two in the morning.

"Yes. You know we need to."

He did. It didn't make it any easier. Cassandra was perhaps the person he hated to let down the most. He had never intended to be called in on her birthday. With Edward Roth approving the party, even sending security, Danny thought he would be safe from having to worry about a subpoena for an investigation their father was conducting.

George didn't tell his family this, but he didn't need to. Danny pieced together on his own that his father didn't have much, if any, real power when it came to the investigations. He was just the face of it, so that those under investigation and called in to testify would be comfortable speaking the truth. The farce of it was almost an open secret that George hadn't done much of anything of his own free will for years now.

George's older children didn't know how to bring it up and Amelia didn't understand. Danny fervently hoped they would be able to keep their conversation to the topic of missing Cassandra's birthday.

Danny tried to keep to that subject by asking if Cassandra wanted her birthday present. He had found a particularly lovely edition of *Lés Miserables* in French. Though Danny had his doubts, he hoped Cassandra would still be able to appreciate it as much as under normal circumstances.

"Not as much as I'd like to know what was going on with you today and, well, for a while now."

Danny knew he could not delay this. He also did not know how to explain, though, to his sister that he was at headquarters because there was a very strong possibility he was going to have to testify before their father. There were committee investigation hearings on not only the failed coup but whisperings about other coups which were to come.

Ultimately, with a deep breath, Danny reasoned his sister was old enough now. The sad reality was that this all could still affect her as well.

As was Cassandra's helpful way, she encouraged her brother along. "Adam told me he saw you at headquarters."

"Yeah, that's what it was. I, um… Cassandra, I may have to testify about the coup."

"I don't understand… you weren't… you weren't involved in it, were you? We all know how you feel, but you wouldn't *actually* get involved in it, would you?" Though it was just the two of them, one could never be too careful, and Cassandra's tone was a hushed one.

"No, I wasn't." Cassandra couldn't breathe a sigh of relief, not yet. "But they think that I might be involved in planning another one."

Cassandra swore that she could feel her heart sink. "Oh, Danny…" Her voice was now barely more than a whisper. "Tell me you're not."

"I'm not. That's all I think I can tell you right now, though, okay?"

Cassandra nodded, trying to blink back not only exhaustion but tears over the circumstances their family had found themselves in. When she let Danny reveal his gift to her, she allowed those tears to fall, especially when they were tears of joy.

In explaining to Danny how the book was just as nice as the locket from Adam, Cassandra realized she had not shown it to him. Both were beyond thoughtful and perfect in their own ways. Danny wondered aloud whether Adam had anything left of his mother's. Cassandra thought the same thing.

Speaking of Adam, Danny was at least relieved he had been able to make it there for Cassandra. Neither of them knew about the incident almost barring him from entering at all. It was just as well.

Brother and sister talked and comforted each other until just before the sun was about to rise. As he saw her out of his room, Danny imparted to his sister that he knew she was worried, and for that he was truly sorry. "I know how much you want to look out for me, all right? It doesn't go unnoticed or unappreciated. You don't have to worry yourself with it all the time, though. I can take care of myself and everything is going to be okay. That's a promise, Cassandra."

Danny was not the only one to make a promise in the earliest hours of the new day. As she nodded her goodnight to her brother, Cassandra promised herself that she would never stop worrying about or caring for Danny.

George was just leaving his brother's apartment after a discussion of finding a lawyer who was still willing and still had the social credit standing left to help Danny. He had not planned on seeing Gregory that night, especially when they were not on speaking terms enough for Gregory to be at his niece's birthday party. As he began the drive home, George made the same promise to himself as Cassandra did. Even if he didn't always show it, he was going to look out for his son, even if it cost him everything—and it very well could.

Making Sense Of That Night

Danny had a problem; there was no other way to regard how the situation came to a head on his sister's birthday. It did not mean, however, that the story was over. Far from it.

As Danny had explained to more people than he ever wanted to, the investigations Edward Roth was ordering his father to conduct were multi-faceted. George was to find out as much information as possible about the previous coup, which Danny had had no involvement in. He was also tasked with keeping a handle on the increasing efforts to have another coup. Not only was Danny involved, he was one of those in charge.

Though George had to step away from Cassandra's birthday party to retrieve him, Danny was spared having to tell his father everything. George had been too angry and not willing to listen much, if at all.

Danny doubted that his father would believe that he was involving himself at such a high level in the coup to protect him, no matter what he said. As much as they fought, often bitterly, Danny wanted to protect George from those who believed he was not forced into the position he was in. Danny also didn't want to think about what would happen to his mother and his sisters if any harm should come to his father at the hands of those carrying out a coup.

He had expected to feel relief over George wanting to just drop their having to discuss the matter. In truth, Danny had never felt more anxious. Danny had been on a mission to protect his father, and yet here he was likely needing that protection—if George even had any more clout to give such protection.

Edward had done the Whitfield family a favor in keeping himself and his family from attending the birthday party. That meant that he was free to question Danny himself.

At about four o'clock that afternoon, Edward Roth sent over his nephew, Scott Ambrose-Roth, and his friend, Howard Forrester, to collect Danny.

Of all the hours Danny was at headquarters, a significant portion was spent waiting. His phone had been confiscated, so using it to update others or pass the time was out of the question. Such tactics were all part of the plan to punish Danny and make him sweat.

When Danny asked if Edward was aware Danny was missing his sister's birthday party for this, Edward relished the opportunity to remind him who was in charge.

"I am in fact aware, Mr. Whitfield. I gave your parents the permission to hold this party in the first place. It was because of my good graces that they get to enjoy planning as much of the party as they have," Edward said. "While it brings me no pleasure to make you miss your sister's birthday party," he continued, though this was not the truth, "that is the price you must pay for these activities the department believes you are involved in to undermine our efforts of keeping the people of this nation safe."

Questioning Danny on the night of his sister's birthday was not merely a lesson for Danny but for his father as well. George had had no idea, but his son had entered headquarters no more than a few minutes after George had left, as planned by Edward.

"You'll never guess who I have been speaking with for the past several hours," Edward started off when telling George it was time for him to pick up his son, his voice dripping with condescension.

It was true that George did not know. In telling Cassandra that her brother was mad at him and that it would be some time before he felt like joining them at the party, George had been bluffing. Moments before arriving home, the party having already begun, he received a frantic message from his wife saying that Danny had been gone for some time and that he had not contacted them with an update. As little as they knew about their son's situation, George and Maria could agree it was best to not further worry Cassandra.

Upon coming to collect his son, George was still told very little. It furthered his humiliation to not know his own son was at his place of work, as it was meant to. His pride was another reason why George didn't push the subject further with Danny on the ride home. They rode in silence.

When they reached the driveway, George warned his son to not further ruin his sister's birthday. It was just as well. Maria did not bring it up, as she did not wish to cause any further disruption.

The father and son still did not talk about it after the harsh words communicated between Danny and his mother.

Unlike her husband, Maria was not going to hold back. She nearly slapped Danny. As she let her son have it, Maria broke down in tears. It was just as well that George did not see the exchange, as nobody would have been better off for the tongue lashing which would have followed. All of that yelling at nearly two o'clock in the morning did nobody any good. The alternative, though, of suffering in silence, had never done anything for them except make it worse.

***

Such an exchange had not been the most heated between the two.

George had just begun his position as Deputy Director and was often gone from home. When he was present, the atmosphere was tense, which Maria told the children was because of stress.

Danny had preferred his uncles' plans to handling his father's position. This was especially since George's plans were nonexistent, other than to follow Edward's orders and claim he had no other choice. Just like Thomas, Danny thought his father was making excuses. Just like Thomas, in words Danny might have meant but would still likely always regret, he let his mother know that, in all likelihood, she had married the wrong man. That Danny would not be there had she not married his father did not make much of a difference to his point.

Maria hadn't said anything in response. It was as if she had been rendered mute. The argument ended then and there since Danny, seeing the damage had been done, didn't dare continue. It was some days before mother and son had gotten over it enough to speak to each other again.

***

While nothing was to be settled the night of Cassandra's birthday, Maria was resolved that it had to at some point and soon. She didn't know if she could bear the family division much longer.

If her son would not talk to her, and he was certainly less likely to talk to his father or sister, Maria hoped Danny would at least confide in Adam.

One could call it anything from productive lunch plans to an intervention. Maria did not care so long as she felt progress was being made on keeping her son safe, and a big part of that meant knowing he could consider himself safe at home.

In one of the instances where they actually discussed the "what ifs" about George's position and fall in social credit status, George promised Maria he would be honest and that he would be all too happy to give her as many positive updates as he had, no matter how trivial. Maria had been waiting on these positive updates for some time now to no avail.

George, however, had at least been able to assure her that he could still keep their son alive and out of prison. He had kept that promise so far.

After dropping out from university with no intention of going back, Danny got a job at a bookstore. It sufficed. It also meant he had a schedule Adam could work with on his lunch hour. Danny's protestations that he wasn't hungry wouldn't do. The look on his mother's face was clear enough.

Danny had intended on staying silent and sulking, but his curiosity got the better of him. "So where are we really going?"

"We're going to lunch, just like your mother asked. Just like I told you we're going."

"Is this an intervention?" Danny asked, half kidding.

"If you want to see it that way, sure." No matter how Danny regarded it, Adam was not joking. Neither was his mother. "But I would hope you can be honest with me and yourself that there are things we have to talk about."

Danny was chafing under the truth. Adam was right. His mother was right. Even his father was right. He hadn't planned on going out to lunch today, though, or on being put on the spot about what was going on. "Where are we going?"

"Wherever you want to go." As Adam started listing off places he had gone to with George before, Danny immediately cut him off. He didn't want to be anywhere his father, or worse, department members might be. Paranoid a thought though it may be, Danny didn't want to take any risks of being spied on. At Danny's request, Adam set off for a "low-key" place. Adam didn't care where they went.

The rest of the ride was silent. Despite the appropriateness of the venue, Danny still found himself looking over his shoulder on multiple occasions. "I'm fine, you know," Danny told Adam.

"You don't seem fine. I wouldn't consider going off on your sister's birthday being fine. I'm your best friend, you should be able to be honest with me, if with no one else. Especially since I care about and want to help you."

After taking a brief moment to order for them both, Adam continued. "You know, this is the place you can tell me something, anything."

"I know." Yet he still resisted.

"I just want to help you, Danny. Your dad wants to help you, too. I can be the middleman between you two, no matter what it is. Things have happened to your family which have affected you personally, yes. But why don't we get to correcting that, especially while we still can?"

As Adam continued, Danny realized he made a compelling case. He likely was the person Danny could trust the most. Danny just didn't know how to explain to anyone who wasn't directly involved, even Adam, that there was a potential coup going on, but that Danny was involved to actually help his dad, not work against him.

"Danny, I'm not here to judge you, no matter what you tell me. I just want to help you."

It wasn't that simple. Danny still appeared conflicted. "I know I can tell you." Adam couldn't celebrate just yet, however. "I don't want to get you all worked up, though."

Adam almost had to laugh, though he stifled the impulse. "I'm not that fragile, Danny."

"Yes, but you work for the department your dad worked for because you actually want to. You work for my dad. I know how much your position means to you." Though he was coming closer to confiding in Adam, Danny still had to get this off his chest. "I need you to know that whatever happens, I don't want you to get hurt."

Adam wasn't sure what exactly Danny meant, only that it was not good. He was determined to let Danny continue, though, even if it was difficult to hear. Once they received their food, Adam waved Danny to go ahead.

"It's about the coup, actually. That's what I've been called in for." Danny spoke so quietly, Adam had to lean in to hear him. When he did hear him, he wasn't sure he had heard him correctly.

"I'm sorry, I'm not sure I heard you correctly. Did you just say it's about..." Even Adam looked around this time before continuing, and lowering his voice even more. "It's about the coup?" Danny just nodded this time. "What on earth are you talking about? What would you have had to do with that? Tell me you weren't involved."

Adam very much doubted Danny was, because Danny was not dead or imprisoned. That he was his father's son wouldn't have even mattered.

"No, I wasn't."

"Oh thank *God.*" Adam could only be relieved for so long, though.

"But, um, there... there might be another one."

Well, shit. Adam didn't know what else to think. Except that Danny was insane, though he couldn't say that and make Danny retreat even further. When he got over the initial shock, Adam had to ask, though part of him would have preferred to not know. "Another one." Danny nodded in confirmation. "And you're involved in it?" Danny sighed, and nodded once more.

Adam figured he had to say something, especially since Danny was likely in some very hot water and would need a friend. "Okay. Right. Wow. Okay." He was repeating himself, but he was filling the silence at least. Danny was relieved not to be the one to speak.

Ultimately, for all the emotions he went through, Adam could not remain surprised. He didn't think anyone could be. It was that much more important, then, that Danny keep a low profile. Now Adam shifted concerns to getting through to his friend as much as he could, as if he might never get another chance.

Once he confirmed Danny was listening, Adam went on. “Right. We can work with this. I still believe your dad can help you, that he wants to do everything in his power and then some, to keep you safe. But you have got to help us out and keep a low profile. Keep denying that you’re involved, or that there even is a coup. No matter what. Promise me you’ll deny it. Please, Danny.”

Danny nodded, and then, with a shaky tone, he asked about Gregory. “Does that mean no more meetings with my Uncle Gregory?”

“That’s… probably for the best,” Adam confirmed, though he hated to have to disappoint his friend. “I am sorry.” Danny just nodded.

Initially Adam feared that Danny was refusing to say more out of anger, but he was instead going with a greater point. “Please believe me that I don’t want you, or even my dad, to get hurt.”

There was very likely going to be some emotional hurt, especially when it came to George, but Adam decided to just assure Danny that he believed him.

Without much else being said, Adam took advantage of how Danny didn’t try harder to insist he could pick up the check. Adam paid, then ushered the two of them out there. It seemed Danny’s paranoia had rubbed off on him as well.

Adam drove Danny home in silence. When Danny did speak up, just as they arrived at the house, his voice was devoid of emotion. “Please don’t tell my dad. He’s got enough on his plate, and, well, I just don’t feel ready enough to talk to him about it. It’ll get done. I don’t know when, but it will. Thanks for the lunch, Adam.”

Danny didn’t even ask Adam about coming inside. Before they made it to the driveway, Adam had told himself that the past few hours were enough. They would have to do, so long as Danny didn't get himself into worse trouble.

***

Danny didn't come down from his bedroom for the rest of the evening. He needed time to process the fact that he would not be having any more contact with his uncle, the man who understood him. Not for the first time, Danny found himself wishing Gregory was his father.

For almost two years now, Danny had been meeting regularly with his uncle. At times he felt guilty that he was keeping it from the rest of the family. George had stopped returning Gregory's messages and phone calls for about the same time, but Maria and the children need not have been cut off from Gregory as much as they were.

In many of these meetings Gregory and Danny behaved as a father and son would, doing things George should have been experiencing as a father. Lately, however, they talked, strategized and planned.

Danny couldn't stand cutting Gregory off without warning, especially since that's more or less what his father did. If there was one quality Danny had to pick that he disliked most about George, it was how much his pride had gotten between him and his own brother.

He was going to make one more phone call and that was it. While George had been under the impression that their phone calls still remained private, Danny could never be too careful. With shaking fingers he called his uncle from the cell phone he used specifically for such calls.

"Danny? What's wrong?" Gregory picked up right away, as he was so good about doing. While Danny had told himself he would be strong in this, he almost broke from the start. For a few moments, all Gregory could hear were the sounds of his adult nephew in tears. He prodded further. "Are you all right, Danny?"

He just nodded at first, but Danny forced himself to speak up that he was all right. It was just as well that he didn't use the video feature; if Gregory couldn't physically comfort him, there was no reason for him to see him like this.

"Yeah. I, um, I talked to Adam."

"Okay. That's good, right? How is he?"

"He's fine. My mom wanted us to talk. Because you know, she's been so worried. And I can't say I blame her, but Gregory?"

"Yes, Danny. What is it, son?"

"I just wonder if I've gotten in too deep in this. I know that it's not… it's not malicious of him in any way, but Adam says with all the department seems to know, that I best lay low. He thinks you and I shouldn't meet up anymore."

Once again, Danny broke down in tears. He didn't even give his uncle a chance to respond right away as he just kept apologizing. When he had finished, what he asked next broke Gregory's heart that much more. "Do you think he's right? Do we have to?"

Gregory took some time to think. What a past few days it had been. He had not been at his own niece's birthday party this year or the year before, yet he had still seen George to talk about the predicament Danny was in, a predicament not necessarily being helped by Gregory, as George put it.

Before he could answer, Danny shared his idea with his uncle. "What if I just stayed with you? My dad would have to come around, I'm sure, but still, we could make it work, couldn't we? I'm an adult and I've been meaning to move out for some time."

"Danny…"

"Right. You don't think it will work. You're right. It was a stupid idea. I'm sorry for wasting time mentioning it."

"No, it's okay. You don't have to apologize for wanting to spend more time with family. I love you, you know that. So does your dad, and your mom, and your sisters and Adam. Which is why I don't think Adam would tell you such a thing if he didn't honestly believe it."

"Okay, I love you too."

The phone call didn't continue for long after that. Gregory made sure Danny was in an okay place and then they parted ways. Danny cried himself to sleep that night.

Just A Conversation

George had not seen or spoken to his brother for over a year when he dialed his brother's line to let Gregory know he was coming by and that they needed to talk. That it was about Danny ensured there would be no arguing. It may have been late, but if he knew two things about his brother, they were that he stayed up late and he cared deeply for Danny.

Showing up on his brother's doorstep in the early hours of the morning was almost more of a difficult move for George than it was for Gregory. For one, George had the stress and pressure of his job and home life and the lengths he would go to to keep his family safe, which, like it or not, involved consulting with his brother. George also was self-aware that the reason he and his brother did not talk was because he was the one who had stopped responding to Gregory's good-faith efforts to reach out.

Though he had not planned on staying very long, George was at his brother's apartment for several hours. Initially, George's approach was to tell his brother how he really felt, even if it meant expressing a sense of blame towards Gregory for getting Danny into whatever mess he was in. Ultimately, however, George just wanted help for his son.

Danny remained withdrawn. Maria said he had talked to Adam, and it seemed to have some kind of an effect, except that Danny wouldn't speak about it. George was too busy to talk to his son even if he had wanted to, and he found himself fearful about what he would find out. Whenever he might have had a free moment to address the situation with Danny, he kept putting it off.

If George did not eventually hear from Danny, however, it was possible that the situation was only going to get worse. There were whispers about subpoenas, which George was trying to keep at bay while attempting to get through with the investigative process.

Normally, as the Deputy Director, George would have had barely any limitations or checks on his power. He had not come to the position through ordinary circumstances, however. As a result, certain files having to do with his brother and his son were blocked off from him.

This reality necessitated George asking Adam to do something he normally would not, to use his own clearance to access the files.

The idea solidified in George's mind the night before, when he brought up to Danny the conversation with Adam he was hoping to hear about. Without another word, Danny got up to empty his mostly-full plate and isolated himself in his bedroom for the rest of the evening. George found himself wishing Danny would yell at him, if only because it would mean that Danny was saying *something.* Instead, it was as if he had closed himself off to the world.

Edward's ever-looming presence did not help George's need for discretion. He would only ask Adam when it was safe to do so. George wouldn't put Adam at too great a risk. Gregory and Danny would not want that. George also did not want to do that to Adam or to the memory of his father.

If Edward was not constantly bothering George and Adam, however, he was hanging around Karl's department, going over the budget. George was sure that Edward had been blackmailing Karl about Tara.

It was thus nearly a week before George felt comfortable broaching the topic. It was another three days before Adam had an update. In truth, this was moving faster than George could have dreamed, though it felt like a lifetime.

The files in question were so classified that a digital copy was not accessible. Adam had removed them from their locked room under the guise of retrieving another set of files, with the claim that his online access code was being reset. It was thus paramount that the files, all of them, be returned before their disappearance was noticed.

Adam would never know that Scott had watched him go into the room and seen him come out with the files. Scott would never say a word about it, not to Adam, his uncle, or even Howard.

George knew better than to mention he hoped such a task was no trouble, for it *was* trouble, especially if Adam was caught with such files.

On that Friday morning, George ushered Adam into his office as if nothing was out of the ordinary, though he did close his door and draw the blinds for good measure. As Adam silently laid the two sets of files out on the desk, initially all George did was stare, taking each of them in.

The files seemed so… inconspicuous, it was hard to imagine that they had risked so much just to access them. In their ordinariness, though, the files had a commanding, almost frightening presence to them, as a physical reminder of what Edward could and was threatening to do to George's family.

For all George knew about his brother, there were still plenty of surprises, namely that he had potentially been an unindicted co-conspirator in a series of planned coups.

Adam hadn't looked at the files, believing it was not his place to do so. He had not seen the note about the subpoena which would be issued in the coming days, or that the file was going through a complete update as leads were coming in, some from Danny's own friends.

At least one thing was clear. The files had to be returned; as much as George could have pored over them all day, he always knew his time with them would be fleeting. He would also have to spend more time talking with his brother and his son than he would reading about them. It was time for George to reconcile that truth which he had neglected for far too long.

"It would seem we have a situation, Director Whitfield, sir."

"It would seem that we do indeed, Adam."

***

George had toyed with the idea of going straight home, of even leaving early so as to get in touch with Gregory. That would have surely aroused suspicion, though, so George had to force himself to remain patient while the hours slowly ticked by.

Yet when it was five o'clock in the evening, George did not go straight home. He instead went to speak with Karl. His secretary, Tara, was not at her desk, which meant that she had either gone home for the day, George thought, or…

The sound of her feminine laughter told him it was the latter. She had been with Karl in his office. Though he couldn't say for certain as to what extent she had actually *been with* him, George was fine with not knowing. He was also very relieved he had not gotten there any earlier, when the risk of interrupting a truly inopportune moment would have been quite high.

"Oh, hello, Deputy Director Whitfield. How may I assist you?" As she exited Karl's office, a bounce in her step, she was ever the picture of beauty and professionalism. It was no wonder why Karl had taken up with her. Tara was not the first secretary Karl had had extramarital affairs with, but she was the one Karl truly loved.

George couldn't help but be nice to Tara. She was so wonderfully likable. She was the youngest one Karl had been with, though George tried not to think about how he was twice her age. Karl had been with Tara the longest he had been with anyone other than his wife. Of all the women Karl had been with who were not Sarah, George supposed he liked Tara best.

"Hello, Miss Wilson. I'm looking for Karl," George said, somewhat sheepishly. "Would it be… would it be all right for me to go speak with him, in his office?"

"Certainly." If Tara felt any kind of unease, she did not show it. She had bested George. After the appropriate well wishes, she sent George in. "And sir, please know that you can call me Tara," she said with a smile.

George knocked before entering. Tara had been completely composed. Karl was another story. He was still fiddling with his tie.

"Pardon me, George. I had not been expecting you."

"It's nothing," George said with a bit of a sigh. It was not exactly 'nothing,' as both men knew, though they went along with it. It was not the time to address why.

As it was clear that George would not be judging him, a relief to Karl no doubt, he decided he had had enough with his tie for now. But, because he had been so concerned with *that* task, he had neglected a more important one.

Karl had not yet noticed the lipstick stains on his mouth and neck.

"What can I do for you, George?" Karl asked as George tried not to laugh.

He would not have noticed them if not for George's reaction.

"Well, Karl, I would recommend that you first do yourself a favor and wipe the lipstick from your lips and your neck." Karl gave George a look, which could only be returned with a shrug, as he went over to the mirror. He managed a word of thanks, though he sounded slightly embarrassed and certainly frazzled.

"Karl, I can come back."

"No, George, I'm perfectly fit for conversation." His voice had a short tone to it, though it was understandable. When he returned to his desk the lipstick was gone, which at least made for a less awkward conversation. "Thank you, by the way. You have spared me from, well, further embarrassment." George nodded knowingly. Once they had that out of the way, George was relieved to see that Karl's expression and tone had changed. "Now, George, how can I be of service?"

George thought for a moment. Karl was in a position to listen as a friend, but he was distracted. Bringing up the concerns he had had with Edward could make Karl more flustered. Still, George had come for something, and it wasn't just to tell his friend that he had his girlfriend's lipstick on his face before he went home to his wife and children.

Karl had been facing his own harassment from Edward. George hoped that by appealing to Karl, perhaps he and his friend could team up. Edward had already taken away Harry from them, but every now and then the flicker of hope to get the nation back on track was alive for his two remaining friends and his son.

George apologized not only for any awkwardness, but for his sounding potentially cryptic. There were not many people he could trust anymore, but he could at least trust Karl and always would. Thus George could relax some. Karl understood and was sympathetic to the vagueness.

"I… As part of my position, I will be conducting investigations and hearings about any previous or potential future coups," George said with a shaky start. "It still remains to be seen how much power I will have in such a role, which matters greatly with how my brother and my son could be at risk."

Karl's change in expression was purposefully slight so as to not alarm George any more than he already was, but it was nevertheless noticeable.

"I am here to inform you that I may need your help in the future. I cannot say for certain what that help will involve, however, or much more, as I myself do not know."

There was no hesitation on Karl's part. "Of course I will help you, George. You say the word and I will be ready at a moment's notice. The hell with whatever Edward has on me." George honored the bravado with a smile, and Karl continued on. "Might I make a suggestion as to someone who might be worthwhile to speak with? I know you and your brother haven't been on speaking terms for quite some time, but perhaps he could help, especially when it comes to Danny?"

George had to chuckle. If only Karl knew how he had already been sneaking off in the middle of the night to meet Gregory. It had indeed come to this.

"Well, I'm a smart man," Karl replied once George explained his reaction, telling him about how the night of Cassandra's birthday did not end with the party. They chuckled together, a sad, almost bitter sound.

Regardless of how he felt about his brother, George found himself talking about Gregory in more instances and with more people in one day than he had in months. George had already thought of calling Gregory from his private line at home. "You should do so, then," Karl assured him.

If anything, Karl and Gregory had been acquaintances. Karl had always been George's friend first and foremost. He knew it made him a hypocrite to not be fond of how Gregory had once been, and quite possibly still was, in love with Maria. At least Karl had never tried to interfere with parenting another man's children as Karl suspected Gregory had when it came to Danny especially.

There was no love lost between Karl and Thomas when Thomas left for the United States. Karl was not too keen to forgive Thomas for his behavior when George was trying to confide in them about their position. He was even less willing to forgive Thomas for sticking his nose in everyone's business, which included Karl's extramarital affairs.

George knew he could count on Karl to not make it a game of choosing sides or reminding George he was being stubborn when it came to having regular contact with Gregory again. He was offering objective advice, as any friend would. At least Karl hoped he could still behave as such, even with Edward breathing down his neck every day.

"How are *you* doing though, George?" Karl asked. "I know this must be weighing on you as well."

George couldn't quite say why, but he was afraid of giving off the hint of emotion. Perhaps it was because he had tried to be unfeeling for so long as a sort of coping mechanism that he accidentally became much better than he had intended.

"I…" The hesitation from George said enough, and Karl's reaction showed. "I'll be just fine, thank you," George concluded with more certainty this time. But then, he *did* give off a hint of emotion, even surprising himself in doing so. "I don't have any other choice but to be. Too much depends on it."

Karl smiled comfortingly at his friend. "Isn't that the truth." He was, in many ways, in the same boat as George, though he would not forget what a blessing it was that he was still in his desired role as Director of the Treasury while George was languishing as Deputy Director and had been doing for years. Still, Karl did believe he was going through enough himself to be able to empathize.

When the timing was suitable, George and Karl walked out of the office together. Tara was still at her desk, patiently waiting for Karl. They would be leaving together, then. George forced himself to have no opinion about it, just as he noticed Karl subtly placing his hand around her waist. He said his proper goodbyes and left.

George did take one more glance before they were completely out of sight. Karl had leaned in closer to Tara. They seemed to be having a moment.

It was a wonder to George and to many others why Karl didn't just divorce Sarah. George felt it was for the sake of their children, especially Emma, who, at fifteen, idolized her father despite everything. Karl could hardly have been a better father to her or her brother, Jack. In many ways, Karl still loved Sarah. It was a most curious affair.

***

In some ways, thinking about Karl proved a welcome distraction. It was, however—and it always would be—only a temporary reprieve from other matters.

Thoughts of Karl and Tara left George as he approached his home. Instead he thought of his brother, of his son, of his wife. *What was he going to tell each of them? Did he dare ask any of them for help in such a way that revealed perhaps George didn't have it all together?*

It saddened George that he had to dread seeing his wife and how concerned she felt, how helpless she was to do much of anything to help him. George did find himself thinking of Karl again, for the briefest of moments. It was wrong to envy him, George knew that, especially when Maria running off with Gregory was at one point a very feasible possibility. He couldn't help thinking though that here Karl was, having his affairs practically out in the open, and it still seemed like Karl's marriage and home life were better than his own.

George had been unable to help his nerves, so he was quite irritable upon entering their home. Maria knew right away something was up. George did not wish to mention his brother in front of the children, or really, at all.

He found himself almost grateful then that the tension which had been hanging over the household for some time now meant there wouldn't be many questions.

George thought about skipping dinner but forced himself to endure it. He was distracted, however, with thoughts as to why he dreaded calling his brother so much. George had made a middle of the night visit to see Gregory, but he didn't expect the need for help to last. This was getting excessive. The more George admitted he needed Gregory, the more he came to terms with just how desperate he was becoming.

During dinner, George barely spoke. Maria and the children followed his lead. As he went upstairs to his office, George asked that he not be bothered unless it was absolutely necessary. When nobody said anything, George took that to mean that there were zero objections.

Maria stared ahead at her husband's spot at the dinner table long after he had left it. George was not the only one who had left things unsaid. Danny soon headed up to his room without another word. Cassandra already knew the answer, so she knew better than to ask her mother if things were all right. She instead focused on cheering up Amelia.

Danny thought, very briefly, of listening up against his father's office door. Even if he had, he would have heard nothing, because George was still resisting calling his brother. He did not wish to confront how close to home his concerns with work were becoming, so for the first hour or so he had to himself he accomplished the work he had been too distracted to complete at the office.

It was inevitable, however, that George would have to call his brother at some point. When it was nearly ten o'clock, George dialed Gregory's number on his private office line. This was something he could do, he *had* to do. It was just a conversation, after all. Despite cutting off contact, even with all the time that had passed, he still knew the number by heart.

The phone rang longer than it should have. It certainly was not too late for Gregory; the man had recently stayed up until nearly five o'clock in the morning speaking with George. Just as George was about to hang up, Gregory answered.

"Hello, George," he said, "this is quite the surprise. I had thought our middle of the night meeting was a one-time thing."

"So did I," George sighed.

"Anyway, what is it this time?" Gregory immediately regretted his tone. He could tell George was bitter, enough so where he wouldn't call unless he felt he absolutely had to. Surely he didn't need Gregory making this more difficult on him. "Is everything all right, George?" Gregory followed up, his voice softer.

"It's… I finally found a way to access your file. And Danny's."

"I imagine it's a cause for concern?" Gregory spoke as if he had a lump in his throat. Naturally there would be a file on him. He could take care of himself, though. For Danny to be exposed in such a way was something else. Gregory never wanted his nephew's involvement to come to this, which is why he had limited Danny's participation in any future coups. At least, that had been his aim.

"Yes, I'm afraid so," George said, his pride slipping away. "Gregory, I'm calling because I'm desperate."

The lack of a response was troubling, but it would have been just as much so if Gregory had said that he wasn't surprised. If George was looking to Gregory for comforting reassurances, he wasn't necessarily looking in the right place.

Still, Gregory could understand and appreciate what had gone into George calling him. "You've been blindsided by all the information, haven't you? It's okay if that's what's going on, George."

Was it? Could George admit to his brother that he knew nothing of another coup, and how foolish he felt for discounting the possibility?

"I... well, yes," George answered, seeing fewer reasons for choosing not to be forthcoming. "Part of me wonders how I could have been so blind to not know about my own brother and son possibly conspiring to overthrow my department with another attempt at a coup, as if the failures of the last one weren't bad enough to keep me awake at night." George took a deep breath before continuing, feeling fortunate that Gregory was in a position to let him do so. "Yet part of me is not surprised in the slightest. Is Thomas involved in this too?"

Gregory bit back his knee-jerk reaction. The point was to help Danny, not to one up George. "Thomas is not. There is no involvement from the United States, of that you can be assured." That was a relief, as the relationship between the current president, Edward Roth, and the Americans was complicated at best. "While Danny and I are involved in some... *choice activities*, as I think is fair to call them, we were never and will never be against you, George."

George couldn't say for certain where the conflicted emotions came from. He hated the position he saw as a punishment and was only still holding it under coercion, if he wanted to continue protecting his family. Perhaps it was because George had never quite gotten over the unproductive meeting with Thomas and Gregory, or that they had hated him working in a position he had loved for the few years that he had it, as if they couldn't distinguish between the well-intentioned but ill-fated Department of Ethics and the Department of Security of Action. Yes, it was definitely that much, especially as George found himself mourning his loss of position, fulfillment and social credit, though he had been doing so silently and on his own. He hadn't even fully let Maria in to understand his grieving; he certainly wasn't going to all of a sudden become best buddies with his younger brother or his obstinate son.

There was another idea, though. Perhaps George was jealous. He had already been jealous of the relationship between his brother and Danny for years, but this was something different. This was a way the three of them could have done something together. Unless they thought he could possibly be on Edward's side, as if he weren't suffering every day as he had been since he lost his position and his best friend all in one year.

Perhaps that was it—how George found himself feeling left out.

"Do you not trust me, Gregory?" he finally asked.

How to answer? *Was it that Gregory did not trust his brother?* He had to admit he could see why George would come to such a conclusion. Even if Gregory trusted his brother, he could not trust his position. He also wanted to protect his brother, though, to save him from culpability.

Yes, that was it. It wasn't that Gregory didn't trust George. It was that he feared Edward very much, and that included what Edward could do to his brother as well as his nephew and himself.

"It's not that at all, George. Please don't think that way. I'm trying to *save* you."

With such passion in his voice, George would have to see what his brother was saying, and he did. That was not all there was to it, however.

"Dare I ask how you're going to be doing so? Will *I* find myself needing to save *you*? In addition to saving my son? Or is this a situation where I'm better off not knowing? It is, isn't it?"

As complicated as the situation was, Gregory could at least feel heartened in how his brother was still able to find humor in what he needed to."

"You've got me there, George. But, as Danny's father, I do feel you deserve to know..." George braced himself for what could very well be the most difficult thing he would have to hear from his brother.

Gregory had felt a closeness to Danny—since before he was born, even. Then as Danny grew up and matured, he was so much like Gregory. How could they not have a connection? It was what came naturally to the both of them, including with their political crusades.

Danny came to Gregory around the time he was dropping out of college. When the last coup had failed, Gregory had lost some close friends. For the first few months, Gregory was prepared to lay low while he figured out his course of action. Thomas begged Gregory to come to the United States with him. While the idea was tempting in some ways, Gregory couldn't bear leaving Danny, Maria or his home behind. Not when there was so much left to do.

The latest coup had actually been the third attempt. It had been the one Gregory was admittedly most hopeful about, which was what brought such disappointment and even fear when it failed so spectacularly. Danny felt the same way. For the first time, Gregory admitted to George that he believed George really had tried not to take sides and thought it had been the best course of action for George to take. It only mattered if Edward agreed, which he did not. As he tried to explain it, Gregory felt for his brother, he truly did. He just didn't know how to show it, especially around Thomas. George didn't know if he felt better or worse about such a revelation from Gregory.

Despite how long Danny and Gregory had been working together for a desperately needed political change, whisperings of another coup had only been going on for months. The holdup, in all honesty, had been to see what

George had made of his position. *Was he going to participate in the wrongdoing he would have to be complicit in, or was he willing and able to resist? Would George be an ally, or would he once again be on nobody's side?* Gregory would appreciate the former and try to be understanding of the latter, but he had to put it out there.

After everything that had just been revealed to him, George answered in a surprisingly quick and sure fashion to remind his brother that he could never actually be so quick and sure when acting. "If only it were that simple," he responded.

Gregory once again emphasized that he understood. "And George?"

"Yes, Gregory?"

"Please believe me when I say I don't want you to get hurt. It was never my intention." Gregory continued on before George could interrupt. "I see what this role does to you. I see how you suffer. If only it were in my power, I would end that."

"Thank you, Gregory. I… I'm glad that I spoke with you. What you told me about my son was quite valuable information. I still must process all of this, but I appreciate it nonetheless. I'll try to speak with him about this and update you as is necessary."

"Of course." Gregory forced himself not to be so disappointed when it came to his brother's lack of emotional reaction. That was what he wanted most for George, actually— just to be able to feel again.

It's A Subpoena

George wondered what it would be like going to work with such newfound information. It turned out to be exactly the same. Not that it was pleasant; far from it. It had merely gotten to the point where there weren't many ways in which it could get worse.

Though there were a few tense days following Adam's finding the files, it seemed like nothing was to come of it. He and George could breathe a sigh of relief, at least for a moment.

Business as usual, however, still meant stress and internal struggle for George.

Any knowledge Edward had of planned coups, he did not share with George. *Then again*, George reasoned, *why would he*? If George had a role in this, it was to not let Edward be the wiser, lest he find ways to further punish the Whitfield family.

One week after the phone call, Scott and Howard came by to collect George. As he and Howard handed George the document entrusted to them, Scott couldn't help taking an extra glance at George's desk. Whatever file he had seen Adam retrieve and bring to George's office was no longer there.

Scott did not have long to think about the files, however. He and Howard had been given strict orders to deliver something of utmost importance, a list of subpoenas to be issued for the investigation hearings. The latest coup was still being investigated, why, George did not know, as so many men and women had been arrested. It was not up to George to ask why, however. He was expected to do as he was told without asking questions, as he had for two years now. If Edward felt an explanation was warranted, he would provide it.

When asking about what the business of having to issue subpoenas was all about, George was merely told by Howard to read it.

It was a subpoena for Danny.

George had had to teach himself to not react in many instances. This was one of them.

Howard confirmed that George understood his son would be called in later that week to testify before the committee hearing, then he and Scott took their leave.

George's hand shook as he held the letter. He read it over and over, as if doing so would change what it contained. The truth of the matter, however, was that he had less than a week before questioning his own son. George doubted the legitimacy of Danny's testifying. *Was it to be a kangaroo court? Was Edward testing George's loyalty?* Both were possible, likely even. *What was to happen afterwards?*

Scott couldn't say why, exactly, but part of him wanted to assure George that it would all work out, even if he couldn't be sure that it would.

Howard would not have allowed it, however. They weren't friends with Danny, far from it. *Why should they care what happened to him, especially if he* was *guilty enough to be brought in for questioning?* It was on George to figure out how he would square this away at home. Howard did not envy George, but it wasn't his job to.

When Adam came in, George was still in this distracted state.

"Sir, I just came to ask if—" Adam cut himself short. "Sir, are you all right?"

The color had completely drained from George's face. Hyperbolic though it might be, he felt in a way as if he had died and gone to Hell. It seemed as plausible an explanation as any as to why he would be forced to issue a subpoena to his son.

"Oh, hello, Adam. I'm sorry you have to see me this way. It's… well, it's best if you read it yourself."

George's hands shook as he passed the letter over to Adam, who was all too willing to take it from him in hopes of relieving his boss of such a burden, if only momentarily.

"What are you going to do with this, sir?" Adam cautiously asked.

"I'm afraid I don't have much of a choice, Adam," George admitted. "The hearing is this week, and it would appear Director Roth believes my son is somehow involved."

Adam didn't know quite what or how much to say. He knew Danny was involved in planning a future coup. The question was whether Edward knew, if he was just trying to seek out information from the young man or just calling Danny in to scare him and test George.

The two were interrupted from saying anything further about it by the telephone ringing. It was Edward himself calling, needing to speak with George.

The dread of being called to Edward's office was not something that lessened over time. Edward either had bad news or simply wished to torture George by gloating about something. He was to bring the letter with him.

"Have a seat, George," Edward said coolly.

George only ever sat if Edward directed him to do so, which usually meant the conversation was going to last for some time. Nevertheless, George was in this instance relieved to be sitting.

"I see that Scott and Howard delivered you this notice of subpoena action?" George meekly nodded, but it was not enough for Edward. "I asked you a question, I would like a full and complete answer, George."

"Yes. Yes, sir, they did deliver me the notice."

"Very well. I take it you were surprised." George hesitated, not sure if he should answer truthfully. "I will try to be sympathetic to the shock this must be for you and not point out further that this conversation is not going very well for you." George had to agree that it was not, though he did not know what, exactly, to say about it. If Edward already knew how surprised he was, he might as well be honest.

"I… yes, sir, I was surprised."

"Well, don't be. This department and you, as its deputy, have full subpoena power. Investigating the previous coup and ensuring that another one does not happen is of the utmost importance. I am willing to investigate whomever and whatever needs to be investigated, and I need to know that you are, too. Think of this as a test, George."

If only Edward realized that George saw every day in the department and every task he was assigned to do as a test, a test of how compliant he was willing to be with so much at stake. He didn't know what good, if any, it would do to try to assure Edward that calling Danny in to testify was unnecessary. George felt he had to try, though.

"Sir, if I may… I could speak with Danny, to assure he has no involvement with any coups."

"Well, that's why he'll be coming in to testify, George," Edward said with that wicked smile of his. George hated that smile. It was perhaps the one thing he truly feared, other than God. "I must admit that the evidence against your son is compelling. I would much prefer the questioning be done in a formal setting. Surely you understand?"

George did understand, but he didn't want to. He knew Danny would try to resist. Maria would be beside herself. Gregory would be worried, and he didn't want to know what Thomas would say.

He had to go about what he was going to say quite carefully.

"Suppose something happens and Danny does not show?"

"Well, then, George," Edward said, leaning in closely, his hands clasped together. "That would be very bad all around. I must really stress the importance of him showing up."

"I will do my best to ensure he shows."

Though Edward smiled, his tone was foreboding. "You had better, George. Because this is not an invitation, or a suggestion. It's a subpoena, which means he has a responsibility to show up or face consequences which I can assure you would be severe. Danny is not an only child. Far from it. He also has a mother, in addition to you as his father. All of you stand to be affected. Am I making myself clear?"

"Yes, sir."

"Good. You are dismissed." Without another word, Edward gestured to the door. George would get no more warnings. Edward had been clear enough. George kept his head up as he walked out, though deep down he felt as if he had been hanging his head in helplessness and shame.

George spent the rest of the day staring at the subpoena. Edward had not even done him the courtesy of giving him much work to do, though George was not allowed to go home early.

As he stole a glance or two from across their offices, Scott thought many times of going to talk to George, but he didn't know where to begin. He couldn't say that it would be okay. He didn't have the power to do so, and truth be told, it likely was not going to be okay. "Besides," Howard reminded him, "it really was not our fucking problem." Even if George didn't, they still had work to do. Howard had already had to give Adam a hard time about being more focused on work than daydreaming. He shouldn't have to do so with Scott.

Was there any way for Danny to avoid testifying? George spent most of the rest of the work day conjuring up scenarios. George had long ago stopped caring about himself and his own life. He also suspected that Danny had a bit of a martyr streak in him, as he did about Gregory. There were still others, though—Maria, for one, and two more children, including one under eighteen. George also wouldn't put it past Edward to target Adam as well and Karl and his family, if he hadn't already.

Enough, George thought to himself. He really was getting himself far too worked up. Or was he? The point was that Danny was not the only one who would be affected if he did not testify. He likely was not the only one affected if he did testify, too, however. George used to go over the idea in his mind to leave, fleeing to the United States even if they had to stay with Thomas. He had given up those thoughts though as outlandish and dangerous fools' errands. He hadn't even mentioned them to Gregory, yet he found himself, if only for a moment, wishing he had.

Thinking *the hell with Howard* as he did so, Adam went to check in on George.

"Sir," he said timidly as he knocked and then entered to find a very frazzled man. "Is there anything I can do for you?"

George's hair was a ruffled mess from how he had literally been tearing at it throughout the day. He had had his head in his hands but did his best to sit up straight once he permitted Adam to enter. "I… thank you, Adam, but no." That was not all he had to say to the disappointingly helpless young man, however. "My family, though, they'll surely need you. Danny especially." George looked up at Adam sheepishly, as if he ever needed to feel embarrassed in front of this young man who practically idolized him. "I must admit I haven't figured out exactly what I'm going to do. I know Danny doesn't want to testify, that he's afraid he'll implicate himself, and that even I won't be able to save him then. But I fear it'll be worse if he does not."

Adam spoke with a smile that tried so hard to be encouraging. "If anyone can figure this out, I believe it's you, sir. With some help, of course." George caught on that he was referring to Gregory.

Adam stayed with George until five o'clock rolled around, at which point Edward chased him out of the office to let George know personally it was time for him to head home. He had important things to discuss with his family, after all.

***

George parked far down near the end of the driveway, trudging up and into the doorway in an almost trance-like state. No rush was needed. Danny was not even home from the bookstore yet. George couldn't say whether he preferred this or not.

Maria *was* home, however, as were the girls.

"Well, George, what is it? Why do you look as if you've seen a ghost."

George supposed he did look that way. Perhaps he should have tried to not look as distressed as he felt. He did not answer right away, instead looking to Cassandra. She was no doubt as eager as her mother, but she could be counted on to take Amelia.

Once she had done so, George was truly out of excuses. "What is it, George? Oh, please tell me, you're frightening me," she pleaded.

"I'm afraid you have reason to be frightened, Maria." George wondered why he said such a thing. She, of course, did not react too well.

"What? What happened? You *must* tell me."

George instead showed her. He took the subpoena out of his breast pocket, already fraying at the creases from the number of times George had held it in his hands as he stared at it.

"I-I don't understand. What is this?"

"You read it, Maria. I shouldn't have to explain it to you." He was losing his patience with her, especially when it looked as if she would force him to repeat what he could not bear to. Her look convinced him he had to speak up. "Oh, fine, dammit! Our son is being subpoenaed to testify before my committee hearing. If you think I have any say in the manner, think again!"

There was a heavy silence, though soon enough George could hear Maria softly crying. "I'm sorry for raising my voice to you," George said, though his tone was still slightly harsh.

Since Maria did not seem fit for much conversation unless it was yelling through tears, George continued on answering what he assumed she would ask. "I did talk to Edward about this. It's… mandatory that Danny show up. He told me there would be consequences for all of us if he doesn't. I-I don't know what to do, Maria! If I thought there was any way to shield our son from this, you know I would. I'm desperate, though, Maria."

"Desperate about what?" Danny walked in at that moment.

For some reason, George began to get angry at Danny. "I'll have you know, young man, that whatever situation you've gotten yourself into has gotten the attention of my department. You'll be testifying. This week. I can try to help you with this, but you *must* speak with me. Otherwise I can't do a damned thing."

Maria put a hand on George's shoulder. He was starting to raise his voice again.

Danny's lip started to quiver. "Are… are you serious? No, you can't be. This has got to be a joke. Oh, we were careful, so careful. And now you want me to tell you what's been going on? When I have to testify? No. No fucking way."

"Danny," Maria chided, not being able to stand that kind of language, no matter the circumstance. It also was likely not to help things with George and his temper.

"No, mom, stop. I have to say this to dad. He wants to hear from me? Okay, here it is. I can't talk to you, or plan with you, or tell you *anything* about my life. It's why I've turned to Uncle Gregory. It's why I've never told you anything. And your job has only made it worse!"

"Danny, you know that with my job I can't–"

Danny was tired of the excuses, though. "Enough! I'm so sick and tired of hearing about this job! I thought if anything it would give us perks, protections. Instead it's just made everything a whole fucking lot worse." Danny had cursed again. "I'm sorry, mom, but really, come *on*."

Maria didn't bother trying to interject anymore.

"I tried to let you talk to me," George pleaded. I know I haven't always been approachable, especially these past two years. But wouldn't talking to me *before* we had a subpoena to deal with been that much more preferable?'

Danny chewed on his lip rather than concede to his father's point. Right as George was, Danny could not acknowledge it. He didn't say anything to protest it, however.

In such a moment, Danny recognized the truth. Perhaps he had waited too long, but that meant it was too late then. If Danny was already going to be forced to speak before the committee in three days' time, then why bother letting his father win with a heart-to-heart conversation now? Danny simply didn't think George deserved the luxury of being privy to what he had planned with Gregory.

Danny also wasn't even sure if he was going to the committee hearing, subpoena be damned. There had to be a way out of this. It wasn't that Danny didn't worry about how his siblings and mother would be affected, so much as he trusted his father to do whatever it took to protect *them* at least.

Yes, Danny was being selfish and stubborn. He could acknowledge that much, but he couldn't be bothered to care much beyond that. He was far too angry and determined.

Was this a bluff? Perhaps it was. Danny was going to let his father decide if he would call it.

"What happens if I don't show up?" Danny finally asked, never answering his father's initial question.

Maria wondered the same thing, though she looked to George to answer the both of them.

George was flummoxed. He had already been through the same question with Edward. George didn't know the answer to that question. What he did know was that none of them would like it. Danny might as well go on the run if he wasn't going to show up for the subpoena. George didn't mention that part though, lest Danny take it seriously.

"Bad things. Very bad things. Why don't you use your imagination if you want to know more than that? I don't know the specifics, but your guess is likely as good as mine." George didn't think he had to say more.

"Fuck you, dad." With that, Danny went up to his room and slammed the door.

Maria was beside herself, though George waved any reactions off. If it meant Danny was going to show up, he would take whatever was thrown at him in the meantime.

"The only other option is he runs away. I think you know that, Maria. That wouldn't be a good thing. Once Edward found him…" Maria just nodded her understanding. She didn't need to hear George remind her how Edward could further threaten their family.

"I need to go call my brother. Feel free to call yours." Without another word, George headed to his office, leaving a distraught and devastated Maria without any comfort or direction.

There was no beating around the bush. George immediately dialed his brother, who fortunately picked up on one of the first rings. "Your nephew will be testifying on Friday. He's been subpoenaed. I had no choice in the matter."

Gregory had barely been able to ask what the reasons for calling were this time. George seemed to be on a mission, and it seemed best to not interrupt.

It was a relief to not have to emphasize imagined consequences. Once George believed Gregory had heard him, he hung up to discuss the matter with Maria. It was inevitable that he would have to talk with his wife, he supposed.

Instead, George came out to discover Cassandra. He had almost forgotten about the girls. She had brought Amelia downstairs to their mother, but Cassandra had hoped for some clarity from her father. Now she would see her gamble pay off.

"You seem awfully distressed, daddy. Are you all right?"

Oh, how thoughtful Cassandra was with her father. Anyone else could say that George was distressed. It was her thoughtful tone and her concern which spoke to him, though.

"I… I will be, my dear. You're too kind to think of me. Thank you, my Cassandra."

He had answered her question, which he knew was genuine, but George also could sense this was her way of politely asking what was going on. They would discuss it at dinner, he assured her.

Dinner that night was a family affair that Danny refused to be a part of. It was just as well not to have to deal with his outbursts and interruptions. George was able to fill Cassandra and Amelia in by explaining that their older brother had to come do something for their father's job. He told his precious girls that he believed he could at least count on them to be good and help their mother out.

George could hardly have been more relieved about dinner. There were no arguments to be had, no shouting or cursing. Cassandra and Amelia merely nodded. Those who were the most calm about the situation were the ones who knew the least. Oh, how George envied them and their innocence. He hoped it was something they could continue to hold onto for years to come, even through this series of hellish situations.

Dinner had begun and ended late, and it was time for the children to go to sleep soon after. Danny was still not gracing them with his presence; he had even ignored Cassandra's knocking at his door. He did the same with Maria, though George supposed he couldn't blame his wife for trying. He figured he would start on making calls to other committee members ahead of the hearing; Danny was not the only one on the list whose testimony they would have to hear.

It was nearly midnight when George joined Maria in bed. She had waited up for him, hoping that the calmer atmosphere would allow him to speak freely. Her reasons were not entirely selfless, as she did expect George to fill her in with more details as to what, exactly, the department had in store for their son.

"He'll come in at about ten o'clock in the morning and stay until there are no more questions. Edward is giving me a list of questions and the direction he wants it to go. I imagine other department members have their own things to ask. Then the senators who are favored enough by the administration will speak. Then the delegates. It… it could go on for many hours, Maria. I want you to be aware of that."

Maria nodded. The lights were out but she was close up against him enough where he could sense her response. She sincerely prayed he would be patient with her as she asked the 'what if.' Maria wasn't trying to make an already impossible situation more difficult on her husband, but she needed to know what their options were, even if they were too terrible to consider further. "What will happen if he doesn't show up, George?"

He sighed. Maria could handle that much, at least. "Edward never told me specifics. But it will be bad for Danny and our family. Failure to show up for a subpoena usually means prison time. I know more than anyone how stubborn our son is, but he *will* eventually have to come before the committee. If Danny refuses to go in, the first place they'll look for him is here, then at Adam's and then possibly even at my brother's. I'm sure Edward will send his nephew and Howard, though he himself may take an interest in personally seeking out Danny. Might as well bypass Edward as much as we possibly can and just pray if we get it over with that this will all go away."

Maria felt disquieted hearing of such scenarios, though its coming from George also comforted her in a sense. "What will you do in all of this, George? Will you help him?"

George was saddened more than he could say, though not entirely surprised that Maria had to ask. "Maria," he said, sitting up and turning towards her. "I will do everything in my power and then some. It is imperative that Danny tells us he has had no involvement with planning any past, present or future coups. He should likely swear off all involvement with my brother and certainly with yours. I may be only one man with my hands tied daily by Edward and the department, but I am his father, and as your husband, I promise you that I will do as much as I can to make sure he gets out of this situation as cleanly as possible.

George did not get to say that he hoped Danny would do his utmost before Maria sat up to kiss him. He didn't need to.

In some ways George was surprised they made love. It had been months since they felt that deep enough connection, despite the shared pain they had. Maria had been trying hard to remind her husband he wasn't as alone as he often felt. George had a feeling it would be the last time before things took an even worse turn.

A Lesson And The Hearing

Danny felt as though he was living a non-existence over the next few days. His father felt the same, yet the two could not unify in their distress. It would take a near-tragedy for that to happen.

It was as a favor to his mother that Danny spoke with George, though ultimately Danny would admit to himself that it was beneficial for them to have their stories straight, namely that he was to deny involvement in any coup, no matter what.

Even if they could not truly be comfortable with one another, they could at least be on the same page, that Danny refusing to show was a non-option. It was too risky. As dreaded as the idea of spending hours testifying was to Danny, the thought of being hunted down by Edward Roth was worse.

If Danny wished for the days to slow down, he was out of luck. Friday came sooner than it ever had for him. Then it was time to show himself before a crowd of people Danny despised. They were the whole reason Danny was actually planning a coup, though he of course could not let a soul be the wiser.

George left early that morning. It didn't matter if the hearing was at ten in the morning or in the evening. He needed to be out of the house and preparing himself for something he dreaded almost as much as Danny did. It was true that the questions were already prepared in advance for George, but any added or omitted questions, any particular tone, *anything* that was a reflection of his free will could land him and his family in hot water.

By seven AM, George was out the door and Maria and Danny were both awake. With a plan to leave the house at nine in the morning, the doorbell's ringing at half past seven was cause for great concern.

Maria tried to shoo Danny away as she answered the door, though he missed any hints.

Scott and Howard were there to pick up Danny. As Danny shrunk back into the parlor, Maria did her best to play dumb.

"I'm sorry, gentlemen, but my husband is not here. He has already left."

"We're not looking for Deputy Director Whitfield," Howard said, expressing annoyance at both the early hour and the time this was taking.

"We've come for your son, Danny. We need him to come with us, Mrs. Whitfield, now." Scott's tone was much more sympathetic, guilt-ridden even, but it didn't change Danny's being caught off-guard.

He had promised his father he would show up to the hearing. He hadn't thought about fleeing in days, yet Danny found himself briefly considering it. *Had they seen him already? If not, would his mother cover for him? How was he supposed to communicate such a plan to her, one he hadn't even fully thought up yet?*

One look at his mother, though, so helpless and desperate, reminded Danny that he couldn't run, he couldn't put her and the girls at risk like that. He would have to go with these men. He would have to show up at headquarters, likely without a moment to prepare.

His mother was able to get Danny five minutes.

It was just enough time to brush his teeth and throw on some clothes. Danny thought about peeking into the girls' rooms so that he could say goodbye, but in the end, he decided otherwise.

His five minutes were up all too soon. Scott had allowed Danny his time to get ready and relented when Mrs. Whitfield asked for a moment to say goodbye to her son. "Then he really must come with us," he reminded her.

Scott wasn't looking forward to the day as it was. He didn't want to have to pull the two of them apart. While it was something Howard would do, Scott hoped it wouldn't come to that.

Danny wished there were something he could say, something he could impart to his mother. As frightened as he was feeling as he embraced her, he wanted to feel strong for her. Saying his goodbyes, Danny told his mother not to worry. The situation would handle itself.

He was not allowed to take his own car to follow them to headquarters. Instead Danny was practically tossed into the backseat. Scott rode up front as Howard drove, speeding out of the driveway like their lives depended on it.

With so many possibilities running through his mind, Danny felt as if he were a lamb being led to the slaughter. Maybe he was; he couldn't say for certain. That was when he began to regret not saying goodbye to his siblings. He even thought, once more, of fleeing, though he didn't know how or when.

The ride to headquarters was a silent one. Danny had known Howard and Scott through high school and some college, and he knew Howard rarely shut up. It was possible it was because it was so early in the morning, but Danny feared the more likely answer was the severity of the situation. What normally took less than an hour to drive from the Whitfield residence to headquarters felt like several.

Being told nothing, Danny assumed he was merely being brought in early for questioning before the committee. So when Howard started to slow down at a side entrance of headquarters, it felt as if alarm bells were going off at full volume.

Danny's demands to know what was going on went unanswered. Danny *knew* they could hear him; Scott's face even wore the slightest amount of conflict. All anyone said to him was to not even think about calling out for help. It actually looked best for Danny to keep his mouth shut.

Except Danny wasn't going to take such advice. "You had better tell me what's going on and where you're taking me, right now," Danny said before any of them could get out of the car.

"Listen real close, asshole, because I'm only going to say this once. Do you hear me?" It wasn't a rhetorical question, and Howard waited until he got confirmation from Danny before continuing. "We came to get you to bring you to headquarters. Yes, the hearing starts at ten, but Director Roth wanted to talk to you beforehand. Call it pre-hearing testimony, if you will."

No. No, this couldn't be happening. They weren't bringing him in to testify, they were bringing him in for an interrogation. *Did his father know about this?* He doubted it. *How long would this last? Would he be late to the hearing? Would that screw everything up? So many questions.*

Howard wasn't going to answer any of them. He had already told Danny plenty, as far as he was concerned, and he elbowed Scott into not saying anything either. Danny would be meeting with Director Roth soon enough. Let *him* answer questions.

"Let's go, then," Howard said as he got out and opened the door for Danny. He also reminded Danny there were ways he could force the youngster to comply if need be, but that it would be easiest, for Danny especially, if he just went with them the first time he was told to, especially since Howard wasn't asking.

Howard was right, though Danny hated to admit it. Any hope he might have had that morning was quickly vanishing. Danny suspected it would be completely gone soon.

The room they led him to was cold and gray. If it didn't look like an interrogation room, Danny didn't know what did. There was a chair in the middle of the room where Danny was told to have a seat. Their job done, Howard and Scott stood off to the side. The show would begin soon, as its star performer, Director Edward Roth, was just arriving.

"Young Mr. Whitfield, so good of you to join us."

"Did I have a choice?" Danny asked, hoping his question wasn't taken as rhetorical.

"Well, no," Edward said as he loosened his tie and rolled up his sleeves. Danny forced himself not to think about why he was doing that. "But you're not putting up a fight does make this easier for everyone. I suspect you'd like things to go easy here, Danny?"

"What I'd like to know is why I'm even here."

Edward thought carefully as to how to answer, pacing around Danny as he did so. It unnerved Danny, though he supposed that was the point. "I know you must know something about the coup, Danny. If not the previously failed one, surely ones in the future. I had thought your father could handle being the one to ask, but I've come to my own conclusions that it's really for the best if it's you and me."

So many thoughts were running through Danny's mind. *Had his father been trying to help him? Was he still going to testify?* Danny finally began to realize how much his father did care for and wish to help him, but it was too late.

"How does that sound, Danny?" The question was not rhetorical.

"Well, I'm sorry to say that I don't know a blessed thing about any of these coups. Even if I did, I wouldn't tell you."

"Well, you're right about one thing," Edward said as he suddenly and without warning slapped Danny across the face. Hard. "You are going to be sorry, especially if you don't give me the answers that I want, and when I want them."

Danny was stunned. No one had ever slapped him before. It was to be the first, but certainly not the last of that day. He didn't look up until Edward made him do so, grabbing Danny's chin so that he was forced to look at the older man. "Tell me what I want to hear and we can forget all about using force, any testifying or anything of the sort."

Though he wasn't looking forward to it, Danny had prepared for this. He was going to stick to his planned script that he knew nothing about any coups in the past or future. He had to, for many lives could depend on it, including Gregory's. Besides, Danny was sure that Edward was lying, lulling him into a false sense of security. Perhaps Danny could have avoided that by being compliant from the start, but there was no guarantee, and it was already too late.

Edward went about answering for Danny then. "I'd say that sounds fair. It's certainly a deal *I* would take."

Danny didn't think before he answered. "Well, too fucking bad. I'm not you." Such a line earned him another slap across the face, harder than the previous one.

"I bet you want to know what that was for," Edward said with a grin as Danny clutched his cheek. As Danny nodded, Edward gave him yet another still harder slap. "Such language will not be tolerated. I'm sure you'll learn your lesson soon enough though, especially with my methods."

Danny could feel his heart sink into the pit of his stomach at such chilling words. He was afraid of this man, yes, but he had to have prepared for that. If he didn't, it was his own fault. He knew of the risks of getting involved, but Danny also knew of the rewards if they succeeded.

Danny would find out soon enough. Besides the chair where Danny was seated, there was a table and in the table was a drawer and in the drawer was a whole damning pile of evidence. The file Adam had gotten George was there, though more complete. There were also pictures of Danny meeting with suspicious characters. The phone records for phone calls made with Gregory Whitfield and Thomas Campbell were perhaps the worst.

"This is what we're dealing with here. This is the evidence I already have right in front of me. This is why I ultimately decided you and I would have a little chat besides the committee getting to have their go at you for a few hours. As head of the department, a department dedicated to keeping our citizens safe, such is my right."

Danny couldn't believe he was talking about rights. "What about *my* rights?" he questioned in another outburst. This time when the slap came he barely even flinched. It still stung, but he was just getting used to it.

"You have the right, no, the *responsibility* to remain truthful, if you want to get out of here."

Danny sighed. He had some thinking to do. It wasn't about if he was going to give up his uncles or any of his friends. He just wouldn't, no matter the evidence against him. *Was there a way though in which Danny could tell Director Roth enough which, despite being nothing, could still sound like something? Once he did, would Danny actually get to say his piece before the committee? Or was it all just a sham?*

In fact, Danny must have been on autopilot when mentioning he didn't believe Roth. "So the hell with you," he even threw in for good measure. That warranted another slap. Danny wondered if his face was going to be as red as it felt by the time he was allowed to see his father.

Edward took a step back, thinking, considering how to proceed. He smiled as he spoke. "Don't you worry, Danny. I'll find a way to break you. If nothing else, I will teach you a lesson. I want to try an easy question here. Now, why don't you tell me when you last spoke with your uncle?"

"My uncle?"

"Yes," he said, losing patience. "Gregory, your father's brother."

Danny told him when. He couldn't have forgotten that phone call if he tried. It would be burned into his memory. Except for whatever reason, even if it was the truth, Edward did not like that. For this time, without warning, he punched Danny in the stomach. He knew he shouldn't have been, but Danny was caught off guard, and was left in pain from a blow that had knocked the wind out of him.

Standing off to the side, Scott and Howard were all but forgotten. Howard was bored, but Scott preferred it this way. He didn't want to be there at all, watching his uncle use threats against anyone else, not after what he had seen and grown up with. No matter what Howard thought, it wasn't because he wanted to be Danny's friend. Scott was just sick and tired of the violence.

"What was that for? I was telling you the truth," Danny whimpered. Again he was punched, the wind knocked out of him once more, just as he had caught his breath. "But I was!"

"Then why," Edward asked, his fists clutching a stack of papers, does it say that you contacted him not even four days ago, hm?" He waved a sheet of paper right in Danny's face. "I assure you, Danny, the questions will only get harder."

So where he had been willing to tell the truth he wasn't believed. It was just as he was feared. Danny began to prepare himself for the worst then. In a way, it gave him a release, though. It was as if somehow God was confirming that he might as well keep lying.

What resulted was pain and anguish. Danny was going to suffer, Edward would see to that.

***

It wasn't Danny losing a tooth that got Edward to let up on him, though Edward decided they could all use a break. It was the sound of a cell phone ringing, not for the first time. It was finally becoming distracting enough. The time was seven minutes past ten o'clock. He may have been there for hours at that point, but Danny was late to the hearing, and George had feared he had failed to show. If only his father knew where he was.

After chastising his nephew for not turning the phone off and handing it over to him before this all began, Edward took the cell phone from Scott.

"Call your father back," Edward said, handing it over to Danny. The boy's hands were trembling so badly he could barely hold the phone, though he managed. Danny had no idea what he would say to his father, as he was no longer able to think that far ahead.

Having no idea that his son was actually in the same building and had been for hours, George was none too happy. "Danny. Where the hell are you?"

Tried as he did to avoid it, Danny couldn't entirely mask his pain. "Dad," he managed to choke out before collapsing into a fit of coughs as he felt the need to spit up more blood than what he had already just gotten rid of.

"Danny? What is it? What's happened to you?" Gone was George's livid tone. He was panic-stricken.

It was Edward who took over answering. "He's been with me, George." Maria's fear had been correct then, George thought, immediately wracked with guilt for how he had ignored her calls and not responded to her text messages. "You see, you failed to inspire enough confidence in your ability to conduct the hearing satisfactorily, so I took matters into my own hands. Danny has been… less than cooperative, to put it politely, and that mouth he has on him. I'm sure your wife does not approve of it. Alas, I've tried to get through to him to see how he could in fact be helping his country instead of acting as a dangerous criminal, but he seems unwilling to be reasoned with."

Edward had put the phone on speaker, for practical reasons as well as to evoke a reaction. George could thus hear his son, sitting there as he cried, tired, beaten and broken down. If his ability to conduct hearings was called into question by Edward, George did not know what hope he had to get his son out of this. That, truly, was George's biggest fear.

"What… what should I do? I'll do anything. Just tell me what to do, Edward, please."

In normal circumstances, Danny would have felt disgust and outrage at the amount his father was fawning over such an evil man. Not too long ago, George would have felt shame for the man he had become. These were anything but normal circumstances, though.

"Call your next witness. There may have been a slight change in the testimony scheduling today, but surely that is something you can handle, George. Your son will be upstairs shortly." Without another word, Edward hung up the phone. "Now," he said, in an almost sickeningly cheerful tone, "why don't we call your mother? I think we shall. I'm sure she'd love to hear from you."

Danny couldn't help it. He burst into tears at the thought of his mother even just hearing him in such a bad way. "Please, no."

"Oh, yes, yes, yes. She's called far too many times already, and we mustn't have her wondering and worrying for much longer." Without another word, Edward went through Danny's phone and into the call log and found his mother.

"Oh, Danny, where are you? I've been so worried. Why haven't you called me back? It's past ten, aren't you supposed to be at the hearing?"

Almost more than the punches and the slaps, Danny felt pain from his mother's worry. She didn't need to tell him; he could just tell she was beside herself.

As much as he wanted to break down, it was necessary that Danny remain composed. Edward signaled for him to tell his mother that the hearing was starting later.

"Mom, I'm going to be going in a little bit later. Things just got switched around a bit. But I'm okay. I'm really okay."

Danny had not provided her with sufficient answers, this he knew. He also wasn't sure if he sounded as okay as he claimed to be. Since Danny was not directed to say anything more, he ended the conversation. He refused to put his mother through any more stress and pain.

Edward likewise picked up on Danny cutting the conversation short, despite not being told to do so. Once Mrs. Whitfield was off the line, however, he wasn't going to bother with getting her back. In deciding what to do with the phone, he gave it to neither Scott nor Danny, but tossed it to the ground, where it got a shiny new crack. Danny would be lucky if it still worked at all, especially if Edward decided Danny wouldn't even be getting the phone back in one piece.

"All right, it's nearly ten-fifteen. Get up, then. Move. Let's go." Danny's weakness mattered not to his tormentors, except for one. Scott very nearly spoke up to point out that the number of times Danny had been hit was bound to slow him down, but with an elbow to his ribs and a pointed glare, Howard warned him to keep quiet.

At such a pace, it was already after half past ten before they made it to the committee hearing. Danny almost had to laugh as to how just hours before he had been trying to decide what he would be wearing. His mother wanted him to wear a button-down shirt. Danny didn't think it quite mattered anymore, as whatever it once had been, it was now blood-stained.

It was not just his father who was going to see Danny like this but a whole committee of men and women hand-selected by Edward Roth, mostly senators, delegates and some department members. Blood was not merely staining his shirt but had come from his nose, his lip and his presently black and partially swollen shut right eye.

Danny also couldn't hold it together. He couldn't stop crying. Everything had just come crashing down so much. Whether Danny spoke the truth or not, he wasn't believed. He was damned if he did, damned if he didn't.

Upon seeing his son in such a state, George wanted nothing more than to envelop Danny in a protective embrace. He was not there for such a purpose, however. He was there to conduct hearings, and that meant banging the gavel to quiet everyone down as he prepared to ask his own son about involvement in past or future coups.

"The upcoming witness will be Daniel Whitfield," George said. His voice just barely shook. Danny was being shoved into the witness chair by Edward.

What followed for the next three and a half hours was the same question, just asked in different ways. Danny continued to deny that he had planned or was planning a coup, that he had had recent contact with either of his uncles or anyone else on a terror watch list. Little did Danny know that his name was at the top of such a similar list. No matter how the question was thrown at him, from whomever it came from, Danny's answer remained the same. Sometimes it came with tears, sometimes with clearer eyes. Sometimes immediately, sometimes with some hesitation, but always the same answer.

George didn't know whether to believe his son, but that wasn't what he cared about. He cared about keeping Danny safe, as he had promised Maria, Cassandra, Gregory and himself he would do.

As was customary, George allowed Danny his closing remarks. "I-I just want to say that I acknowledge my remarks and sentiments against this department may have caused such suspicion. But I am not involved with, nor have I ever been involved with, planning a coup against Director Edward Roth or Deputy Director George Whitfield, my own father. I've never wanted anyone to get hurt, I do mean that with all my heart." Danny was beginning to tear up now. "I've said my piece, and I'd really just like to go… if… if that's all right."

No matter how the hearing ended, Danny couldn't bear even just the thought of returning to being interrogated by Edward Roth. He didn't think he could afford to have to worry about losing any more teeth. *His father wouldn't let that happen, would he?*

George couldn't do anything to turn back the clock and save Danny from those abuses hours prior. He could make sure there would be no more.

Finished with closing statements, George quickly adjourned the meeting and rushed over to Danny, embracing him as he had wished to do so many hours ago. Fortunately the physical contact wasn't too oppressive on Danny's body. It was even welcoming.

Danny was terrified of letting go of his father, though he eventually did. Of all his thoughts about his father's career, Danny prayed in such a moment George would be able to use his position to help him, as his son.

If Danny wanted to get out of there in no worse shape, he was going to have to provide some answers, ones which Edward wanted to hear. He could look at it as living to fight another day. That meant providing names of other possible conspirators and soon, with the possibility of continued informing.

Had Danny been brought up with such an idea hours earlier, he would have said thank you very much, but no fucking way. Presently at the top of Danny's mind was getting out of there. They could stand around in the committee chambers all day long, but Edward was not releasing Danny until he received assurances.

Danny fervently wished he could have the counsel of Gregory, Thomas or Adam. Right now all he had was his father, who was telling him to take the deal.

Had he been facing the same situation days, even hours earlier, it was possible Danny would have had the audacity to laugh in Edward's face. That was before he was made to realize just how little his status as his father's son meant, especially when Edward was able to broach the subject as being about preventing a future coup and thus about national security. George knew that Edward had been given full discretion for interrogation methods from the president; never did he think, though, that they'd be used against his own son. They had both been fooled, and yet George figured he shouldn't have been as surprised as he was. Heartbroken, yes, but not surprised.

Feeling ashamed in addition to broken and bloody, Danny promised to inform. It was just as well he'd stopped talking to his uncles. They'd never get anything on Gregory and Thomas—not from Danny, at least. Yet he never believed he would end up even agreeing to such a deal. That was before Director Edward Roth had taught him a lesson.

Such A Day Makes For A Harrowing Evening

It was still afternoon when Danny was released. He had had no concept of time or day. George feared a concussion, but Danny swore off being bothered with medical intervention.

Once he was released, there was only one place Danny wanted to go. It was Adam's.

Danny knew his father would want him home, that his mother was worried sick. Danny could barely think straight but he knew he just wanted to be with Adam. He needed a place to figure out his thoughts, and right now Adam's was the best place for that. Even though Edward had released him, Danny still had a feeling that Edward could change his mind, have Danny picked up again in just a few short hours and then for God knows how long. Danny realized he was likely being paranoid, but he didn't care. He had to get to Adam's.

Adam had been sent home early by Edward, which at the time was inexplicable to him, though it would come to make sense. Edward did not wish for Danny to have even a hint of Adam's comforting presence.

Danny did not care how he got to Adam's. He would walk if he had to, though he hoped it would not be necessary. George was willing to take Danny anywhere he wanted to go.

Part of Danny worried about getting blood all over his father's car, as he had where he been sitting while testifying and then in his father's office. That was why Edward had them meeting in George's office. Danny muttered something to the effect of how he felt bad, but

George hushed him. After confirming that Danny did not wish to go to the hospital and definitely did not wish to go home, George agreed to take him to Adam's. Danny gave him the okay to call first.

It was a short drive from headquarters to Adam's, where he lived in the house his parents had left to him when he was just barely an adult. George hadn't said much during the phone call, which almost made it more alarming.

"There's been an incident. Danny is hurt. He wants to come to you." Adam had barely said okay before George hung up. There were no questions.

Part of the reason for such a quick conversation, besides how Adam would soon see Danny for himself, was because Maria had tried calling yet again. George made sure to pick up this time. He had no fewer than ten missed calls from her. He chided himself for not calling her right away, but George, too, had been unable to think clearly.

"Where is my son?" she practically sobbed to her husband. "Where is he? What's going on? Oh, George, how could this have happened?"

Maria didn't need to say it, for George already knew. He was very likely to blame.

"There… there has been an incident. He's all right now, though. He's safe with me. I'm taking him to Adam's." George tried to keep his voice calm and steady, difficult though that was. His knuckles were practically white from clutching the steering wheel so tightly.

"Adam's? Why not here?" Her voice was becoming hysterical once more.

Fortunately, Danny spared his father from answering. He had to clear his throat, even though the strain greatly pained him. He could not bear letting his mother worry any further. "It's okay, mom. I asked dad to take me. I need… that's where I need to be. Please, mom, *please* try to understand."

There was a moment of silence. George hoped it would end soon.

Maria did for him. "I will have you home, safe and sound, where you belong, by tomorrow morning. Is that understood?" Danny quietly murmured it was, though that was not enough for Maria. "Is that understood, Danny? George?"

"Yes," both men answered her. "Maria, I will call once I've dropped him off," George relayed, and then, he hung up.

Adam was waiting at the end of his driveway when George pulled up.

Practically jumping out of the car, George went to let Danny out, wanting his son to exert himself as little as possible.

Adam had prepared himself, or so he thought. But Danny looked *bad.* Something had indeed happened to his friend. From the looks of how fresh Danny's injuries had been, it had been practically right under Adam's nose, while he worked, unaware. Honestly, the prospect terrified him. He did not have time to revel in his thoughts, however. His friend needed him. As he looked at George, Adam could sense that his boss needed him and his calm presence as well. He would save his questions for another time.

George wanted to go in with them, but Danny insisted his father had done enough. It wasn't that he was angry at his father or blamed him, even if George couldn't help blaming himself. It was simply that he wanted to be around Adam and only Adam.

Adam searched for the words as George looked helplessly on, though he eventually recovered himself. "Go ahead," Adam said. "We'll be in touch later."

The first order of business for Adam was getting Danny inside. He was such a wreck that Adam half-feared he would pass out on the stoop. Like George, Adam found himself wishing Danny would let him take him to the hospital, but he knew it would be pointless to ask.

"You'll be safe here," Adam reassured Danny as he coaxed him inside.

"I know. That's why I came," Danny said.

***

Edward had not only sought to teach Danny a lesson but to send a message to George. That message was received. The title that George had was merely that, a title. He had been punished with being forced to relocate, with a drop in social credit status, and now his son had to pay the price for being involved with yet another coup. George cursed aloud in the car. Edward had made his life, at work and now home too, such a living Hell. Edward had seen George's ambition and squashed it like a bug.

George didn't dwell much on the attempted coup, especially since he truly had had nothing to do with it on either side. He found himself thinking of it now, however, and wondered what would have happened if he had agreed to help Edward snuff out any dissent. *Would he have succeeded? Would he himself have been targeted? Or would Edward still have found some reason to see him punished?* George told himself it was likely the latter, which was why he barely entertained such notions and hadn't in years.

Now that George *was* thinking of involving himself, it had to be when his own son was involved. Though he hoped Danny would at least consider the deal of providing Edward with information about the latest coup, deep down George knew that Danny was likely just saying so to be released. He would probably have said anything to get himself out of there. His son hadn't had his wits about him.

While George wished Danny would come home with him, he knew that his son was safe with Adam. He was more focused on his wife and daughters now anyway.

***

As Adam helped his friend into the house, Danny did all he could to avoid seeing any reflection of himself. He hadn't seen what he looked like while still at headquarters. He didn't want to know. Danny realized he couldn't go as long as he wished without coming into contact with a mirror, but for right now, he was determined.

Adam had been striving to not overreact lest it make Danny more nervous. His friend was a sight to see. Adam could hardly be more enraged at the bastards who had done this. What made Adam all the more fitting a person to care for him at this time, though, was how Adam was used to himself looking as Danny looked now, from getting picked on at school and from being an outlet for his father at home. This thought crossed Danny's mind, but only briefly. He did not wish to think of anything more unpleasant than what was already before them.

After a painfully long amount of time, Adam and Danny reached the couch. "Would you like to get cleaned up first, or would you like to explain to me what's happened?" Adam asked, emphasizing Danny did have choices. "You do look banged up, but I believe you'll start to look better in no time," Adam said, sharing a bit of honesty. What he left out was that the emotional scars would likely take longer to heal.

Danny examined himself for any fresh remnants of blood. "I'm not bleeding all over your couch, am I?"

Adam did his own examination and confirmed Danny was not. It wouldn't have mattered anyway. "It's just a couch," Adam assured his friend. "Would you prefer to get cleaned up in the bathroom, though?"

Even though the blood had dried, Danny's fingers, two of which were broken, had been particularly painful but were now almost numb.

Getting cleaned up now, though, in the bathroom where the first aid supplies meant that Danny would have to come across his reflection in the mirror that hung there. While Danny didn't feel entirely ready, he also didn't know, when, or if, he would be, and he reasoned it was best to just get it over with.

Adam once more helped guide Danny, this time to the bathroom. Danny could see himself quite clearly in the mirror; his eye, at least, wasn't swollen enough to prevent that. The face staring back at him was still enough to bring fresh tears to his eyes.

***

George dreaded arriving home, though his wife was stronger than he anticipated. Nevertheless, Maria still demanded to know what happened.

"Let's talk about this inside, please," George practically begged of Maria when she came outside to meet him.

"So long as you tell me right now where my son is and assure me that he is safe," she pleaded back.

"He is. He is safe. He's at Adam's." Maria nodded through the tears as they walked back up to the house.

George has not cleared the final hurdle yet. Amelia and Cassandra were inside, anxious and in anticipation for news. His daughters and his wife all looked as if they had been crying at some point.

"Right, we have a lot to discuss," George said, addressing them.

Such a day would indeed make for a harrowing evening, George thought, for neither the first nor the last time.

***

As Adam cleaned Danny up, he found out what had happened in the basement beneath him, all while he worked in his office, none the wiser. Even if he had had no way of knowing, that still didn't change how terrible Adam felt.

Danny told him he could barely remember the last time he was at home, which had been about half past seven that morning. He explained how Scott and Howard came to his house, how his mother answered the door and that she couldn't say no to him going with them. Danny nearly teared up as he implored Adam to believe him, as if there were a chance he wouldn't, that he was going to show up on his own. He was.

"I know, Danny. I know," Adam assured his friend, even though they both knew, deep down, what Adam thought didn't matter to Director Roth.

As Adam applied ointment around Danny's eye, nose and mouth, he tried to be gentle, though the young man still winced, mostly on reflex. "I'm sorry."

"It's okay. You have nothing to be sorry for, Adam. I don't see how you could ever be. You didn't do this."

"Edward Roth did, though," Adam quietly asked.

Danny nodded. "He let Howard give it a go at me, though Scott didn't want any part of it."

Adam closed his eyes against such a painful thought. Though Howard had never raised a fist to him personally, it was not something he wished to experience. The way Danny shared such details, it was almost as if Adam had been right there with him but powerless to stop any of the blows.

Adam could not let his mind wander even if he wanted to. Danny had more to tell him and it was important. Edward knew that Danny was involved in a potential coup, but worse, he thought there was a chance Danny had been involved in the previous one, when he had not been. He had had nothing to do with it. Edward also wanted names, as in he wanted Danny to incriminate his uncles, as if he could ever do such a thing. Even under great duress, Danny would not give them up, at least he didn't think so. He hoped to never get to the point of finding out, though Danny wasn't sure that was too likely. Adam assured Danny he knew this. He knew how loyal Danny was to his uncles, especially to Gregory. Things hadn't ended there for Danny, though. The only reason he was allowed to leave following the hearing was because he promised to inform for Director Roth. Danny was still trying to figure out how to get out of that one, though Adam alerted him he need not trouble himself in such a way, at least not now. That Danny could be brought in again or arrested if he did not give up names was a detail not forgotten, however.

There was a break in conversation as Adam went to tend to Danny's fingers. "Are you sure you don't want to go to the hospital," Adam asked, though he already knew the answer. Danny merely gave him a look. Though Adam apologized, it was not for looking out for his friend's best interest.

What Danny said next was enough to change Adam's focus. "You know, I think I really ought to turn to my dad for help."

While Danny may have been loath to admit such a revelation, Adam could hardly have been more relieved, especially since Danny had come to such a conclusion on his own. Danny could see how it affected his friend to hear that, for he knew how closely Adam and his father worked together. Adam worked under George, but it was much more than a boss and employee relationship. It was something deeper, like a friendship.

Danny was distracted from further thoughts about his dad and his best friend when he marveled at how quickly and effectively Adam had bandaged him up, something to be quite grateful for. Danny realized it was such an unpleasant, almost disturbing thought, because there was likely a reason behind Adam's precision. Danny wondered how many times Adam had had to clean himself up before with his own incidents. Danny didn't ask.

***

The first thing George did upon walking in to see his daughters expectedly waiting for him was to emphasize to them that Danny was safe at Adam's. He would figure it out with Adam when their brother would be home, which they all could hope would be in the morning.

Cassandra was a sensitive but also a wise soul. She would likely weep for her brother, but she could also be trusted to know the truth. At Amelia's tender age, George wasn't as certain what to tell his youngest child.

Sure enough, though, they wanted answers.

"Why is he at Adam's, though? What happened?"

"Please tell us, daddy," Cassandra chimed in. "Please. We just woke up to find him gone."

Regardless of what he said, George had to tell them something. "Your brother," he began, "had to go into where I work today and answer a lot of difficult questions for many hours. It was a very tiring experience for him, and he prefers to rest at Adam's. As I said, though, I do hope to have him home by tomorrow morning." Such statements did not constitute George lying, though he conveniently left out how their brother had been interrogated to the point of being in a sorry state.

Amelia merely nodded her understanding. The way in which Cassandra and Amelia looked up at George suggested they likely had an idea what he was hinting at.

George didn't know what more to say, and he found himself suddenly feeling most awkward and terribly self-conscious. He was thus going to go make some phone calls to Adam about when they could be expecting Danny at home, but also around headquarters, to see if anyone had any prior knowledge and, most importantly, to make sure that this never happened again. Before Maria could even ask, George let her know he wouldn't be at dinner that night. Such was expected, though disappointing.

"I'm going to make some phone calls. If you want me to fix this, as I know you do, then I'll need to be left alone." It was too late for George to decide if his tone and words had been necessary, for they were already said.

For some time, George just sat and stared at his phone. He was feeling bad, almost as if he had abandoned Maria and the girls when they were all concerned for Danny. The truth was, though, that George didn't wish for them to see him this way—anxious, guilty and feeling like a failure.

If he was going to try to settle this, he needed to be alone, however. He needed the space to think and the quiet to make his calls, which he would make. Which he *had* to make. It was also a moment's peace from any likely commotion. It wasn't merely Danny's interrogation which was the issue. Other troubling matters were affecting the family as well, including George fighting with Maria more than ever and in front of the children.

Please God, George couldn't help praying, even though he hardly prayed anymore. *Please, help me save my son. Help me be a good father and a good husband.*

Once that prayer was said, the first person George called was Adam. It went to voicemail, though that wasn't surprising. He was likely tending to Danny.

George next tried to call Karl. What he knew about the hearing would have been little, with working in another building. He certainly would not have known about the interrogation. George grimly thought how Karl was far away enough to where George no longer saw him on a regular basis, but he was still close by enough for Edward to harass.

Karl at least did George the service of coming to the phone, and George believed him when Karl said he had only just found out about the subpoena a few days prior. He knew nothing about Edward conducting an interrogation of Danny, though he promised to call if he found out anything further. He was at home that night, with Sarah, Jack and Emma. George hadn't asked, but was glad to hear that his friend was spending time with his wife and children.

It took a moment before George felt brave enough to call Edward's line. Though it was his office line, there was the possibility Edward would still be at work and would answer it. Then George would have to speak to the man who had not only issued a subpoena for his son but interrogated and beat him. What would George say? George wondered if he had had the courage to tell Edward that this was unacceptable, that he was not going to stand for such treatment, especially as the deputy director. It was because George was his deputy director, though, a job forced upon him, that he did not know if he could find such strength. Not for the first time that evening, George felt shame.

As it turned out, however, George would not be put to the test—not yet, at least. Edward, somewhat predictably, didn't pick up. George was brave enough, however, to leave a message requesting that Edward call him back.

Would George ever have the strength, the courage, in person or even over the phone? He would have to, he told himself, *if he wanted to be a good father, a good husband, a good provider*. He truly wanted to.

As George sat reflecting on this, he knew there was one more person he had to call. He had just called his brother earlier in the week, so he didn't see why it seemed like such an anxious prospect now. Perhaps it was because George feared Gregory would think him a failure as a father, for this especially, though not necessarily only for this.

George was stopped from calling Gregory at the first moment he considered doing so and thus was given a few more minutes to put it off. His phone rang. He was so surprised he almost jumped out of his seat. George only let it ring for a moment before answering.

"Yes, this is George Whitfield. Hello?" He had been too excited to check to see who was calling before he answered.

"Director Whitfield, sir, it's Adam. I'm sorry I missed your call."

"It's quite all right. How is he?"

Little did George know that just the moment before, Adam had to talk Danny out of a near panic attack at the thought of Adam calling his father. It was almost as if George didn't already know, as if what had happened was some great shame to be hidden away. Danny wished he could hide at Adam's forever, impractical though that would be.

Adam talked Danny down though, promising he wouldn't divulge any details to his father that Danny wasn't comfortable with. Adam had missed a call from George though while they were in the bathroom, and he figured he owed George the courtesy of calling back, especially when things were harried at home.

He put the call on speaker. Danny didn't have to participate unless he wanted to, and he could at least hear what Adam was telling his father.

"We're… he's going to be okay, Director Whitfield, sir," Adam said, hoping he was conveying even just the slightest amount of hope.

"Good. Thank God, Adam. And thank *you*. When do you think he'll be home? I'm sure Maria and the girls will want to know."

Adam nodded to Danny, who nodded back, before offering he would be bringing Danny home in the morning. "He really doesn't want to come home tonight, I'm sorry to say. He hopes you can all understand that."

George was disappointed but not surprised. "Ah, yes, I can understand. You're sure he'll be all right, Adam?"

Reasoning it would not take too much to answer, Danny spared Adam from having to do so. "I'm hanging in there, dad."

Such was as honest an answer as Danny could provide. He *was* hanging in there. He wasn't okay, but he would be. He had to believe that. Especially when having his father take him to Adam's had been the right decision.

George became emotional at hearing his son's voice. It was still hoarse from the hours spent at headquarters under less than ideal conditions. It was not just from crying out in pain and frustration, but from having to repeat the line, over and over, that he was not involved in any kind of coup against the department. His voice was starting to come back now, a good sign. George wished momentarily Adam had done a video call, so that he could soon his son. He had already seen him in the aftermath of Edward's questioning; any other instance of seeing him was surely to be an improvement. That would perhaps be too much for Danny, though.

"That… that's good to hear, Danny." George had to remind himself to speak up, lest they think he had hung up. "I love you, son."

Adam said he would call with any update, and then let Danny answer.

"Okay, dad." He thought about it and then he added in an "I love you too." Adam smiled at that before indicating he was hanging up. Such was just fine with Danny. He had nothing more to say. He was shocked he had spoken up as much as he did.

Even after Adam hung up, Danny sat, staring at the phone for a little while. Adam let him have his time. When a few minutes had gone by, Adam offered his friend a chance to eat something and take a shower, which Danny agreed to.

At first, he just concentrated on chewing his food. Adam was able to see how conflicted he felt.

"You okay, Danny? And I don't mean about your face or your fingers. Was the phone call too much?"

Danny looked up at him. For a moment he merely stared. Just as Adam was beginning to feel uneasy, he got an answer. "No, I mean I'm fine. The phone call wasn't too much. Thanks for asking. Is it okay if I take a shower now? Hopefully it'll have me feeling a little less, well, out of it."

Adam let him go without another word.

***

George could have rushed to tell Maria and the girls he had heard from Adam, from Danny, but he still had to call Gregory. One dreaded put-off task replaced another. The news wasn't necessarily bad; it could have been worse. Danny would be home tomorrow morning, a few hours away at this point. Still, he knew Maria, Cassandra and Amelia wanted to see their son and brother, the sooner the better.

Though he knew it would do no good, George tried to think whether he could have prevented this from happening to Danny. Not only if but when. Down the rabbit hole George went. *Enough*, he decided. He was going to call his brother. He would just have to hope that the words would come to him.

"Hello."

"Gregory, it's George again."

Gregory was able to sense something was going on. "George, what's wrong? Something happened to Danny this time, didn't it?" Gregory didn't even ask; he knew it to be true already.

His voice was shaky. "Yes." George tried to clear his throat but knew he couldn't fool his brother. "They came and took him this morning, hours before he was going to testify. He hasn't been home since."

"Okay. Do you know where he is now?"

"Yes. I dropped him off at Adam's, which is where he insisted he wanted to be. He's spending the night."

"It's all right, George. He'll be safe with Adam. We both know this."

"Yes, thank goodness for Adam, at least." Still, even with knowing that, the pressure was too much. He admitted to his brother how he really felt. "I don't know if Edward thought there was a chance he wouldn't show? He was going to, though." Gregory confirmed he knew this. "I should have talked to more people, to Danny and Edward. I could have prevented this. I should have. And my son had to pay the price."

Gregory felt terribly conflicted for his brother. He hadn't said so enough but with time and understanding, he had come to understand what George was going through as a result of being forced into such a position. He had even been speaking to Thomas about coming around.

"George, I'm sorry. I'm sorry for Danny that this had to happen to him. But I'm even more sorry for you in a way, for your guilt. This is Edward's fault. No matter what you may think or what anyone may tell you, this isn't on you."

"Thank you, Gregory. That means more than you could know. Regardless of who may be at fault, I still can't help thinking about what this means for my failings as a father."

Both brothers were taken back to the family barbecue held several years before, when George was announcing the creation of the Department of Ethics and that he would lead it.

Gregory and Thomas, being the best friends that they were, especially back then, had been by each other for most of the barbecue. George had tried to forget them, drinking heavily beside Karl and Harry, but eventually his brother and brother-in-law could be ignored no longer.

Thomas addressed George first. From the start, he showed he wasn't going to hold back. He set the tone then. "Oh, hello there, George. We were just congratulating you on your position."

George, who would recall from that moment on what a pompous asshole he thought Thomas was, knew that he was doing no such thing. Such was hardly a disappointment. It was that his brother was standing there, even if it should not have been surprising.

As unsurprising as it was, seeing his brother and brother-in-law standing opposite him was enough to get to George. Ignoring Thomas, he sought to address Gregory first.

"Were you also 'congratulating' me, Gregory?"

Thomas still needed the attention to focus on him though. "I'm sorry, George." It was doubtful he was. "I think you know you've done wrong. Good for you if you're happy. But there are other people at stake here. This doesn't merely concern you, but my sister, my nieces and nephew. If you won't think about them, we will."

His words did concern George. "You have no business telling me what is right for *my* family, and in my own home, too. I don't give a damn what you or anyone else thinks. I do want what's best for my family, and I will be the one to decide what that is."

Gregory was conflicted, though he had still said nothing. George tried once more to reach out to him.

"What is it, Gregory? What's so wrong with this? I'm not trying to be a bad husband. I'm not trying to be a bad father." George had struck a chord with that last line, and he knew it. Gregory's eyes had lit up. "That's it. You do think I'm a bad father, then. I'm sure this doesn't help in your mind."

His brother did step forward then, after whispering something to Thomas. "George, it's just that…"

"It's just that what, Gregory?"

He couldn't say it, and so George would have to hear from Thomas, again. Gregory had been too afraid to say what Thomas was not. Thomas' voice was quiet as he told George that this wasn't helping. His ambitions had gone too far.

George didn't respond. He merely asked Thomas if he was done. Then George told his brother-in-law it was time to leave.

Thomas did not put up any kind of a fight, fortunately. He did have to have the last word though, as he declared their relationship would never be the same. So far he had been correct.

That was fine, if Thomas wanted to leave in such a dramatic way. He left almost immediately. Then Gregory tried to approach George once more.

The look he had on his face meant he would have liked to apologize. At least maybe they could have talked it out in a less tense manner without Thomas. George should have given his brother the chance; how George wished he had. George was too upset and angry, though.

George was also afraid. He was afraid that his own brother was going to say what Thomas had said. Not even their father was able to make him behave more reasonably.

He didn't even let him try. "Gregory, if you feel the same, then you should just leave too."

George could tell Gregory was trying to hold onto his composure while they were still under the watchful eyes of many others. "George, come on. Don't listen to Thomas; he shouldn't be saying those things to you."

Even if he hadn't intended it, his words had enough of a hurtful connotation to them. "And you should? As if you haven't done so enough? Perhaps I wasn't being clear enough the first time when I told you to get out."

Their father was right there when George kicked his own brother out, something George had never done before. He had come close to it, but had always stopped himself. This time, though, he had been drinking, and there had already been so much tension.

Despite being the only one considered for the position, the politics of it all still meant it took a few months before George was confirmed. His father didn't live to see him start. George had thus, even now, always wondered—and regretted—if the stress of the situation worsened the older Whitfield's health enough to eventually kill him.

While he was too proud to back down, George didn't actually want Gregory, and certainly not their father, to leave. He had hoped Gregory would try again harder. Perhaps their father could have taken them aside and tried to fix it. Instead, his brother respected his wishes and left, taking their father with him.

Gregory and Philip still said goodbye to George. Philip nearly made his older son cry when he said he was proud of him, that he hoped it all worked out for the best.

Such was one of the last memories they had of not only their father, but of Thomas, Gregory, and George all at the same place. It was not necessarily a happy one, as Gregory had not been able to say he did not consider George a bad father. He now, once again, though without the undue influence of Thomas, had the opportunity to share what he thought of the delicate subject.

Gregory had not said anything for several minutes, as he had been lost in thought. George had to confirm his brother was still there. Just as he had done several years ago, he was hesitating.

"Yes, right, sorry, I'm still here." This time the delay came not because Gregory did not know how to say his brother was a bad father, but because he was trying to find the words to assure him he was a *good* father.

"There have certainly been worse than you, George," Gregory began. "I perhaps would have been a different father than you, but the truth is you're Danny's father and I'm not. Maria had children with you, not me." His words only got gentler from there. "You are in a difficult, arguably impossible situation. One of the things I have been meaning to say to you is that you deserve a lot more credit than what you are giving yourself. If you need to look at it in such a way, think of this, that at least you've realized how much you care for your son. I truly believe you do, George, and I am sorry I haven't said so enough."

George thought his brother had certainly been honest, but also comforting. "Thank you, Gregory. I do appreciate that." His tone was calmer now.

"Of course, George. That isn't all, though, is it?"

"No, it's not." Although he did not have a set plan for the conversation, George still did not feel as if he was ready to end there. In fact, he found it going into an interesting place. It was rare for George to be speaking with his brother, never mind multiple times in one week, and to ask for advice or share ideas. He was determined to put all that aside and stand by his son as well as what was right by him and the whole family.

George hadn't really thought of asking his brother for advice before, but maybe it was time to gain his perspective on what was going on. Situations around him were crazy enough that turning to his brother was not so bizarre anymore. "I'm hoping that we could work together. I'm serious. Whatever I have to do, and it may involve making some questionable decisions, I am going to find a way to help out my son and my family."

"Well, George, I hope you fully understand the risks in this. As your brother, I would be grateful for any assistance and of course will try and provide you with whatever *I* can provide. I hope you realize the possible ramifications for this?"

"Oh, I do. I am even prepared to incriminate myself. I probably have not helped things just by calling you. Though at this point, having contact and assistance is worth it. Goodness knows that this certainly won't be the only way to ruin things for myself as of late. There was a time when they wouldn't have traced the phone calls I've made from my personal office phone here at home, but they probably will soon if they don't already. I do want to let you know that I am willing to do whatever I can. I mean that, and I hope future results will show that there can be some good between us."

"If you're serious, George, then this will mean a great deal to me."

"I am serious, Gregory. And I hope it's enough thanks for how good of a brother you've been. I'm sorry for not realizing that."

"It's fine. And believe me, you've been a better father, and a better brother, than you realize."

Speaking to Gregory brought up potentially riskier situations and painful memories for George, but he still was glad for the call. It felt like he had actually done something, instead of languishing in his circumstances. If it took having his son taken away to be questioned and beaten up for him to realize how to be a better father and brother, then Gregory was right. At least there was a lesson learned.

Upon hanging up this time, George only remained in his office briefly. He was in a position to go be with and comfort his wife and his daughters, if they were still up. Checking his watch, he discovered he had been upstairs for many more hours than he realized.

As he opened the door, George was somewhat surprised to find Cassandra sitting there, seemingly troubled. Once she saw her father standing there, she immediately launched into an apology.

"I'm sorry, daddy. I hope you didn't think I was eavesdropping. I just came to talk to you and heard you on the phone and well, I didn't want to interrupt. Mom and Amelia are already in bed." That his wife and youngest daughter had turned in didn't surprise George, though his sweet Cassandra's apology was unnecessary and saddened him. He was not angry and hoped he did not appear so.

George's stunned silence was taken by Cassandra to mean he had been disappointed in her. "Please don't be angry with me. I've just felt so lonely and so worried about Danny." She finally began to cry then.

To see his daughter in such a way broke George's already troubled heart. While he had not meant for her to hear the conversation between himself and Gregory, he could never be angry with her for her concern, especially now. Truth be told, if there was anyone George could trust and confide in, it was likely Cassandra. That she came seeking information about her brother, especially when they were the only two left awake, was understandable. George had been meaning to talk with Cassandra about what was going on, and, just like most everything else lately, had put it off for far too long.

Still in the hallway, George welcomed her with open arms, as she quietly cried. He assured her, his dear daughter, that he was far from angry or disappointed with her, though he did wish to know what it was that she heard. Only so that he might better explain, not because she was in trouble.

"Not much, I promise, daddy. I was feeling so worried and so curious and wanted to stop by your office to see if you had any information yet. Since I could hear you were on the phone, I didn't want to interrupt you, so I waited outside. When I heard you mention Uncle Gregory's name, I became interested. It was only for a brief moment, though. I heard you say you were serious and that you were sorry for not realizing something."

She had only heard the end of the conversation, then. There was even less for George to worry about. It made sense that Cassandra would be intrigued to hear her father talking to Gregory.

"Daddy," she asked, with some hesitation. "Do you think we'll get to see Uncle Gregory anytime soon? I understand that things are, well, complicated, but I can't help but wonder, especially with you two talking."

George thought of something he had not thought of while talking with his brother, though it could become necessary, and sooner than he would have liked. There was, it turned out, a chance they would see Gregory, but that it would be without George. If anything happened to George, he wanted his wife and children to be safe, and despite their differences, George always knew they would be safe with his brother.

"That is quite an interesting question, my dear. It is one which has, I am afraid, an answer which is not as simple as I would like it to be."

"You can tell me. I promise."

"I know I can, Cassandra," he said with a smile. Just as soon as it had appeared, the smile disappeared. "It may come about that you, your mother and your siblings will spend some time with your Uncle Gregory, while I take care of things to do with the department and my position, and, above all, to make sure that you are safe, all of you."

Cassandra thought about what her father had just said. George was glad she had not launched into a tearful and passionate plea that they stay together, especially when George was realizing it was not entirely a sure thing for much longer, especially after Edward had personally interrogated Danny.

"Does it have to do with what happened with Danny?" Cassandra finally asked.

Such was a thoughtful question. "In a way it does," George answered her. "Cassandra, would you like me to tell you what happened to your brother?"

"If you think I can handle it, daddy."

Cassandra had brought up such a wonderful point, and George wasn't sure if she meant to. Of anyone, though, Cassandra could be counted on for George to tell. While Cassandra cared deeply for her brother and did not wish harm to come to him, she was not so delicate or young for George to have to keep things from her. Besides, it would be a relief to finally confide in someone.

"I do, my dear," George said, trying not to seem too distressed. "Cassandra, your brother was taken away this morning, by order of the Security and Action department. I'm sorry to say that he was interrogated and treated very badly. He is staying with Adam tonight, who has agreed to update me." Upon hearing Adam's name, Cassandra relaxed. "So while it may have seemed as if I have failed in dealing with this situation effectively, I promise you, your sister, your brother, your mother, Adam and anyone and everyone else, that I will do a better job this time at protecting Danny. I hope that you'll believe and trust in me, Cassandra."

As Cassandra looked up at her father, she couldn't believe there was any way he could think otherwise. She had a feeling he doubted and was too hard on himself, though Cassandra could never know for sure, since her father kept so much, too much, inside.

"Of course, daddy," she exclaimed, throwing her arms around her father in a tight and loving embrace. She hoped to always be the kind of relief for her father as she was right now. Though Cassandra did not ask to be his favorite child, she still took the responsibility seriously. This was especially the case when her parents had been so sadly distant. It was not that Cassandra was replacing her mother, far from such a thing. She did wonder what their going with Gregory meant for her parents' floundering marriage, though.

"What will this mean for you and mom?"

George sighed. "I don't know, Cassandra. I honestly don't." He was done trying to dress up the truth for her. That didn't mean that the truth had to be all bad, however. "But I have no intention of divorcing or separating from your mother for any other reasons than the safety of all of you."

"That's good, daddy. And before you even have to ask, I believe you."

"You know, my dear," George said as they sat together in his office. "I do believe your brother stayed with Adam for the night not just because he needed a break and a rest, but to protect us, your mother especially. While it was good of your brother to want to protect your mother, I am sorry that I have not looked out for her, you and your sister as I should have. That's another thing I'm determined to do better on, starting now."

"It's okay. I understand what you're going through as well. At least I try to." George knew that she did. "Should we wake mom?" Cassandra asked.

"I will do so in a few moments, I assure you. For now, would you like me to walk you back to your bedroom?" Even at eighteen, Cassandra did like that. After a hug and a kiss goodnight, and a kiss on the head of the sleeping Amelia, George prepared himself to go speak to his wife.

For a moment, George thought of returning to his office. *Perhaps Adam would call?* No, George had gotten the impression that Adam would call in the morning. *What about Edward?* If Edward was going to do him the courtesy of returning his call, he would have done so already. *Or Karl?* George thought it best to let him be with his family, on the rare occasion that he actually was. There was no more reason to put off telling Maria they could expect Danny home the next morning, a few hours from now. He had kept it from her long enough.

Quietly, he headed over to their bedroom. Sure enough, she was asleep. It looked though as if she had been trying to wait up for him. Seeing her there like this, alone on their bed, with sorrow and worry etched on her face, made him sadder than George imagined it would. He almost thought of not waking her at all, but then he reminded himself that she would want to know.

He gently shook her. "Maria? It's George. Wake up, dear."

"George, what is it?"

"I have some news about Danny."

As soon as George said the name, she was more alert. "Oh, you do? Is he coming home tonight after all? Is he all right?"

"He will be with Adam for the night."

Maria looked relieved, but then also confused. George knew that she had wanted to see him home safe and sound, and desperately so. "Is he…"

"He's in rough shape, physically and also emotionally. I promise you that I will get to the bottom of it. Most importantly though, I promise you that I will be a better father to our children and a better husband to you. I am so sorry for all of this, Maria." He truly was.

"Oh, George." As tired and as worried as she had been, Maria was kind enough to caress his face. "I do trust you to fix this, I do. And I still do love you, no matter what."

Such words, from his daughter and now his wife, meant much to George. He was a man who had not felt encouraged or as though he had a purpose for two years now, and it was beginning to bring life crashing down around him. He wondered how his wife or his daughters, his brother, even his son, had what faith and trust they had in him. They still saw some good in him, and for that he could thank God.

***

Danny had tried for several hours to sleep, though it evaded him. He wondered if that was a blessing in a sense, for he was sure his dreams that night, and possibly for many more to come, would be haunted by what had transpired earlier.

After taking a shower, Danny felt much more fit to speak with Adam about how he was okay with him bringing him home the next morning; he had finally accepted that he couldn't hide out from his family forever. Adam certainly thought that was good of his friend, and he was proud of such progress Danny had made.

Now that he was in a calmer state, Adam felt comfortable bringing up to Danny how deeply the near panic attack had frightened him. He hadn't meant to set that off. He never would knowingly do such a thing. He had just wished for George to know when his son would be coming home. Danny could understand that.

"I'm going to talk to my dad. I'm going to tell him everything."

Adam had almost fallen out of his seat, he had not expected such a revelation, especially one as good as this. Perhaps this was the silver lining to come out of it.

Though Adam had not said such a thing out loud, it was a shared thought between the two. Danny thought of this as he lay in Adam's bed, as Adam had insisted Danny would have the bed while he would sleep on the couch. Neither of them dared suggest Adam would sleep in his parents' room.

While he appreciated the gesture, the reality was Danny simply could not sleep. It was not that the bed was uncomfortable so much as it was the fear of dreams and memories. They would quite likely be there regardless, but it was possible, hopeful even, that they wouldn't be so bad if Danny was closer to his friend. Taking a blanket from the bed, he crept into the living room. Though the lights were out, Adam was still awake.

"Are you all right? Do you need something?"

"Do you want to watch a movie?"

If Adam was shocked at his friend wanting to start a movie at one o'clock in the morning, he did not say it. "Sure. What do you want to watch?"

"Literally anything."

The two friends laughed as Adam scrolled through the channels. Danny had gotten what he needed in coming to Adam's, not just a place to clean up or rest, not a break, but a return to normalcy. Here, he could almost have that again. Almost.

He's Home

Though they had stayed up rather late, Danny and Adam were up early the next morning, each anxious for their own reasons. Mercifully, Danny did not remember his dreams, though the longer he slept, the greater the chance he would remember something he didn't want to.

The reasons Danny had wanted to put off going home hadn't changed, not only for himself, but his family. He still felt the need to protect his mother and sisters. Danny and Adam both knew Maria would have engaged in the appropriate amount of fussing before she cleaned Danny up. Adam's own mother had been too afraid to help him clean up unless Harry had already gone to bed. Just as Danny had memories he wished not to remember, though, so did Adam.

As they silently made breakfast together, Adam on pancakes and Danny scrambling eggs and frying bacon, Adam's thoughts moved on to Director Whitfield. He hoped there might be a silver lining to come out of this, that his boss could properly involve himself once Danny had told him what he needed to. Adam, more than most, understood that George was in a difficult position with both his career and his family life. Danny was his best friend, but Adam knew he didn't make things easy on his father.

Adam was loyal to Danny to the point of death, but he wanted to be able to accomplish enough before that time came. He just wasn't cut out to save Danny all on his own; he needed help, and George was on a mission to provide that help.

This did not mean Adam blamed George. Far from it. He didn't know if he blamed the man for anything, which seemed a necessary reprieve considering the man had enough blame from his brother and brother-in-law. As was his way, Adam blamed himself in some small part. It was true that George and Danny needed to talk and it was something he should have pushed for sooner. Still, there was nothing he could do about what had already happened. Adam knew from his parents' deaths that wishing hard enough could not undo the past. He would just have to do his best with the current circumstances.

There was much to think about yet not much to say, as both young men were each lost in their own thoughts. Last night had had its fond moments; Danny had even been able to forget about his injuries, especially through staying up late watching movies, talking and laughing, but that was hours ago. It was now time to prepare himself to go home, prepare himself to re-enter real life.

Adam let breakfast last for as long as he could. As it got closer to ten, however, and he and Danny both had received text messages wondering when they would be arriving, Adam went to take a shower so that they could be ready for Danny to head home.

While most of the car ride was silent, Danny remembered himself just in time. As anxious as he was to be home, he was still grateful for the time with Adam. He didn't think he had emphasized that enough. Danny doubted he even could, but he could say thank you.

"I can't tell you enough how much I appreciate last night, Adam," Danny said, his voice already full of emotion at the start of what was to be an involving day.

"It's what I'm here for, as a friend to you and your family," Adam said with a small smile. He was delighted to see Danny return it.

Adam did not go in with Danny, who was initially disappointed but understanding. It was a time for them to talk about what had happened and what would happen going forward as a family, though Adam assured Danny he was a phone call, text or visit away. After watching his friend slowly walk inside, turn and wave, Adam pulled away, left to wonder on his own what would become of the Whitfield family.

***

Maria had been thinking the same anxious thoughts, that Danny should have talked to his father before it came to this. That he hadn't was systemic of other concerns, of her son turning to his uncles instead of his father, of how she and George were fighting more often in front of the children.

The time for pointing out such things would be later, however. For now she just wished to hold and comfort her son.

They had all been up early. George prayed his family slept less fitfully than he did, though the chances weren't likely. Cassandra and Amelia had been looking out the window ever since Adam had texted he was bringing Danny home.

With Adam informing them that he and Danny had made themselves breakfast, the rest of them ate without him. That it was a quiet affair made it no different from recent meals.

When Danny was still not home after breakfast, Maria took it upon herself to clean the kitchen, even when it was already relatively spotless and when Danny didn't care for an immaculate home. Still, it was something to do and George wasn't about to argue with her. He didn't even bother to point out when Maria had cleaned the same spot three times.

The girls were glued to looking out the window, and with Maria not seeming fit for conversation, George knew not to press it. The only sound, besides the faint noise of the car pulling into the long driveway, was Amelia announcing her brother's presence. "He's home," she said as they all took their place gathering in the parlor by the front door.

With the dishes and the dish towel put away, Maria now had a free hand to grasp George's. Just as they heard him on the porch, about to turn the handle, Maria briefly closed her eyes. George surmised she was praying.

His parents and sisters had expected Danny to be in a sorry state, physically and emotionally. He did live up to that. He had one black eye while the other looked at least bruised. There was bruising around his nose and his lip was swollen. His fingers were also bandaged. He did not have trouble walking, though he did slouch. At least it was a relief he did not look worse. Maria's hand briefly shook in her husband's, but she was able to compose herself enough to embrace their son.

Danny was responsive, though a bit delayed, and he was stiff in his movements. It was as if he was still trying to come to terms with how all of this was real. He was no longer in the safe haven that was Adam's, but he could also be thankful he was not at headquarters.

It was not merely Danny who was relieved at this. For George, the hearing had gone worse than he could have feared; he doubted he'd be able to forget the sight of his son in the witness chair. There had also been countless hours of questioning witnesses, all of them terrified men and women who swore they knew nothing of another coup and yet were still at the mercy of the department. Nobody had envied George for some years now, but he also did not envy the unfortunate souls before him that harrowing day.

Maria took her time with their son, as George expected her to. She took a good look at him and smoothed out his hair. There were tears, but she managed to smile. "Oh, Danny. It's so good to have you home."

As timid as Danny was, he was at least able to respond to his mother. "Thanks, mom." Though his voice was mechanical, that wasn't what stuck with anyone.

They had prepared Amelia before Danny got home. Fortunately, Adam had also done a superb job of cleaning him up. Seeing her older brother in such a state was not as shocking or frightening for the young girl as everyone had feared.

The most emotional reaction came from Cassandra. Tears welled up as she hugged her older brother, one of her best friends, whom she normally thought of as so tough, but who now looked so broken before her. Even she was able to get it together, though. The conversation she had with her father the night before had helped.

Then Danny faced his father. While Danny did not blame his father, he also had not reached out as much as George wished he had.

"Hi, dad."

"Hello, Danny. We're all so glad to have you home, where you belong." Maria murmured an agreement.

"You're not working today, dad?"

"No, I'm not. I felt it was important to stay home with you, your mother and your sisters today." Even though it was Saturday, George had hardly had the day off since he started working with Security and Action. While George didn't believe in working his employees six or seven days a week as the Director of Ethics, Edward was not of the same mind, especially when it came to those he needed to exert tighter control over.

While Cassandra offered to do Amelia's hair in her bedroom, Danny sat with his parents at the kitchen table. Though he had already eaten and his mother was aware of this, she asked him if he wanted anything heated up. He did not. He did not want anything to drink, either. Danny was relieved when his mother stopped asking him. He didn't want to snap at her, but he didn't want to answer so many needless questions, either.

George was thankful he had already discussed with Cassandra that he was considering sending her along with her siblings and her mother to Gregory, because he was about to bring the idea up to Danny and Maria. Without the girls around, George hoped Maria would be able to react honestly. It might also be welcoming news to Danny, who might then feel compelled to share more with his father.

"I… realize that this might be some shocking news, which will be explained to the girls in due time, but I have been in contact with my brother and I—"

George was prevented from continuing any further as Danny burst into tears.

Though George wanted to ask what was the matter, Maria was preventing him by holding their son, now rocking in his mother's arms. "George, what on earth did you say?" He shook his head and shrugged that he did not know.

For a few moments, Danny just preferred to be held by his mother. George's patient persistence paid off, though.

When Danny first spoke, his voice trembled. "I'm sure that you were just trying to help, dad." George nodded that he was. "I'm sure you didn't have any idea, that you couldn't possibly understand, but dad?"

"Yes, son, what is it? Please, Danny, know that you can tell me. I just want to be able to make this right." Maria nodded her agreement, as she looked to George, pleading for him to fix this.

"When I was… when I was downstairs at headquarters yesterday, I… they asked me about all the times I had talked with Gregory. And I couldn't understand it at first. Because they had all these times listed that I swore to them I didn't talk to him, but they didn't believe me."

This was a lot to take in. Not only for Danny, who realized the painful truth, but for Maria as well, who would have to temper her happiness at her husband talking with his brother, especially at the price it came with. George was learning that not only had he damned his son, but that his calls were being traced. It shouldn't have been a shock.

For a time there was no sound but that of Danny crying as he went back to the comfort of his mother's arms. George sat, starting straight in front of him. He couldn't believe he had done this to his son. He was surprised that Maria wasn't standing up to curse and blame him outright, unless, of course, that was to come later. Here he had been trying to help, yet it had spectacularly backfired. *Did Danny's denials earn him that black eye, the swollen lip, the broken fingers?* George almost couldn't bear to know.

Then George felt a hand on his shoulder. It was his wife's. "George, it's okay," she murmured. *God bless this woman for how strong she was*, George thought. He wondered what he had done to be lucky enough to deserve her.

It was enough. She was enough. Her kindness and understanding was enough. It was all enough for George to say what he should have told their son before any of this happened.

"Danny, I truly am so sorry for how I have failed you. For this recent situation, but for the past as well. I want you to know that I am trying to start a conversation between us now not to punish you, but to help you. I do mean it, that from now on I want to help you. I called Gregory for that purpose, and I am so sorry that as a result of doing so I caused you further pain and trouble, no matter what I intended. Hopefully I can get a hold of those phone records. I guess you could say that I am in a bit of shock and denial that it has come to this, though in reality, I shouldn't be all that surprised with how things have been going." Realizing that he was going on a bit of a rant, George let Danny process what he had just said.

There was still more on his mind, however. Maria was interested and Danny wasn't bothered; his tears had ceased. George was speaking not only to his wife and his son, but to himself in a way. "I've been hiding behind my job a lot lately, I know. It's gotten a whole lot worse than it ever was. I thank God every day for Adam's help, but I just… Edward makes it so difficult. That is why I have always seemed too tired or busy or in foul moods. But you should always be able to come home, to talk to me, because I love you and want to help you, and I am determined, as long as I have even an ounce of clout, to help you."

The words he heard next caused Danny to lift his head. They were so simple, yet so powerful. "I love you, Danny. I'm proud to call you my son." Such words were true. George was proud of his son; Danny worked for a cause George only wished he could be a part of. He would like to say so more often.

"You do?"

Maria's face nearly crumpled to hear their son, though she could sympathize with both men.

"Yes, Danny, I really do, and I'm truly sorry for how my efforts, no matter how well-intentioned, made things worse for you in any way."

Danny sighed through the tears. "It's okay. You couldn't have known. And you know, maybe I needed to realize that these past few years haven't been easy on you, either."

It was through such an admission that Danny realized he needed to come clean to his parents, especially when his father's words rang so true. He didn't know where to begin, so they told him to start at the beginning. With a deep breath, Danny did. It wasn't easy for any of them, but it was necessary.

It went back to the most recent coup, just over two years ago. Danny had dropped out of college to work full-time with his uncles, though he hadn't realized how involved he would become. When he first heard about the coup, Danny's first concern was for Gregory and Thomas, as it sounded like something they'd both be involved in.

Both men were questioned but ultimately deemed uninvolved. Not even George had known this. Gregory and Thomas each had their own reasons for not telling him.

Gregory and Thomas had not involved themselves in such a coup because, as they saw it, it was bound to fail. That its principal actor was a senator meant it was someone far too close to the process it was trying to dismantle. It was no wonder that it was unsuccessful.

While they had not been involved in it, Gregory, Thomas and Danny were still all hoping the coup would be successful—if not that one, then another one. Very little time went by before they realized it would likely have to come from them, from those outside of the political class.

Danny wasn't entirely sure how Director Roth knew enough to have him called in. It wasn't known why Edward knew a lot of what he knew, unless one believed he had spies everywhere. Danny's disappearances, including on Cassandra's birthday, were in part because of being questioned. He was also going to meetings, some led by Gregory and some delegated for Danny to be in charge of, though he himself did not know all the details.

When it came to being questioned, Danny refused to give up such information, as George himself knew from the hearing. Those other witnesses, Danny explained, were also part of such meetings. Which meant Edward knew enough that Danny could possibly be in danger, as could Gregory. Thomas was thankfully safe in the United States, but it also meant it was too dangerous for him to make contact. Danny had not told his father, because, and it pained him to admit, he didn't know how much he could trust George.

His brother-in-law was the least of George's concerns. His son and his brother were planning a coup against his own department. Granted, it was a department he had been forced to be a part of, but it still meant George could be caught up. The same went for Adam, who was part of the department by choice and thus could be in an even more dangerous position.

If George and Adam teamed up with Danny and Gregory, if George let bygones be bygones when it came to his brother and Thomas, they would have an invaluable resource on their side. It would also serve to protect all of them when the time for a successful coup came.

That was something to think about. By the next time he spoke to Edward, likely at the office on Monday, George would have to know what he was saying, to make sure no further harm came to his son.

There was also the issue that Danny would have to start informing and soon. As he had left headquarters and the hearing in a sorry state, Danny had made a promise that he would give names of those more involved than himself. Otherwise he could expect to be brought in more often, and for visits which made the one he just came from look tame in comparison.

Ultimately, Danny felt he was going to be arrested anyway. At least it would be for the right cause and while keeping his uncles safe, he hoped. If he could stay out of prison and didn't have to go to any more interrogations or hearings, well, that would be appreciated, and George was determined to see what he could do. He assured both his wife and son of this.

Danny laughed to himself before he nearly started crying again. "You know what?"

"What's that, son?" George asked, looking right at Danny.

"I thought that this could really be a cause which would be worth dying for, and yet… and yet I'm afraid that I am going to be killed for this."

Maria started tearing up at the thought, and even George almost did as well. "I will make sure that that doesn't happen. You have my word, Danny. I promise you that that will not happen. I'll do everything in my power.

I'll give my last breath to make sure that that doesn't happen."

"Thanks, dad. I'm… I'm glad we talked."

For a moment the three of them just held each other close. George and Maria made eye contact. He could tell that his wife saw him in a different light, for the better. "So am I, Danny, so am I."

***

The next day was Sunday, a time to be with family in every sense of the word. When Monday rolled around, though, George had to go back into work. He still had not heard from Edward. Karl had not returned his calls either, though. George hoped it was because he was enjoying the time with his own family for once, though George didn't know if he could afford to hope so much.

Since he had not even received the courtesy of a returned phone call, George was determined to seek out and speak to Edward, preferably first thing. It was not meant to be, for as he entered, the first thing he saw was Adam at his desk. George was surprised to see that the young man had not only already arrived but was asleep. He wondered, then, when on earth the younger man had gotten there.

"Adam," George asked, considering gently shaking him awake. It had been unnecessary. Adam snapped to attention.

"I'm sorry, sir. I hope I have not kept you waiting. Is there anything I can do for you?"

"No, Adam, I'm quite fine." George was sure his voice reflected how sad and tired he himself was. He had done nothing to hide it. "I just got here myself. I'm sorry I didn't make it in the other day. I hope my absence was not felt too deeply."

"It's okay, sir, it was understood."

"Good." Now that that had been addressed, George hoped to get to the bottom of what Adam was doing sleeping at his desk. *So help me, God,* George thought. *If Edward has forced me to address something else…*

"I suppose I should explain why I'm here so early."

"Yes, that would be helpful, Adam." George was trying not to take it out on Adam. It wasn't his fault.

Director Roth had wanted him in early to have a talk with him. That talk had so far yet to happen. Adam, unfortunately, couldn't answer as to whether George was to be involved in that. George did not react; he did not wish to upset Adam any more than was necessary. It might as well involve him, though, George figured, since he was aiming to speak with Edward already.

"What time did you get in here? Dare I ask?" Adam's hesitation was answer enough. "Never mind, I don't want to know." Adam closed his mouth.

This was going to be a difficult day, not that it already hadn't been. George would be lying if he said he wasn't anxious about returning to work. He had to speak with Edward about what was going to happen to Danny, whether that was a difficult conversation or not. Now there was whatever had to be discussed involving Adam. *Did Edward know that Adam had accessed files? Was he in some sort of trouble? Was George going to have to fire Adam just as he had fired Harry?* Too many questions, each with an answer George wasn't sure he wanted.

With no time like the present and with Adam reluctantly following in tow, George began the dreaded walk over to Edward's office.

What they found, however, was Edward just about to leave his office, on his way to speak with Karl.

"Hello, George, Adam. What may I help you with?" From his tone, one would never know the connection he had with the two of them or that he was about to harass a third man.

"I was thinking we would have that talk." George beckoned to Adam. "Since he works directly under me, I was hoping I could be privy to your conversation with Adam."

A thin smile appeared, one of Edward's most eerie. "Be that as it may, might I remind you that *I* am Adam's boss, just as I am yours. You are merely my deputy."

George had a choice. He could hang his head and bow down to Edward's technically correct point. Or he could respond in kind. "Be that as it may, sir, I feel I have much to contribute to this discussion with Adam, especially since I had already been hoping to speak with you. I see you are leaving your office though. Perhaps we could all go?"

"Perhaps we could." Just like that, Edward blinked. George had more to dread, though, with what Edward said next. "I was just on my way to Bradford's office." Suddenly the walk became much worse than it had been, the awaited discussion more dreaded.

They walked in silence, with Adam and George every once in a while exchanging furtive glances. Edward's presence had a formidable role, since anyone and everyone quickly got out of their way. As they entered the Treasury and approached his office, Karl wore an unmistakably aggrieved look.

"Hello, Edward, George, Adam," Karl said, nodding at the three men who had come to accost him before he even set foot in his office. "It's nice to have you back, George." Karl's words carried with it a specific tone, as he hoped to be letting his friend know his displeasure was not with him.

What Karl craved more than anything was a moment's peace. He was certainly not going to get it from work, which once had been a safe haven. Like many other things he meddled in, however, Edward had destroyed that. Instead, three men were making their way into his office, one whom had been hounding him nearly every day on rearranging funding for a supposed war on domestic terrorism, which is how Edward regarded the coups.

"I do hope you'll pardon the intrusion, Karl." Edward's words were merely a formality. Karl's response showed that he had no choice but to not mind. He certainly could not be asked to be left alone, not with Edward's influence, even if he was Karl's equal. "We have much to discuss though, all of us. And while perhaps your matter is best discussed privately between you and me, George insisted on coming along with Adam." Karl looked mortified at the possibility of such a conversation.

Here Edward was, doing what he did best, twisting the situation to turn friends against one another. In normal circumstances, George would have considered speaking up, but he had to trust Karl would know better, and he did. "I am hoping that that conversation can wait and that I might discuss with you my son."

Edward had taken it upon himself to sit in Karl's chair. His smile lingered over a picture of Jack and Emma and even longer over the tiny picture of Tara and himself Karl dared to have on his desk.

"Well, I certainly did not think we would be here to discuss Jack." With that comment and his smirk, Edward managed to make the situation worse. Karl shut his eyes, Adam prayed, and George counted to ten.

George was desperate but refused to show any more signs of weaknesses. "Edward, I don't believe I have ever been more serious in my life, and I am here, humbly, to ask what I may do so that my son never finds himself in such a situation ever again."

It was as if it was just the two of them. At least it felt that way to George. Edward didn't care if he had an audience or not. "Yes, you are here 'humbly,' because you do not have a choice, George. You made the decision to no longer have a choice when you decided not to help me strike down that coup. Now you've gone and raised a son who could very well be plotting a coup against my—*our*—department, one which his father and best friend are a part of." He gestured to Adam, who tried to look anywhere else. "You want to know what you may do?" Not knowing if it was a rhetorical question or not, George decided to risk affirming that he did. "Make sure he informs, unless you want someone else informing on *him.* Because I don't care whose son or brother or friend I have to arrest. I *am* taking down this coup."

Edward had not given George an opportunity to respond, as he was not yet finished. "You were there at the hearing, you saw how I had to quite literally beat your son into submission. He needed it, believe you me. And lest you think that he is the only one, think again. I have a nephew. Harry had Adam. We must all do our best, yet I feel I am the only one doing so."

To mention Harry, who could not defend himself, and in front of Adam, was going too far. Edward could see it from the moment George stood up, made himself taller, had that fire burning in his eyes, even clenched his hands into fists.

"What, George? What are you going to do?" He once more had that smirk on his face, for he knew George would not do anything. The time to do something had not only been long before Danny's interrogation and hearing, but before George even took on such a position. Had George decided to use his influence to help Edward in subduing that and any other coups, he could enjoy his freedom. Now, however, with the choices he made, he would keep paying the price for as long as Edward deemed necessary.

It wasn't George who responded but Karl. "Nothing. He's not going to do a thing. George, perhaps you should take it easy."

George was not pained by Karl's reaction. If anything, he felt for his friend. Perhaps he had said his piece. George would likely have to turn to other measures. Though he might dread it, it was the price to pay for saving his son.

"George, I think it's time you went home for the day. You and I will be having a talk later, rest assured. We can talk about Adam, too."

Adam. The young man had been forgotten, he had been so quiet, even when Edward evoked his father's name and talked about Adam as if he had not been there.

"George, I don't like to ask twice."

George looked to Karl on this, as he collected Adam. "Go, George. We'll talk later."

Without another word until they exited the office, George and Adam left. "I'm sorry for involving you in that back there," George said once they were safely out of earshot.

"It's okay, sir, it's nothing I'm not used to." George was so taken aback he actually stopped walking. "What, Director Whitfield. What is it, sir?"

"It's not something you should be used to. Once I've made sure my family is safe, that is my next aim, to make sure that you are respected always."

"Thank you, sir. Though I hope and trust you'll look out for your family first and foremost." Such was Adam's polite way of saying that he could endure whatever came from Director Roth.

***

Before leaving what had been a rather short and unpleasant return to work, George decided he needed to see his friend. Unlike previous encounters, George was not interrupting a sexual escapade. It was almost worse.

As he approached Karl's office, George realized he did not see Tara. In fact, George had not seen her in several days.

The office had an overall despondent feel to it. The mood was not helped by the fact that Edward was there, just walking out the office door.

"It *is* necessary, Karl. Because I say it is, and you will do well to remember how much power, and over what and whom I have." The door to the office was open, and George was thus privy to the end of what had been an uncomfortable conversation.

Then Edward saw George. Gone was his attitude from earlier. Though to a naive person this would have been welcoming, George knew better. Edward was scheming and calculating. "Good day to you, George. I'm sure you and I will be having another discussion in no time."

George nodded. He had to get to Karl while he still could. He should not have been surprised to see his friend pouring himself a Scotch.

"I'm sure you're sorry to see me this way, George." Karl uttered a weak laugh. "There're no lipstick stains for you to warn me about this time."

"Should I be, though? Warning you, I mean, Karl. Have I been such a terrible friend that I can't see what's been going on? Edward has blackmailed you, hasn't he?"

Karl hung his head for some time. He wished to be fit for conversation, even if there was very little he could share with George. "I do not see it that way. You have not been a terrible friend, but rather an admirable father and husband. I look up to you, George. I hope you see that." Though Karl had not answered the question, George no longer expected him to. "Please don't see this as me pushing you out, but rather encouraging you to go home to your family."

George knew his friend was asking him to leave as politely as he could. It wasn't the time to press the issue. He instead nodded and began his leave. "Take care, old friend."

"You do the same, George."

It was just as well that George left at an appropriate time, for he had to speak with Gregory at least one more time. A plan was brewing in George's mind and there was much for them to discuss.

***

George's family was trying to carry on as normally as possible. Several revelations had come which Maria was now pondering at the kitchen table while Amelia worked on her school assignments. She only had a few weeks left; Cassandra had already graduated and was in the parlor, talking to Danny. Maria was glad the brother and sister had one another, even with the recent tension.

Something had happened to her son. More accurately, something had been happening for some time now. Though it only caused more stress and concern for him, Maria did believe George was trying his best.

As Maria was pondering their plight, she found herself thinking, not for the first time, that perhaps it was not such a terrible idea to go to the United States. There was still some bad blood between Thomas and George, but she hoped the men would get over their differences, especially with all the work George was putting into to protect them.

Despite how Danny had paid for the phone calls, Maria was thankful George and Gregory were on speaking terms. There was also another part of her, however, which feared George putting aside their differences to plan something with his brother. She wondered when he would be honest with her.

Maria would have these questions answered sooner than she expected, for Cassandra's remark was too startling to ignore. "Why is daddy home so early?"

It was not yet noon. George had never come home before six, and at times recently had stayed out until

Amelia was asleep. He had even stayed the night at his office before. For the first time in many months, George had failed to go in on a Saturday. Now he was coming home before noon.

Maria simply shook her head to indicate that she didn't know. Instead of chastising the children for lining up to meet their father the moment he walked in the door, she joined them.

Tired as he was, George still tried to approach his family with love and warmth. This was especially when he had been preparing himself, with guidance from Gregory, to not see his family for some time.

"Hello, everyone," George said with a weary smile.

Though she appreciated his attempts at cheerfulness, Maria thought her husband looked as if he had aged a decade. "Hello, George, dear. Is everything all right?" Maria realized she was perhaps taking a risk asking this in front of the children.

"Yes, Maria." George thought about what he would say, but he didn't actually say anything until they reached the kitchen. The children dutifully remained quiet.

"George, would it be better if we spoke in private?" Perhaps that was why he had not said anything yet. She was prepared to send the children upstairs. Cassandra could especially be counted on to help.

"Not necessarily." Such a response, and a cryptic one at that, was maddening. The children all looked silently to each other, not daring to say a word in case their father spoke.

Maria pressed him for more. "What is it, then? What's happened? What's going on, George?" She was getting too anxious. She tried to calm herself, but so much, too much had happened.

"I was sent home early," George said, his voice coming out in an odd tone. "Though I'll likely have to go back in. There was a... discussion at work, between

Edward and me. Things got slightly heated." George searched for a way to explain, and then decided to just come out with it.

"I fear this situation has come to a head. Danny could end up being arrested." Amelia gasped but Cassandra quickly embraced her, letting their father continue. "I therefore think it would be best for you to take the children and go to your brother's. I'll have Adam and Gregory join you."

"And what about you?" Maria asked what was on all of their minds, a question George hated having to answer though he must.

"That's what I've been talking to my brother about on the way here. He plans to call Thomas and fill him in as well. But… I will be staying here. Perhaps, someday, soon, the opportunity will present itself for me to join you, or for you to come back home. I have to stay here though. Edward needs me."

"Are you planning on sacrificing yourself for that man, George?"

In a way, George was. Such had been the plan he came up with in the car, when speaking to his brother. It had not been a pleasant one, but it was necessary, and therefore easily decided. It was too important that Danny not be arrested, which was never a guarantee. It was with a heavy heart that George planned to come forward and tell Edward that it was not Danny who had been planning the coup with Gregory, but him. Would Edward believe it? Considering that he never got over George not helping him shut down the last one, it was possible.

George had not been able to admit the full details yet, not with them so fresh, and in front of the children. "I… Yes, Maria, in a way you could say that. I completely understand your reaction and appreciate your concern." It pained him to say the words which came next. "Very soon it may just be you and Danny left to make that decision.

You won't have to worry about me anymore, and my position. There should be no hesitation about you being free to go."

Maria dropped the plate she had been washing in a frenzy. She nearly slapped George, though managed to stop herself. "How could you say that? How could you imply such a thing, to me, your wife, in front of your children?"

She gave him no opportunity to answer as she stormed off to their bedroom. Maria had barely made it before she closed the door and collapsed, sobbing up against the frame. She didn't know what to do. She didn't know what to think. She had dared to hope, for so long, that one day George could get along with her brother and his own, especially if they were to see the strain of his working under Edward. It had backfired, however. Now that George was making plans with Gregory, however, it was for a reason she feared was consequential.

When George had made his way to their bedroom to approach her, Maria could not say that she minded. Something told her she would likely not have much more time with him.

"Maria, I'm so sorry. Please, forgive me for not realizing the effect this situation has had on you."

As part of making the most of what time they had together left, Maria was quick to forgive. She had to be. "Of course I forgive you, George. I love you. I know you love me, and you've made so many sacrifices."

At least she could see it that way. George thanked God for that. "You have no idea how sorry I am, Maria. I'm trying to do what's best for this family, as I always have, and in this instance especially, I'm afraid it isn't very pleasant."

"Oh, George, I can see that. Please, forgive *me* for not being more understanding."

"There's nothing to forgive." George waited only a moment before continuing with what he had to get on with telling her. They would decide, together, how to tell the children. "I do have to tell you something, though. Something I wasn't ready for earlier, which I may never be ready for. It needs to be said, though."

Maria nodded she was listening. George hesitated then. "George, what is it? You don't have to hide anything from me, no matter how unpleasant. I'm ready to hear it. I'm your wife. You should be able to tell me these things."

George cupped her face lovingly in his hands. "I know. I wish I didn't have to say this, but I'm afraid the situation really is going to get worse."

He told his wife then, his beloved partner, his great love, of his plan. He explained to her how Edward had indicated enough that he was not likely to leave Danny alone, not when he still thought Danny had something to do with the coup. That was, unless he had someone to arrest. It was a likely enough story that George would have felt slighted with his forced position, and that it was he who had been helping Gregory plan the coup, that he was hiding behind their son.

"George, dear, when did you come up with this?"

"Just since I left the office. I fear Edward will work quickly, so I needed to work quicker."

Maria was nearly dizzy with concern. She didn't think she had loved her husband more than in that moment. She would not be losing her son, thanks to her husband, but she would be losing George, and they couldn't know when they would be together again.

George was doing this for Maria, who had been begging him, pleading with him, fighting him to do something for Danny. He was finally doing something, because he loved her, but because he also loved their son. Maria tried not to cry. She was determined to remain strong.

They made love in the few precious moments they had together.

***

As much as they wished to spend every minute together, Maria and George agreed it was not becoming to leave the children downstairs alone for much longer.

As they reached the bottom of the steps, Maria asked what they should tell the children. They would surely be confused, especially if George was taken away and didn't come back. Still, part of her was unsure about whether they should really explain it all to them.

"I'll figure something out." He looked at her so lovingly that she couldn't help but trust him. "If that's all right with you."

"Of course it is." George gave her one last kiss before they headed into the kitchen. If the children knew anything, they didn't show it.

Maria desperately wanted to enjoy the rest of this day. Now that she actually knew what was happening, she was finding it increasingly difficult not to let her emotions show. She frequently felt how lucky she was that George was there, strong, by her side, willing to help.

By the time dinner rolled around, Maria felt uneasy again. She wanted their last meal together to be perfect. It got closer to the hour when they would come for George. The children seemed to be overwhelmed. Maria would be surprised if Danny and Cassandra didn't sense anything. Amelia might even have sensed something. The only one perfectly at peace with this seemed to be George. Gone were any trace of his nerves.

When they did make conversation, dinner wasn't too horrible. Cassandra and George at least attempted to make an effort, and for that Maria was grateful.

As she got the pie that she had baked for dessert and brought it to the table, she touched George's shoulder. He looked at her for a moment with a look almost of despair in his eyes, though only for just a second. Although the interaction was brief, she could still sense that it had alerted Danny and that it wouldn't be long before Cassandra and Amelia figured it out as well.

"What is it? What's wrong, mom?"

"Take some pie, Danny." She wanted to give George his own time to tell the children, but she also didn't think it wise to ignore Danny's question. He was quite uneasy as it was. "Your father has something to say, and he will tell us when he is ready to do so."

George took the pie Maria offered him, to eat later. "No, I've waited too long to tell them as it is."

As he began to tell their children, George reached for his wife's hand. She took it, but was also saddened by how this gesture made the children more confused.

"I don't want any of you to be afraid of what may come. We just need to handle whatever—"

Normally Maria would be strict with the children for interrupting, but this time she could not blame them.

"What are you talking about, dad?" Danny asked.

"Daddy, what is it?" Cassandra questioned. Please, tell us it's something not too terrible. I don't mean to interrupt, but..."

"Yes, what is it, daddy?" Amelia asked as she timidly joined in.

George looked at Maria. As she nodded that he could do this, he suddenly became his brave self.

"It's likely at this point that the situation cannot be helped. I just want you all to remain calm while I explain it, which I will do if you give me the chance."

All the children nodded, although Cassandra looked as if she was about to cry. George continued.

"Too many things have come up at work about our home, about my brother, about Danny. In order for all of you to be safe, I need to go and take care of a few things. Before you ask, I don't know when I'll be back and unfortunately I will most likely leave tonight."

Cassandra allowed herself to cry with her brother comforting her, though with little success. Danny himself was about as unfeeling as could be, no doubt struggling with how to react. Amelia could see her older sister crying and did her best to avoid looking at Cassandra. She couldn't help a glance, though, and burst into tears.

Maria looked at George sadly, though she couldn't blame him for the way he went about this. He did the best he could. All they could do was hold each other and wait for the children to stop crying.

Amelia and Cassandra both got up to hug their father, each clinging onto him for dear life and trying to get him to promise that he'd be back soon, even though they knew he couldn't.

Danny, however, reacted differently. He didn't get up. Rather, his look of unfeeling turned to anger, then hurt, then shock. He was slowly grasping the nature of the situation.

"Dad, can I actually talk to you in the other room?" Tears were threatening to spill and as Danny spoke, he began to choke up.

"I think that may be a good idea."

George led Danny to the parlor then. Maria tried not to listen, though it was hard not to. Danny had figured out that George was to be arrested in his place. George was explaining to him that he was to be the man of the house now and would help his mother in making decisions.

Danny was still crying when they got back to the kitchen.

As if time could not be any crueler, the doorbell then rang.

A Father's Sacrifice

Edward had seen no need to waste any time speaking to George. He thought of having his nephew and Howard bring George in, but that would likely be too much of a production, not to mention that Edward didn't wish to deal with any objections Scott had. He would send Karl and Adam, who could be counted on to make sure George complied without too much fuss.

Karl and Adam also had very little choice. With Karl being blackmailed and Adam reminded on a regular basis of his status, both men were expected to do as they were told.

Each was painfully aware that it was dinner time; Karl was missing dinner with his own family, though that was not unusual. They did not know what had just taken place between George and his children, especially Danny. It would not be overly optimistic to say that the relationship between father and son had changed.

Feeling it best to not make whoever was at the door wait, George quickly answered. He was, admittedly, surprised to see Karl and Adam, though he did not know whom he expected to see. As he welcomed them inside, Maria and the children were already standing in anticipation in the parlor. While George was adept at hiding his emotions, Danny was not.

"What are you doing here, Adam? Have you come to arrest my dad?"

There was an awkward silence. Adam was hopelessly confused but still wanted to be able to answer his friend. The truth was, as George had suspected, that Adam knew very little.

As George went to answer for Adam, Danny refused to let him. "No, dad. I want to hear it from Adam. Why is he here? And what is Karl doing here? Doesn't he have a family, or is that no longer a thing?" Adam was looking more hopeless by the minute.

George thought of asking Danny if he would rather Howard and Scott came to the house, or Edward himself. It wouldn't be very appropriate though, and it would be unhelpful, especially in their last moments together.

Adam found his voice, though, to assure his friend he was not there to arrest his father and never would be. The same went for Karl, who murmured an agreement. The line about his family could go unaddressed; Danny was not himself.

When George spoke this time, Danny allowed him to do so, in part because Maria had come over to him.

"Adam and Karl are not here to arrest me. If it does come to that, and remember, it very well could, it won't have anything to do with these two. For now, a discussion will likely be taking place, though I don't know what is to happen from there."

Karl stepped forward to speak and echo what George said. He was able to do so with a pleasant expression despite Danny's sullen one. "Yes. Tonight, at least, we shall all just be having a talk."

They had been fortunate in that Danny allowed as much to be said. He was still confused though. George didn't feel as if he was able to leave him yet.

George excused himself to speak once more with Danny, to emphasize that tonight would just be a talk with Edward, and that he truly believed he would be all right. What tomorrow would bring, he didn't know, but he was resolved to be calm.

Blinking back tears, Danny mentioned he understood. He even apologized to Adam and Karl, especially for the comment about Karl's family. Karl saw it as nothing.

George felt odd saying goodbye as he prepared to leave. He didn't know when he would be back home or see any of them again. Still, he could at least be at peace with how he was leaving things.

Once the three men were outside, Karl did not comment about Danny's behavior, as George half-expected him to. Karl was set in not judging the young man in such a situation. He did mention that he hoped it was all right with George if Adam had come along, as Karl had been the one to suggest it, with Edward agreeing on the hopes it would make George more compliant.

Adam and George were to ride over in George's car, while Karl took his own. He wanted George to have some comfort and time to catch up with Adam, which Karl was sure he would be doing with George later. George realized this was Karl admitting something was up, though he would say no more about it yet.

With just the two of them, George could address how anxious Adam was. He realized that Adam knew even less than he originally thought, especially if it was Karl's idea to bring him along.

Initially, George had hoped to be the one finding out information, but it looked like he would be the one to give it. "Adam?"

"Yes, Director Whitfield, sir?"

"Why don't you tell me what you know?"

As George suspected, Adam barely knew anything. Edward had talked to him about the importance of following orders. The vagueness concerned George greatly. He had not even been home, since in addition to coming in early he had stayed late, and it was just as he was about to head home that Karl asked if George wished to go with him.

Karl, Adam explained, had not mentioned anything about an arrest. He likely had no idea. The only ones who knew were Gregory and Edward.

George did not know if the drive to headquarters would be sufficient, but he tried to explain to Adam what was likely about to take place. He owed that to Adam and to Karl, whom he would find time to explain it to if they had a few moments alone.

"I do believe Edward plans ultimately on arresting Danny."

Adam became quiet quickly, and quite uncomfortable. "But you've got a plan, don't you, sir?"

"I do, Adam." Taking a deep breath, George continued on. "Edward believes my son is part of the coup. After careful consideration with Gregory, I plan on revealing it was all me."

Adam was quiet for some time. "Do you think it will work?"

"I have to try."

It made sense to Adam. Which brought him to his more difficult question. "What do you think will happen to you?"

George sighed. "I don't know. It's possible I'll have to resign, though since I've hated this position from the start, I doubt that Edward will do me the favor. It's possible I'll be arrested or detained. I've been trying to prepare my family. I told them the best I knew how. I trust Maria will be strong for the children."

"When did you think of this, sir? We were just speaking to Director Roth and I didn't catch on to you bringing up any such thing…"

"You're correct. I spoke to my brother on the way home from work earlier today."

"Oh."

George had to give a small chuckle. Such was a normal, expected reaction. Gregory had not been surprised to hear from George anymore. Nothing surprised him anymore. He had always believed George wanted to be a good father, and now he was doing something about it.

George worried about Gregory in this plan, but Gregory just told him to do whatever it took.

The ride was quiet for a few moments until Adam began to laugh. George figured it was simply a nervous reaction and was willing to pay it no mind. Adam seemed embarrassed.

"I'm sorry, sir. You must think me inappropriate."

"I actually don't, Adam. May I ask what you were laughing about? I understand if you do not wish to share, but I could use a reason to laugh."

"Of course, sir." Adam found it only fitting. "Though it isn't exactly a funny joke I was recalling." George gave his blessing for him to continue. "I couldn't help thinking of how I remember you and my dad talking about how you were going to run for president. You discussed it often over the years, and though you talked about it less and less, it was sometimes still mentioned, up until his death, that is. And now look at the position you're in. It's… different, sir."

George understood why Adam was laughing. For if he was not laughing, he'd probably be crying. There had been too much crying recently, as there would be for the following days.

Adam's memory had served him well. While George had hoped to lead the up-and-coming Department of Ethics for a few years, he planned to someday be president. He had the backing of Karl and Harry, especially with the promise he would give them cabinet positions and not just because they were his friends, but because they were qualified. George would deal with those in his family who disagreed in time. Besides, having the honor and privilege of being elected, of bringing about change, would be worthwhile.

Once George was forced into his position as Edward's deputy, the dream became increasingly faint. Harry still brought up such a hope for George to become president, and so George indulged him. It was one of the few things that gave his friend hope. George was willing to entertain his friend until the bitter end, especially because he did hope to someday achieve such a dream.

Though that dream had, in a way, died with Harry and Leah, this was the final straw, especially if George was to be imprisoned in some way.

Adam was ready to move on soon enough in the conversation, which forced George out of such dreams for the last time. "Sir, if I may share more of what is on my mind?"

"You may."

"And sir, may I speak plainly?"

"Of course, Adam."

"Right, sir. Well I do know that it is perhaps rash and immature thinking on my part, but you see, sir, I cannot help but think that, well, you're letting them win."

Adam did speak plainly. George could understand his hesitancy to come out with it. He appreciated having Adam look out for him, in a way. As a husband, father and protector, though, George could not afford to think so selfishly. He appreciated Adam taking on such thoughts then, and in the sadness, he felt it wasn't merely the sadness at losing his friend, but for the kind of burden Adam was taking on. Both men, however, were able to agree that if Danny was kept safe, it was well worth it whatever else came. Adam did hope that George didn't mind his lamenting. George didn't mind in the slightest. He was grateful someone could give the past the attention it was due.

George wished to talk to Adam about his continued role in the department. He had had a feeling Edward was looking to change that, and it was one of the things that sat most unwell with George.

"I do not yet know of my fate, of my position, of my role as your boss. I thus can't know, at least not yet, what is to become of your position. Such a great uncertainty does worry me."

Adam appreciated such thoughts but did not take his role lightly. "Sir, whatever happens to me or my position, so long as you and your family are safe, I will take whatever comes. And I wish you to know that I will never stop fighting for your family."

George was thankful he had Adam as not only a trusted employee but a dear friend. He didn't know what else to say. Yet this was enough. Time demanded it be, for they had arrived.

Karl pulled up behind them soon after. Just as they all stepped out, George reminded Adam that he truly appreciated what Adam was doing for his family, and that he hoped that Adam would accept that George would do what he could for the younger man. Luckily, Adam understood and each of them had said their piece.

George thought to himself how he had, for several years, sometimes six or seven days a week, gone into this building. Back then, it was just a building. Today it represented something more. George thought of making such a point to Karl, but they were no longer in his parlor at home, and Karl's demeanor had significantly changed like incoming storm clouds.

Karl seemed set on heading to Edward's office. Every moment seemed a struggle to keep it together. George was glad he had not said anything, for it likely would have distressed his friend further. Karl had still said nothing after knocking on the office door.

When Edward answered, Karl hoped very much to pass George along and get out of there. Such signs of weakness, however, led Edward to draw out the discomfort.

"I see you have brought George. It's good to see you did as asked!"

"Yes. May I go now, please?"

Even Edward was shocked at the amount of pleading from Karl. He sent Karl and Adam off, adding they would need to be ready at a moment's notice.

While George was not looking forward to time with Edward, it was unavoidable, and it at least gave his friends, particularly Karl, temporary peace. George was not only relieved for his friends, but the prospect of getting this dreaded process over with.

Edward had a way of bringing up topics of conversation. Drawing the process out, so as to inflict stress, tension and have an advantage over his victim, was one such method. It was not a method he employed tonight.

"I suppose you know why you're here?"

"Yes. I think you and I need to have a conversation about my son."

"Ah." Edward folded his hands and sat upright. "George, I'll be frank. I think you need to prepare yourself and your family for your son's serving time. Anything else, I'm afraid, would be a mix up of priorities."

Before George could state his case against his son's imprisonment, Edward had more to say before he dropped quite the bombshell.

"You're not the only one who has had to straighten out his priorities. Karl has his own issues." George assumed he was referring to Tara. "You know, George, I am sure many men here have engaged in extra-marital affairs with their secretaries. I wouldn't be surprised to find you and I were in the minority who have not. But few have gotten said secretary pregnant and then been so stubborn about it."

George could not believe he was hearing such news. It made sense though, that this was what Edward had on Karl.

Edward pulled George out of his thoughts. "Oh, you didn't know?" The look on his face had given it away. "Well, now you do. It's going to come out, no matter that he was foolishly trying to keep it a secret."

It was time for George to drop a bombshell of his own. "I am well aware you plan on arresting my son. I also recall you mentioning something else."

"And what would that be, George?"

"You said you would be bringing in someone, you didn't say it definitely had to be my son."

Edward was growing impatient. "George, I did wish to call you in here to prepare you for your son's arrest in the coming weeks, since I've assumed your son has yet to have someone to inform on. I hope I do not need to say that pleading and begging will do nothing but wound your pride. If you *have* found some other unlucky soul to turn in, I suppose I can hear it."

George thought Edward underestimated him at his own peril. "Right. Well I can do better for you. I have further information about a coup."

Edward's face turned to stone. "Then you had best bring it forth, George."

Suddenly, George had a sense of power over Edward. He had something Edward wanted, even if it would lead to George's own downfall. He could only revel in it for a moment.

George merely had this prepared for a few hours, but he needed to sound convincing. "I'm the one who's been working on a coup. I hid behind my son, I am ashamed to say. I not only believed I had the skill and position to get away with it but the motivation." This next part was not an act. "I've been far too tired with how things are going, since the position change, since Harry's death, with Adam's role in the department micromanaged."

What Edward said next caused George to feel quite guilty. "What I am curious about is why you waited so long to come forward with it, when it could have spared your son hours of interrogation."

The emotion in George's voice was genuine. "Yes, well, I'm not proud of hiding behind my son for as long as I did. I'm coming out with it now, though."

Edward was puzzled as he tried to decide if this made sense. "I suppose it's all plausible. I'll have to decide what this all means, though, so don't clean out your office just yet. Oh, no. I intend to keep you working. Releasing you from this position would be a reward, not a punishment to you. As I'm sure you've expected, the same deal still stands from the last time. You stay where I tell you, and your wife doesn't become a widow."

George had expected this. He had only the slightest hope he would be released from his position, and it was a hope that was completely destroyed now. Edward could do as he wished with George, though, so long as Danny was safe.

There were a few moments of silence. Edward realized he could not stay quiet. "You want to know what this means for your son, then."

"I very much do, Edward." George saw no need to hide his anticipation. Regardless, he was unable to control it.

Edward had begun tapping his fingers on the desk, though he at least answered George. "Fine. Very well. With this newfound information, I can deal with him remaining at home. Make no mistake, George, I will have my eye on him." Such was expected. George could understand. "Your son could very well still end up finding himself arrested. You've been forewarned." George would have to hope his son would be aware of this. "George, I do hope your son is worth it to you."

Edward was right. In some ways, George thought back to Adam's comments about his presidential ambitions, about how he was still stuck in this position. George did care about his family enough, though, even Danny, to put all that aside and do what he must for them.

"He is, Edward."

Edward nodded, and that was all there was to say on the matter. George agreed to stay the night in his office, and then he was dismissed.

George had more to mention, however. "I do hope Adam will be left unharmed in this."

"We shall see about that, George. Do send him in."

That was all George was given on the matter. He would try again, but it would have to be some other time.

With a heavy heart and head, George returned to his office. Adam and Karl were waiting there.

"Adam, Director Roth needs to see you." George couldn't hide the guilt in his voice.

"Then I'll go to him," Adam said dutifully. He left his boss and Director Bradford to have time to talk. He was sure they would have much to discuss.

***

Danny had already learned from a young age that the world was unfair, yet he was still fixated on how just as he was beginning to have a relationship with his father, their family dynamic was about to change.

It had only been a few hours since George had left, though it felt like days. At least the last time George saw his family involved comforting them. It was a bittersweet memory, though, and slightly more bitter than sweet because of unfair timing.

Danny hoped that in time, whether it took months or years, he could look back at this time differently. Perhaps it wouldn't be permanently marred by such hell as he had gone through. He had to have hope about that, even if the future seemed so uncertain.

The worst for Danny was the internal conflict. His father had told him that whatever happened, he did not want Danny to blame himself. George had made the decision willingly, and he hoped it gave Danny comfort to know that he had Gregory's help.

George also reiterated that it was his duty not only as a father, but as a good person. Danny thought of trying to come up with a name for informing, but George didn't wish to put that pressure on him. As much as Danny understood and appreciated it, he still felt responsible for ripping away a father and a husband from his family.

Maria assured Danny that she had not put George up to this, that it was all of his own accord. Danny didn't need her to tell him such things, though he could understand why she did. Not too long ago it would have been necessary.

As difficult as it may have been to keep things together, Danny reminded himself he was the man of the house. He intended to fully appreciate the sacrifices his father had made.

Danny would need to pray for peace. That's what his father would have wanted, for him to finally have peace after so long. Such was the last thing Danny had said to his father, that he would strive for it.

After George left with Karl and Adam, those left behind went back into the kitchen to clean up. All were silent as they put food and dishes away.

Cassandra offered to go upstairs with Amelia, so Danny could have time with their mother. Despite having the whole downstairs, Danny couldn't bring himself to leave the kitchen table. Maria was all too happy to remain by Danny's side, wherever he wished to be.

At the kitchen table, at least, Danny could enjoy some of his mother's pie. Danny hoped to cheer her up by asking for some. Though he wasn't that hungry, seeing how delighted his mother was made it worthwhile.

Besides, she wasn't prying. Maria truly wished to be there for him. Danny responded that he was enjoying the pie, which brought genuine smiles to both of their faces.

Maria asked how Danny was feeling, and as she asked, she could already see how Danny was still struggling emotionally from the interrogation as well as George's leaving.

"You can be honest with me, Danny," she said. "I know we've already talked, and I don't mean to pressure you in any way, but I want you to know you don't have to hide your feelings from me." It was as if she had read her son's mind. She was his mother, though, after all. "Whatever you decide to share, know that I'm here for you."

Danny took the hand she had stretched out on the table and gave it the most loving and confident squeeze he could manage. "It's been difficult, mom." She nodded that she understood but didn't interrupt. "So much has happened over a short period of time. It's been so confusing and painful and, well, the ways in which I've hung back, I suppose I've done in order to spare you."

Maria had always tried to remain strong for her husband and children, particularly since George had been forced into his position. Whatever side Gregory and Thomas were on, however she had felt about either man in her life, she was committed to standing beside her husband, especially when he was looking out for their family. Maria was sorry to say she had faltered in that lately, as she and George had increasingly fought and then stopped talking. As sorry as she was to see George go that night, and as frightened as she was, Maria trusted and was grateful towards George for doing what he ultimately thought best, even if it meant sacrificing himself.

Maria hoped to impart some of that to her son. "I can only imagine how conflicting this must be for you. I'm sure it's a lot to deal with, but your feelings are normal.

And I cannot say this enough, that your father loves you. He knows that you love him." She reached for her son's hand grateful that he took hers. "You are loved and you are worth saving, Danny."

These words coming from his mother, in such a firm but loving way helped Danny realize perhaps he could make it through this after all.

***

George had expected Karl to be embarrassed, but then he recalled the awkward truth. Karl did not know yet that George had been told about the pregnancy.

As George went about figuring how to bring it up, Karl was the first to speak.

"I'm sorry, George, for leaving you with Edward. I wouldn't have done it had I any choice."

"I know that, Karl. Besides, I'm relieved you and Adam had each other. These past few days haven't been easy for any of us."

On the matter of Tara, George only knew what Edward had told him, and he was sure that there was more to the story. He did not wish to gossip or pry, but to remind Karl he could open up to him, as his friend.

"Karl, please know that I am not judging you…"

Karl sighed as he clutched the bridge of his nose. "You want to know what's been going on."

Though he felt awkward doing so, George owed it to his friend to admit he already knew.

"Tara is pregnant." Karl's face sunk in shock, dejection and ultimately resignation. "Edward told me."

"Oh." Karl didn't say anything else for a moment. Though George knew it was best to have told his friend right away, he still felt for his friend.

"Karl, I'm so sorry. I can only imagine what you're going through." It was important for George to show compassion rather than expressing any kind of opinion on the matter. "I'm also sorry that Edward, of all people, told me. I completely understand if you wish to keep this between Tara and you, but I'm here for you in any way I can help, even if there's not much I can do."

It was some moments before Karl responded. He mostly just went on sighing. George found it rude to check his watch, so he could only assume some minutes had gone by. "I… thank you for that, George." Quietly, George responded that it was nothing. "So, my secret is out. You know that Tara is pregnant, then." He laughed to himself a bit, though George knew he saw the situation as serious. "Did he also mention she's keeping the baby?"

George thought back to Edward and his less-than-delicate phrasing. "He did mention that, yes."

Had he been in a similar situation, though he had never even had a mistress, George knew he would have thought the same. It wasn't the child's fault. The two men had discussed the issue before, when it came to a vote which ultimately passed in the Senate. Still, even with such views, George would let Karl talk to him, if he wished.

He did. Karl had much to say.

"You know, George, I realize this is not the most… ideal situation. Tara and I were not careful, though I cannot blame her in this. It's of course my fault. I should have known better than to put her in this situation."

George found himself agreeing, but allowed his friend to continue. "We cannot just 'get rid of it,' as Edward wishes. Tara is even more set than I am."

What he said next almost brought Karl to tears. "I must admit something. I hope you won't think less of me." George beckoned for him to go on. "I admit it would be quite tempting to just 'take care of the situation.' Edward has been so persuasive."

George decided to step in to keep his friend from beating himself up any further. "It's because Edward has blackmailed you. You can acknowledge it."

Karl nodded, sighing once more. "He has. He also plans on telling Sarah and leaking the news to the press." He went on to mention the abortion. "The only thing that could stop him from doing so is if Tara has the abortion performed by someone of his choosing, so he's able to ensure it's done."

Mentioning Sarah was, in many ways, the most tragic. She was a woman completely blameless, who still loved her husband despite his failings, the affairs being the chief among them. Her love wasn't enough, though, not when Karl had Tara.

"I know she won't be happy about Tara being pregnant. How could she be? I believe she got through it all by pretending none of this was happening. But now, well, nobody is going to be able to pretend anymore."

Though George was curious as to how Edward had found out, he would have to wait and instead focus on comforting his friend.

"He's even going to tell her not just that Tara is pregnant, but that I'm going to run away with her. Forgive me, George, I know you have your own situation to deal with, but this can't be good."

Karl was right, and from the sound of it, George was piecing together that he was likely not the only one to be separated from his family. Worse for his friend, he knew even less about his situation than George knew about his.

In deciding what to say, George mentioned his point from earlier. "First of all, you don't need to convince me you and Tara wouldn't have the abortion." Such assurances seemed to calm Karl. "Please know I can sympathize with having much to handle."

Both men recalled how George had not yet told Karl of his own fate.

"I won't be able to go home myself. I took the blame for Danny, so I'll be brought in in his place." Karl immediately looked sympathetic, but such was not the reason for George mentioning this.

If there was a way to impart hope, George was going to take it. "I have to have hope that Adam will have a better fate. Perhaps he can continue with our plans and goals then." Adam could also be counted on for familial assistance. "You know that Adam would never pass judgement. He will help us as he knows how to, I'm sure."

George could not pretend to play God. None of them could, yet he had to have trust and faith in the Lord. He hoped such a reminder would comfort his friend.

Karl did not remain silent. "Thank you, George. Thank you for your friendship, for all you've done for me, whether I deserved it or not." George explained that it was nothing, that he only wished he could do more for Karl.

With the present calm, George found it to be the right time to ask how it happened Edward found out.

"Karl, if I may ask something?"

"You want to know how he found out."

George answered that he did. He figured Karl wished to keep the matter as private as possible, with Edward likely the last person to involve.

"Recall you coming to the office at the end of that day?" George did. "Tara told me then. She was hoping to tell me after I came out with you. I wish I had been more serious, that I had realized this could always happen."

Fortunately Karl did not beat himself up for long. "Once you had left and she told me there was something she had to tell me, we decided it was perhaps best if we talked about it in my office. She was nervous to tell me at first. Honestly, George, I thought she was preparing to leave me, and I'll admit the thought troubled me."

Despite how problematic the affair—any affair—was, Karl truly did love Tara. He recognized it was best for them not to be together, but he had trouble letting her go.

"That was when Tara told me she was pregnant. I didn't know how to react, so I didn't. She burst into tears then. She thought I was angry with her about the situation. Tara knew it wasn't proper, but she couldn't help being excited. She asked me to forgive her, George, and then she said she loved me."

Karl wasn't exactly sure when Edward came by or how much he heard, but it had been enough. Karl and Tara were foolish for thinking they had privacy.

They didn't realize that Edward was there until Tara went to leave. She let out a little start of surprise, but Edward put on his usual charm as he assured her that he had just gotten there. He claimed that he was about to knock when she opened the door herself, and she believed him.

Tara wasn't always so naive, Karl explained. In this case, it could be understood, though. Once Tara's back was turned, Karl could tell Edward knew. His face said it all.

Sure enough, Karl was called to Edward's office the very next morning. It was strongly recommended that they 'get rid of it.' In the coming days the pressure only increased.

After he finished, Karl just stared ahead. Sharing so much had exhausted him, physically and emotionally.

When he spoke again, it was to acknowledge that the whole thing had just now hit him and hit him hard. George was somewhat surprised he was sharing so much after being quiet for so long, but he was more than willing to listen.

Karl hadn't been able to bring himself to tell Tara that Edward knew, that he wanted her to have an abortion. Tara had mentioned her refusal to have one all on her own. He knew he would eventually have to tell her, he just didn't know how or when.

Karl had kept the news not only from Tara but from Sarah, which was why he had been so anxious about

Edward making such a thing known. He was ashamed to say he couldn't bear to face her, his own wife.

The situation was, in many ways, pathetic, and pathetic was exactly how Karl felt. George could see it. Such was the nature of getting wrapped up in affairs. That was not to say his friend did not deserve mercy, that his already complicated life needed to be worsened by Edward.

Karl asked if he could discuss George's situation for a moment. George felt his friend had relived his own predicament enough and that it was perfectly acceptable to move on.

Edward had been asking Karl about George, about Danny, about Adam. "I was distant with you because I wanted to be honest when I said I didn't know anything. I'm sorry if that came off differently." Karl had more to admit. "I also wished to speak with Edward as little as possible, selfish though that may be." Knowing Edward, George didn't find it selfish at all. Karl was facing his own troubles.

Though both were concerned about Adam, they couldn't do very much about how long he was with Edward. George took the time to speak his mind then.

"I can't go home." George could feel Karl looking at him. "I said that already. I'm sorry."

Actually turning to Karl, though, he could see how sympathetic and understanding his friend appeared to be. "You of all people, George, hardly need to apologize."

George continued on then. His thoughts would not quit. "I just hope my efforts to keep Danny out of prison actually work. Edward mentioned it didn't have to come to this, that we could have picked any person to take his place."

Karl listened politely, took a moment to choose his words, then set out, determined to reassure his friend. "George, I can only imagine how difficult this is for you and your family. But you are a good, moral man, and that is why you didn't send some poor random soul."

While it was still just the two of them, George wished to bring up the role and duties they had as fathers. "I just can't help thinking how this affects my role as a father, especially since it seemed to have taken such a long and dramatic occurrence to really feel like I could connect with Danny."

Karl had been present at the barbecue where Gregory and Thomas confronted him about not only his taking on the position of Director of Ethics but as a father. Though George didn't often talk about it, Karl could see how much it affected him, and he hated Thomas for what he had done to his own brother-in-law. "You have been a good father, George. I don't know if I could ever impress that upon you enough, but I do mean it. With all your children."

"I certainly hope so, Karl. But yes, this has been a difficult time for Danny. Please excuse his behavior."

Karl waved it off as nothing, even smiled. "Of course. I have a son of my own."

Ah, yes, Jack. Though George could not know everything about Karl's family life, what he did know, besides the affairs, seemed picturesque in a way. "You know, Karl, I had often envied you for the relationship you had with Jack. You have a fine son."

The mention of the son whom he did not know when he would next see brought tears to Karl's eyes. They were, in a way, happy tears, for Karl could hardly be prouder of his son. "Thank you for that, George. I think the name of the game, for all of us to some degree, has been about appearances. Even Harry knew that. I know you think about him, even if you don't say it. I do, too. So much did not come to light until after the fact." Karl was trying, as he had ever since Harry's death, to tell George not to blame himself.

It was on that note that the two decided it was time to check up on Adam.

George couldn't help his nerves or that his stomach was in knots. It didn't help that they could hear Edward's voice as they got closer.

Looking to Karl, who nodded, George loudly knocked. He had not been heard, though, on account of all the yelling, which caused George to cringe. Fortunately, that soon subsided and so George knocked again.

The door was answered so suddenly, it almost banged against the wall. "What?" Edward appeared irritated, his face red. Realizing they were there about Adam, he didn't even give them a chance to speak before he shoved the young man out the door. Adam was shaken up but not hurt.

It was expected that Edward would merely shut the door in their faces. Before ultimately doing so, however, he made it clear that nobody was going anywhere but their offices for the rest of the night. He would be speaking to them in the morning.

Seeing no reason to stand there, the three men made their way back to George's office.

George quickly thought to ask if Adam was all right.

"Yes, I'm fine, sir."

George was not so sure. "Adam, if you would like to talk about the matter with either of us." Karl nodded in encouragement.

"Thank you, both of you. But I'd much rather know what I can do for you, Director Whitfield."

Karl agreed with Adam. George was outnumbered then, and he figured he might as well accept what help he could get, while he could still get it. This included with organizing his office, but also something more.

"I think it's best if we all pray tonight like we have never prayed before. We're certainly going to need all the divine intervention we can get."

***

Danny had stayed up for hours talking with his mother. It had been a much needed talk about his father, and how Danny could appreciate what George had done for him. There was also discussion about more trivial matters, which helped Danny to relax.

The hours spent with his mother reminded Danny how it felt like it had been long, too long, since he had really gotten to catch up with Cassandra. It was after midnight, but if she was still awake, he told himself, he would check up on her.

He stopped by her room, but she was not there. Instead she was in Danny's room, sitting on his bed. When she saw her brother, though, she suddenly felt meek and apologized as she made her way out.

"Cassandra, wait, please."

As soon as she stopped and Danny took a real look at her, he could see there were tears in her eyes. He held her then, hoping it communicated how sorry he truly was for everything, especially when it came to pushing her away.

Upon letting her go, Danny emphasized that he wanted them to be always able to go to each other. He didn't know when their father was coming home, and he was afraid about the future. It was okay for her to be, too. They could only live out each day with the hope that it would be better than the last one. Cassandra could agree there.

Though he only just recently became close with their father, Danny was well aware how close Cassandra was with George. His sister had always tried to be strong, perhaps too strong.

"I'm sorry I got dad sent away," Danny said, his voice suddenly almost choked with tears.

"Oh, Danny, please don't blame yourself." Cassandra meant this more than she meant anything. She refused to choose between her brother and their father. "I do hope you understand now how much he loves you. Besides, we'll always have each other, you and I. I do believe that."

He, too, believed.

The two talked until it was late enough that Cassandra decided to sleep in Danny's room, in the bed Adam had slept on during his time with them. Perhaps tonight didn't have to be all bad then.

Suddenly, Amelia appeared in the doorway. She was half-asleep and frightened. Asking if Cassandra was there, she explained that she had had a bad dream. She hadn't had her glasses on, and as dark as it was, she hadn't seen her sister.

"I'm right here, Amelia." Cassandra went over to her.

As she was comforted by Cassandra, Amelia felt instantly better upon hearing the suggestion she sleep in there with them. It was a big enough room that they could include their younger sister.

While they fell asleep, Cassandra and Danny told Amelia stories of how they used to have sleepovers all the time, sometimes with Adam. Amelia was excited to hear about it and hoped they wouldn't spare any exciting details.

The situation was far from perfect, but it was ideal in its own way. At least for that night, the Whitfield siblings could be together.

A Matter Of Loyalty

George woke Adam up that next morning. It was nine o'clock, rather late considering what Edward had planned for that day, though Adam was still groggy. He had slept terribly and fitfully, knowing that no matter what happened that day, it would likely not turn out well for any of them.

Before they left for the Whitfield residence, Edward had wanted to speak with Adam once again. Adam had been lucky to only receive a warning and a threat for accessing the files to pass along to George, but topics far more involving and dire needed to be discussed.

Lest Adam feel any excitement or anticipation because he was privy to secret information, another warning was in order.

For his admitted part in aiding and abetting those planning a coup against their own department, George Whitfield was to be under close confinement in one of the rooms at headquarters. He would not be officially removed from his position, however. Adam's predictable confusion did not go unnoticed.

Edward felt it necessary to explain the reasoning behind George's situation, in part because Edward wanted to make it clear how George could consider himself lucky.

"If there's one man I don't want to make a martyr out of, it's George Whitfield. I will come up with a further suitable punishment, but in the meantime, he still holds enough trust from other key allies, and I plan to put that to good use. With any hope, we can snuff out any coup attempts even faster than the last time," Edward explained.

It was true that Edward could just place a phone call or send his nephew and Howard to deliver a message. He was going with George, though, sending him home, however briefly, to send that message. Such an announcement was meant to have a far-reaching effect. Edward needed it to, which meant Adam was to do exactly as he was told, and that meant not deviating or causing any kind of trouble or inconvenience. Otherwise, the consequences could be dire for all involved.

As nervous as he was, Adam was on high alert to pay attention.

"We will be leaving shortly to go over there, and you will be coming with us. Now as I said, this entails a warning. You will do as you are told. Is that understood, Adam?"

Adam dutifully nodded. It was just easiest to do as he was commanded in that moment. He could reassess later.

"Very well, Adam," Director Roth said. "If all goes well, you can trust that no unnecessary harm will result."

Adam didn't trust that for a moment. He kept that to himself, though.

Before being dismissed, Adam was told to let George know to come in as well. While he did not want to be in Director Roth's presence more than necessary, the lack of clarity about the day's events was not welcome. It brought anxieties of its own, even. Edward was done with him, though, and so that was all the time Adam was to be granted with him.

George's meeting with Edward was even more brief and terse. He had been given the same warning. Notably, he had not been given the same assurances Adam had.

From there, things moved quickly. Adam and George were to say their goodbyes to Karl. He was dismissed for the day to sort out his affairs.

Everyone had been updated as much as they were going to be. Edward wanted everyone to move on quickly with such things. He normally had no patience for time-wasting, but especially not on this day.

"You are doing a great service to my friend and his family. Thank you for that and take heart," Karl said, leaning in close so only Adam could hear his words.

Karl patted Adam on the shoulder. It was time to go. Scott and Howard were to come along. Scott dreaded the assignment before he even knew what it involved. He was not privy to the same information Adam and George were but was expected even more to follow orders. Whatever it entailed, Scott knew enough to realize it would not be pleasant.

Initially Adam was to go with the other two young employees. That way the dread would consume him even sooner than Adam feared it would. Adam knew he had little say or influence, especially on something that was so inconsequential to Director Roth.

Fortunately for Adam, George had enough clout on such matters. He was permitted to drive with Adam while Edward took his nephew and Howard along.

It meant several more free moments together. In many ways, it meant the world.

The drive that morning was somewhat similar to the night before. Adam had been more naive, though, and because of it, sheltered from unpleasant truths he would soon have to reckon with. He longed for it to be that previous night.

George offered to drive, sensing Adam's nerves. In addition to the anxiety and dread, Adam felt guilt. He felt like the Whitfields belonged to him in a way, with how much he owed his life to them.

"Adam, I can see how anxious you are. You don't have to pretend." Anyone could see how anxious he was. Director Whitfield was merely being polite with his comforting tone. "I myself don't know what is going to happen today to any of us. Whatever happens, though, and

I do mean this, nothing is your fault. Whatever Director Roth says or my son may say in anger, or Scott or Howard, you are blameless." They were stopped at a light. "Promise me you understand and will take this into consideration."

Adam felt more conflict when it came to the man who, yes, was his boss, but had done so much more for him. If he said he understood, he didn't want to be lying.

"Yes, sir, I do. I understand. I'll… try."

George gave him a sad but knowing look as the light changed. "Good. That's all I can ask you to do."

They were no longer looking at each other, as George had his eyes on the road. Adam, not for the first time, had a very particular feeling about the possibility of intervening in some way.

The rest of the ride proceeded mostly in silence. If Adam wished to say anything more, his chance was slipping away. Even when they arrived and he still had nothing sufficient to say, they got to the house far too soon for Adam's liking. He felt as if he was going to his death, though it wasn't himself Adam was concerned for.

Edward signaled for them to park at the very end of the driveway. He had Howard park right beside them. Just as they were about to get out, Adam thought of it. He had split seconds to decide if he was going to speak.

"Director Whitfield, sir?" He always called him that when it was the two of them, even if his title was Deputy Director.

"Yes, Adam?"

"Whatever happens, sir, please forgive me if I can't do enough."

Had they privacy and time, George would have embraced and held Adam close to him like he would his own son. They had neither luxury, however, and so a muttered "of course" would have to do.

It didn't calm Adam completely, but it was enough to allow him to get out of the car.

Edward didn't even address them right away. He had told Adam a brief enough plan, mostly just directing him to not get involved. Howard and Scott were to have more to do with today, whether Scott liked it or not.

Adam found it odd that Howard was trying to speak with Scott, who was barely even giving him the time of day. He seemed almost as perturbed as Adam about what was to come. Adam had neither the closeness with Scott nor the time to ask if he knew something he didn't know.

All of that was stopped by Edward speaking at the moment.

"I have something more to mention, if I may, Adam."

It should have been simple enough, but Adam still felt his voice quavering. "Yes, sir?"

"Right. I don't think that I need to remind you of the little discussion we had just earlier this morning, do I?"

Adam had been hoping that Edward wouldn't do this, but he couldn't be surprised. He still had to answer. "No, sir. Of course not. I remember what you said."

Edward and Howard exchanged a pointed look. Adam knew he couldn't very well react, though. "Good," Edward said. "Fortunately, you have a way to prove yourself. You are to retrieve the Whitfields, all of them, and bring them out here to the driveway." His tone was pleasant, but wouldn't be for long, especially when he expected Adam to act immediately.

Adam did not know what made him hesitate. It did not go unnoticed. "Adam, may I ask what the holdup is?" His tone reflected a vanishing patience.

"No, sir, everything is fine."

"Did you just say no to me, Adam?" Though Howard was laughing as Edward spoke, he was the only one.

Adam closed his eyes in an attempt to regain calm and composure. "No, sir. I-I didn't mean it that way. My utmost apologies, Director Roth, sir. What I meant to say is that I'll get right on it, sir."

"Fantastic!" Edward's tone was once more cheerful, despite the nature of the task. "On you go, then."

Though he finally set off, Adam was not fast enough. That he dared to make eye contact with George didn't help, either. While he didn't say anything, the sigh released from Edward was not comforting. If Director Roth wasn't going to do anything, Howard decided he would. "What the hell are you waiting for? You heard the man! Go get the goddamn family, Adam," he urged with a push.

It was the push Adam needed. Fearing Howard or their boss would become violent, Adam took the advice to heart. Scott didn't see why it had been necessary, but Howard pointed out that it at least worked. Adam knew better than to let anything else distract him, though, and so the conversation between Howard and Scott quickly went out of mind.

The long walk up the driveway gave Adam time to think. He didn't want to be alone in his thoughts, though, as he was already conjuring up ideas of what was about to happen, none of them pleasant. If they continued to occupy his mind, Adam was concerned they would consume him completely. When he did reach the doorstep, it was with a heavy heart and hand that he rang the doorbell.

Maria came to the door immediately. Adam was a welcome sight, and made it easier for her to be more bright and cheerful. Adam wished she wouldn't be so optimistic.

Before Adam could break the news that she and her children were needed outside, Maria had pulled him in. He was led to the kitchen, where the children were all patiently waiting in expectation. They looked as if they had been up for hours. Nobody had slept late that morning.

Adam had still not yet said that they were needed out there, and so Maria took the lead in asking if there was any news. Adam was paying more attention to the situation now.

"I actually need you all to come outside with me, and I'm afraid I need you to do so right now."

Nobody moved despite Adam's clear instructions. Everyone looked rather confused and unhappy, and while it broke Adam's heart, he couldn't blame them. Danny decided he wasn't having any of it.

"What the hell are you talking about, Adam? I mean, I was able to get over you coming here last night, which was bad enough." Adam knew to not interrupt to say he understood that. Danny likely wouldn't let Adam get a word in edgewise. "You come here this morning now, though, just show up at my house unannounced, and tell me that I have to go outside with you. What exactly do you think you're trying to do here?"

It was a great question. Danny's guess was as good as Adam's, for Adam didn't know. He was trying to help the friends who were like family to him, but he didn't know how to do so in the way he had been forced into, if he even could help them.

Adam didn't know what else to say. "I'm just trying to follow orders, Danny. And I think that the sooner you all come outside, then—"

Danny was not going to let Adam finish his sentence as he became angry enough to throw him up against the wall. His anger management was one more thing Danny needed to work on. As unexpected as it was, Adam was determined not to show he was in pain.

For a moment everyone was too shocked at Danny to do anything. His mother and sisters tried to get him to ease up, but he ignored them. As far as Danny was concerned, it was just him and Adam.

"I can't believe you, Adam! I can't believe how you could turn your back on this family after all we've done for you." Danny pressed Adam against the wall even harder, but his words hurt worse than the physical pain. Adam could see exactly why Danny would feel this way, and he had no idea how to earn back Danny's trust, trust he probably didn't deserve.

"Who's out there?" Danny demanded, all of a sudden.

As he explained that Danny's father was out there, along with Director Roth, Howard, and Scott, Adam tried to find confidence in his voice. More than anything he wished to relay that everything was going to be okay, but there was much Adam was failing at on such a day, this included.

Danny's reactions were not helping. He threw up his hands, proclaiming that Adam was obviously sending them all out there to their deaths. Amelia let out a frightened gasp and Cassandra seemed to be taken aback as well.

During the stunned silence, Maria took a moment to jump in, and she did not sound happy.

"That is enough! If Adam is asking us to go outside, then we'll go outside! Danny, I understand how you must be feeling right now. If we give Adam a chance, though, it will hopefully not turn out so bad."

Adam did not know whether to agree with her. He hoped she could be right, that he could have some of that confidence, because he didn't feel any good or useful to anyone. Adam realized then that Danny still had him up against the wall. Danny looked poised to let him go, which would be a welcome reprieve for them all, least of all Adam's back. Danny only tightened his grip, though, as he called Adam out for his weakness and bad lying. Adam could hardly have agreed more.

Though Adam could not fight Danny physically, a sudden inspiration stirred within Adam to fight Danny on tone. He ended up surprising himself.

"Well, I don't know what the hell you want from me. Is it possible that something bad may happen out there? Yes! There you go, okay? I've admitted it. I don't have a choice in this matter, though, which is what I've been trying to tell you. I don't know what's in store for you and I pray it's not bad, but the truth is that I don't know, and you have no *idea* how much it's eating me up inside."

Danny loosened his grip and his expression softened. Adam continued on. "Every second we keep fighting is a waste, and the more time we waste, I'm afraid to say, the worse it could be. I don't know if you really want to see what happens if you just continue to attack me here. Maybe it's not the best feeling in the world to have your best friend being part of all this. I get that. But you want the truth? Well, you don't have a choice, either."

Adam had been harsh, but he needed to be. Fortunately, his words had an effect on Danny, an immediate one at that.

"Fine, you're right. Let's go, then."

Without another word Danny released Adam, who led the way outside.

From the moment they stepped outside, it was clear the scene had dramatically changed. To Adam, it was as if he had fallen into a nightmare. George was on his knees in the driveway, with Edward standing not too far away. Howard and Scott were by his side, their guns quite visible.

Such a scene was the last thing Adam wanted to happen, the last thing the Whitfield family should have to experience. He had already experienced enough pain at the hands of Director Roth when it came to his father's firing which led to the worsened alcoholism, the physical abuse, and ultimately murder-suicide. Yet here Director Roth was, causing unimaginable pain again for him all over again.

Before Adam could attempt to assure the family it hadn't been like this before, he was pulled out of his thoughts with a rough slap across the face from Edward.

"That was for taking too long," Director Roth said with not an ounce of fake cheer. "You are not off to the best of starts, Adam, I'm afraid to say."

Cassandra whimpered and Adam felt the need to quickly reassure her that he was fine without seeming as if he didn't appreciate her concern. Still, Cassandra was a strong young woman and Adam believed she would understand that he needed to focus on her brother, who was presently yelling once more at him.

Adam wondered why Director Roth didn't step in, and then, he realized that Edward must be relishing the division between the young men. Danny harped on why Adam hadn't warned them of this. If only he knew.

It was possible Adam would have little or no chance of success explaining, but he still wished to try. "Danny, I didn't know, I swear. It wasn't like this at all when I went in to get you. I know it may be tough for you to believe me right now, but that's the truth."

Given the state Danny was in, Adam doubted he would be believed. He was right. Yet for all the yelling and verbal abuse Danny hurled at him, Adam could understand.

If he had the chance, Adam would have been all too happy to let Danny shout his concerns until he was blue in the face. They had no such luxury, however.

Even if it was a fool's errand, Adam still felt a duty to try as hard as he could with Danny. Their lives could depend on it.

"Danny, please. I'm on your side. I swear on my mother's grave that nothing was like this when I went in to get you. I understand that it must all be very confusing right now. You may not know what to think or who to believe, but I really am on your side."

George soon felt sad and desperate enough to speak up. "Danny, son, if you can't believe Adam, I hope you'll at least believe me. He had nothing to do with any of this."

Edward stepped back in. Danny still hadn't indicated whether he'd listen to George.

"All right, enough is enough. I was content to have the two of you fight it out, but you were told not to interfere, George." Director Whitfield hung his head in shame. Edward had more to add, though. It was a purposeful attempt to drive Danny even further from believing Adam.

"I appreciate your efforts, Adam, but I'd say so far we are not doing a very good job with crowd control."

Danny heard what he wanted to. As far as he was concerned, Adam was as good as working with Edward Roth against Danny and his family.

Edward was pleasantly surprised not to be interrupted. Continuing on, there were a few announcements to be made.

"After his admitted confession, I have decided that George will be kept at headquarters. I am not having him publicly resign, as the last thing I wish to do is turn him into a martyr. Besides, he may still prove to be useful, as Danny might be."

Edward looked directly at Danny as he spoke next. "It is only because of my good graces you are not languishing in a cell right now. We will continue to monitor the situation, which is all the warning you need. That is, if you want your father's actions to actually mean something."

With a nod, Edward directed Howard to stand by Adam. Just as he could figure Adam likely did not trust him, Edward could not trust Adam. "Consider this your own warning," he told Adam, nodding to Howard once more. "I shouldn't need to remind you that you agreed to go along with whatever I asked of you, but it appears I do." Howard had his gun aimed at Adam, daring him to make another move.

Though Adam would not have the opportunity to get any closer to them, he was standing near enough to hear Danny proclaim he couldn't believe Adam could have made a deal with that man. Try as he would to think of Director Whitfield's reminder that this was not his fault, the words still stung.

Ultimately, Adam had nothing to say in return. Not just because of Howard's gun, though Adam did not want to get shot, to be sure. He just didn't know if anything he said would do any good anymore. Still, the silence wasn't helping with Danny. Adam wished he knew what to do.

Edward sought further ways to work against Adam. "If you prove yourself willing and cooperative, I will perhaps go easier on you."

Adam figured he was damned either way then. He had reason to be beside himself. That sense of righteous indignation wasn't going away, either. If Adam was on a mission, it was to convince Danny that he, Adam, was on Danny's side, that Edward was working against both of them. This wasn't a matter of following orders, it was a matter of loyalty.

Edward had not been anticipating a response, as evidenced by his turning around to speak to Scott. He had already been worrying about Adam, and he didn't want the same concern to exist with his nephew.

Adam couldn't see Edward's reaction when he spoke up, but Scott's shocked face was clearly visible.

"I know you'll never go easy on me. It wasn't about that. I'm here to help this family, whatever it takes, whatever you throw at me."

For a moment it was almost as if it was just Adam and Edward. Adam couldn't forget Howard for too long, though, not with that gun pointed at his back. Howard continued to hold it there as Edward approached. Edward didn't say anything, but then again Adam didn't really expect him to. The backhand slap he received across the face, hard as it was, wasn't surprising either.

Danny became his next target. While there was no gun pointed at him, not yet at least, Adam knew better than to feel at all relieved.

"It is true that your friend has been involved in some rather complicated and morally conflicting situations."

"He." Danny was breathing too harshly to finish in one sentence. "Is not my friend anymore. Not after what he's done."

Adam knew that any amount of sympathy Director Roth had was all just an act. Edward was still going with that act to sow discord.

"Well, regardless of what you consider him to be, and if I may offer my take, I'm not surprised you feel that way, he's in a tight spot. It's so tight that you mustn't be surprised with whatever Adam will do to get out of it."

Danny was in quite a state and had been for the past several days, but Adam did not understand how he couldn't see what Edward Roth was trying to do there.

When Adam tried to say more, though, Howard jabbed the gun into his back. "Jesus Christ, Adam, just shut the fuck up."

George tried once more to speak up. His voice was quiet and scratchy at first, but it got clearer as he continued on. "Danny, please, just trust Adam. He wants to help you, truly. You've been best friends your whole life. He hasn't turned on you yet and I don't understand how he could be capable of doing such a thing now."

Danny looked over at Adam as he considered his father's words. His softened expression actually gave Adam hope, only for Edward to squash it with what he said next.

"Yes, well, that does not mean he isn't capable, George. More importantly though, I think you forget what I said earlier. And now, just as I promised, there will be no more warnings."

As Edward continued on, Adam had no choice but to listen, though his attention did slightly wander over to Cassandra and Amelia, both of them understandably terrified. That Adam attempted to make eye contact with Cassandra, his face still red from the slap, upset her even more and she turned away completely.

Edward continued on. "As I said, George will be at headquarters, but all of you will be staying exactly put. There will be rules and regulations dictated, and I do not need to be hunting you all down. Lest I need to be blunt, you don't need that, either."

Maria thought of stepping in as Edward approached Danny, but she was waved away by her son. He did not need to see anyone else punished.

"I don't need to remind you, young man, that there is an open file on you which could at any point turn into an open investigation if I don't get information from you which satisfies me. Is that clear?" As soon as Danny nodded, Edward had moved on to Maria. Adam wished he could do something to help this woman and her family, but he knew better than to act out at such a moment. It still maddened him to no end to see such a helpless, innocent, kind person harassed.

"Now, if I may give you some advice, Mrs. Whitfield." His tone started off friendly enough but quickly became impatient, especially because she was softly crying. "I highly advise against you taking your children and fleeing to your brother or brother-in-law. We will find you, and there will be consequences. In such an event, I will make certain that the next time you see your son, it will be to identify his body." Edward had her clarify that she heard and understood him. Adam had to marvel at her managing to nod through her tears, but it was not enough for Edward. He needed her to clarify once more she was sure.

Adam was becoming increasingly anxious once more. It pained him to see Edward make this as difficult as he possibly could. There was no reason for this other than to torture and torment.

He sighed. That was all he did, yet such behavior from Adam was enough to cause a reaction. Howard must have felt it and sent a signal to Edward, who came marching over, wearing the angriest face Adam had seen on him yet. Though he could not see Howard's expression, Adam could make out Scott's anxiety and George's devastation.

"Is there a problem here, Adam?" Edward expected an answer, one which Adam did not know how to give. Of course there was a problem. None of this was necessary. The family had been alerted to George's fate and Danny was reminded of the deal. They should have been able to leave the family in as much peace as possible.

If Adam was going to need some coaching, Edward would provide it. "I can see that there is much you wish to say, so why don't you say it?" While Adam was hesitating, Director Roth took out his own gun, and placed it right up against Adam's mouth. Cassandra whimpered so loudly Adam could hear it from where he was standing.

"Say it, Adam. I'm sure you'd rather come out with it than have this family see me blow you away in their driveway." Cassandra began to cry.

It provided the motivation Adam needed. "F-fine. You need to leave this woman alone. She has done nothing wrong and you're abusing her and her children like common criminals."

Despite Adam doing as he asked, Edward did not move his gun. Adam shut his eyes, preparing to brace himself in case he really was going to be shot and killed.

He didn't. Instead, Edward mentioned that it appeared Adam would not be taking him up on his offer after all. This time, Edward was certainly being rhetorical.

He mentioned for Howard to watch Adam, and then walked away.

Adam had found his voice to become outspoken. "You'd have to be out of your mind to think I would take you up on that offer."

Edward told his nephew not to look like such a moron and marched back over to Adam. "It seems like we weren't done running our mouth, were we?"

With as close as they were standing to each other, Adam was rightfully afraid to even blink in front of Director Roth. Considering it was possible that this was the end, Adam let Edward know that indeed he was not done speaking.

Edward was not surprised, as Adam was his father's son, after all. Deciding Adam had said enough even if Adam had not yet decided so, he told Howard to move aside. Adam continued to brace himself, while Cassandra was audibly crying.

"I hope that you have said your piece, Adam. One more outburst out of you, and I *will* use this gun. Is that understood?" he asked, whispering in Adam's ear.

It was clear. Edward did not say who he would use the gun on. Adam didn't dare wish to put anyone else in any further danger. He quickly and dutifully answered that he understood.

Before walking away for good, after a moment's thought, Edward decided Adam did need to face some sort of consequence. It wasn't with a bullet, though it still involved his gun as he deftly used the butt of the gun to hit Adam in the back of the head. It was enough to draw blood and knock Adam out.

Adam opened his eyes fairly quickly. Still, he had been out long enough for Cassandra to come running over to him. While he was thankful for her concern, Adam very much feared for her and how she could be used by Edward Roth.

He did not brush her away to be cruel. Far from it; Adam thought first of Cassandra's safety. Touching the back of his head and seeing how much he bled did not help with the pain and it certainly did not help Cassandra. Still, Adam knew he had to get her to back off.

Before Adam was able to depend on Danny to come collect his sister, Edward was already pulling the two apart. Adam felt the most helpless he had yet that day to hear that Edward decided Cassandra would be going back to headquarters with them for a yet-to-be-determined amount of time. Edward was doing so in retaliation to Adam's and George's outbursts, as using the young woman seemed to be the best way to punish both men.

"This is one more way in which I can make sure you know I mean business," Edward announced. "Cassandra will be coming back with us then. I'll keep her for a day, maybe two. It all depends on my mood."

What followed was a scene. Maria was literally begging Edward for mercy as was George, though he was even more helpless. Neither of them made any progress; both of them were ignored.

When Danny tried to offer himself up instead, Edward looked for a moment as if he would consider bringing him along, but then remembered he already had something in mind for Danny.

Adam couldn't help blaming himself and his outburst. Perhaps if he had kept his damn mouth shut, he wouldn't have been knocked out and Cassandra wouldn't have come running over in concern, providing the idea for Edward. *Was Cassandra inevitably bound to have done so regardless? Especially if Edward had found some other reason to target Adam?* Perhaps. Adam couldn't know for sure, and the not knowing was what maddened him, especially as he looked over to see George hang his head. He didn't know if he had ever seen the man more devastated before.

Edward, feeling enough damage had been done in addition to communicating what he had been there to say, found himself ready to go. Another Whitfield family member had something else in mind, however.

As Maria tried to explain as best as she could to the ten year old that she had to say goodbye to her father and sister, and that she did not know when she'd be seeing them again but that it would hopefully be soon, Amelia was not having it.

She desperately ran over to clutch onto her father, as if she could shield him and her sister from being sent away. Nobody could reason with her to do otherwise. Not her mother, father or sister could get her to understand, because as far as she was concerned, it wasn't she who needed to understand. These men who had come to their home, had hurt Adam and confused her brother and made her mother and sister cry needed to leave them alone. Amelia didn't think Cassandra had ever done anything wrong in her life, especially not something to warrant her being punished by this man.

Amelia finally obliged when she was told she could hug them goodbye. As she went to embrace her sister, however, she refused to let go. She wasn't going to go anywhere unless they made her.

It wasn't someone who ultimately pulled Amelia away, but something. Initially after Edward fired his gun, it was as if time had stopped for those few minutes. The shot had been the only audible noise, then came a horrible scream. Initially Adam thought it had been Mrs. Whitfield who had been shot, but it was Amelia, an innocent child who hadn't even fully understood the situation at hand. Her mother was merely reacting. He was too distracted to notice that Howard had stepped in front of him now.

Adam had been able to see it all unfolding before him, yet he couldn't do anything to stop it, not a thing. As he tried to run over to Amelia, Adam felt another kind of shock. It wasn't outward at the chaotic scene going on, but down. A knife was sticking out of his stomach, stuck there by Howard.

***

Edward ushered George and a sobbing Cassandra into George's car and drove off. He would let his nephew and Howard deal with the mess and with bringing Adam back to headquarters. Edward did not need to stick around to know that the child was going to die. It was unfortunate, but it was also preventable. He had only meant to fire his gun as a warning shot, it wasn't his fault if she ran straight into the bullet's path. If it was anyone's fault, it was that of her parents and her older siblings who should have been able to contain her.

As Edward drove the car, George sat in the back, doing his best to console his surviving daughter. She kept asking over and over how this could have happened. He wished he had an answer for her, but none seemed to suffice.

Cassandra wondered not only at the cruelty of this man who had hurt Adam and shot her sister, but at how her father was able to be as strong as he was. To her, her father was the strongest man she knew, especially in such an instance. She hoped he would be able to impart some of that to her. If only George, for all of his recent failings and conflicts, knew just how much his daughter looked up to him, he might have gotten through the past two and a half years as less of a shell of a man.

While he was compassionate and strong for his Cassandra, George was not impractical. Once she had calmed down, George explained to Cassandra what she already knew, that time had unfortunately likely run out for Amelia. It had not, Cassandra reminded him, run out for Adam.

Edward spoke up then to remind George if he did not want any more dead children on his hands, he would do exactly as he was told. Edward did emphasize that he did not mean Cassandra, and that she was merely being used as a bargaining chip for the next few days. Cassandra was hardly relieved, as she was still worried about her brother. Edward Roth certainly had not offered any reassurances about him.

Cassandra was not the only one to mention Adam, however. "It was a foolish thing Adam did, trying to intervene," Edward said. Cassandra dearly hoped that Adam would not be blamed for Amelia's death. Though he wasn't, what Edward said next caused her to worry all over again. "He, of course, did not help himself, not with your son and certainly not with me. He has committed acts of insubordination for which he must be punished. I've yet to draw up plans, but know that I will."

She did not know why she bothered whispering, as that cruel man was likely to hear her regardless. Speaking softly as she could, though, Cassandra implored her father to commit to doing something for Adam. She did not know how he would actually need it.

***

As he heard the sobs coming from Mrs. Whitfield, Adam knew that he needed to get over to them, even if all he would be able to provide was useless comfort. He refused to stand there and do nothing, though.

He still had that knife sticking out of him though.

Nevertheless, Adam had enough adrenaline to push past Howard and run over to where an innocent child was dying. At least he thought he did. Howard would not have it. He had an order to keep Adam where he was and intended on carrying it through, no matter what.

It was then Adam realized that this was likely calculated between Director Roth and Howard, at least to the extent that Adam would be prevented from intervening. In preventing Adam from going over to Amelia, it looked as if Adam was just standing by doing nothing, the one thing he had promised himself would not happen. Adam couldn't blame Danny for his righteous indignation.

Amelia was dead, yet Howard was still unrelenting. Finally, he took the knife out. He was not supposed to kill Adam, but perhaps Howard had gotten ahead of himself, though he had fortunately missed vital organs. It still looked like they would have to account for Adam needing medical attention then. Howard ordered Adam to stay put while he talked things over with Scott and the Whitfields.

Though he was left completely alone, Adam was too much in shock and too weakened to do what he had just tried moments before. It was why Howard left him there with complete confidence.

As much pain as he had caused, Howard had also been what was holding Adam upright. Without him, Adam collapsed onto the ground. He could fight back the curses which almost left his mouth, but not the wince in pain. The driveway was perhaps the worst place he could be, so with what strength he had left, Adam crawled onto the grass, rolled onto his back and waited, praying no more harm would come to any of them.

It was the first time all day Adam was alone with his thoughts. He was not meant to be for long, however. Adam turned to see a yelling match between Howard and Danny, who had gone to push Howard before Scott stepped in. Maria was still crying as she held Amelia's lifeless body.

Once the situation had calmed down enough, Howard tried once more to address them. Adam could make out that they were talking about him. He could see Maria hesitate and then nod. Danny, on the other hand, was not so quiet.

"I don't know how clear I can make it to you people that he is *not* my friend. I'm sure as hell not going to be doing him any favors."

They had been told they were not permitted to help Adam. Though he wasn't surprised by them, Danny's words almost hurt Adam as much as the knife.

Adam finally looked down at where he had been stabbed. He wasn't dying. At least he didn't think he was dying. There was still a lot of blood. Adam finally got the idea to apply pressure to the area with his hand, wishing he had thought to do so sooner, especially when his vision was starting to become blurry. The tears didn't help. Adam could just barely make out Danny going inside, carrying Amelia's lifeless body. As he was heading in, Danny hadn't noticed his friend had been stabbed, though Adam didn't think he would care even if he had.

Howard came back over, ordering Adam to get up. He even threatened to get out the knife again, not believing that Adam was having trouble moving.

Adam heard Scott speak up for the first time that day. His voice sounded strange. "Jesus, Howard. Give him a minute, would you?" Surprisingly but fortunately, Howard listened. He grumbled to himself, but at least he put the knife away.

Maria started to make her way over. Howard, still short-tempered and none too happy, noticed right away. "What the fuck is she doing here?" Scott was just as surprised as he was. He hadn't even talked to her, never mind told her to come. Adam knew even less about what she was doing there.

"I just wanted to say goodbye to Adam, please." She was no longer crying and had a calm complacency to her.

As he convinced Howard that Mrs. Whitfield had already been through enough, Scott got him to relent. Howard did order them to be quick, however.

Maria had been too distracted to react to Adam's condition. He couldn't really blame her considering she had just lost her husband and both daughters, one of them permanently.

When Maria did come over to Adam, she was nearly in hysterics once more. It was at that moment that Adam was prevented from telling her he was fine, even when he most certainly was not, on account of the gasp of pain that escaped his lips, no matter how hard he tried otherwise.

As Maria was trying to figure out what to do, Howard took advantage of the time to get them moving, especially since it would take a while with Adam's pace.

Maria wasn't having it, though. "No wonder you hadn't come over for Amelia. You couldn't." Adam nodded as he blinked back tears. "I'm not letting you leave with them. I won't!"

Adam would rather be comforted by Mrs. Whitfield, but Scott and Howard had their orders. Adam broke the news to her that he had to return to headquarters.

Adam hated to have to disappoint her. Scott was the one to finalize their parting. "All right, Mrs. Whitfield. I'm really very sorry, but it is time to say your goodbyes." That he apologized did not go unnoticed by Howard, who wanted to know what business it was for Scott to even say he was sorry. Scott shut him down with a warning look not to undermine him.

Howard dragged Adam along as they made their way to the car. It took Adam considerable self-control for him to not cry out in pain. He didn't wish this to be any worse than it had to be for Mrs. Whitfield.

Mrs. Whitfield called out desperately for them to wait just as they were about to the car. "I'm not letting you take him anywhere until I'm sure that he'll get medical attention."

Howard just shrugged. "I can assure you he will, Mrs. Whitfield," Scott said, making a mental note that Adam did look bad.

With a nod from Mrs. Whitfield, it was time for the three of them to leave.

"Goodbye, Adam. I trust that God will protect and keep you."

"Goodbye, Mrs. Whitfield." Adam's voice almost caught. He was determined to not let it. "Thank you for all you've done for me. I won't forget it." Such goodbyes, Adam thought, could almost be signaling the last time they would see each other. He fervently prayed this was not the case.

Howard was about to pull away before Adam remembered one more thing. Miraculously he waited.

"Mrs. Whitfield, please do me one thing?"

"Yes, dear? What is it?"

"Don't tell Danny about this. Please." Maria quickly pieced together he meant the stabbing. Adam didn't want anyone else knowing. The less people found out, the better. Though she couldn't quite understand his reasoning, Maria promised she would oblige.

With one last word of thanks and a final wave from Adam, Howard sped off. They had already delayed beyond what was necessary, and he couldn't believe all the apologizing Scott had done or even the sympathy he had shown.

Scott surprised all of them, even himself, when he shouted at Howard a reminder that an innocent little girl had just been killed a few minutes ago. He wasn't going to take any shit from him about that or anything else for the rest of the day.

Checking his watch for the first time all day, Adam was surprised to see that it was just past noon. What a tragedy it had managed to be in those first few hours he had been awake.

The Suit Jacket

Cassandra quietly sobbed into her father's chest as Edward drove them to headquarters. Her father was being arrested, her brother had been interrogated and her little sister had been killed. God only knew what would happen to Adam. While Cassandra was not completely naive to the events of the last few years surrounding her father's change in title, she had never expected this to happen.

Though she was afraid, her father's presence did give her peace of mind. There was no one she'd rather have by her side throughout all of this tragedy, though she wished he hadn't been affected for several years now.

They were pulling up to headquarters then. The gates opened automatically for Edward's car. Cassandra wondered if anyone would see them or dare come to her aid. The thought lasted only for a moment, though. Nobody would be the wiser about the true nature of her presence there. *Even if they did, who was to say they'd intervene?*

Edward did not need to use his gun or even take it out, but just knowing that he had it was enough to get George and Cassandra to do exactly as they were told.

Though Cassandra felt comfort in taking her father's hand in hers, it was not meant to last. Not long after they entered the building, they stopped in front of a door. This would be where Cassandra was to spend the next few days then, to be used as a bargaining chip.

She was afraid. Cassandra could admit as much to herself. She would be strong and brave though, especially for her father. Speaking of George, he was the one having a difficult time letting go. Cassandra wished she could make it easier on him, though she did not know how.

Edward was patient, knowing that he was getting Cassandra into that room no matter what. He shouldn't have to be, though; he knew George knew better. "George, come now," he said almost sweetly, which made him all the more frightening. "There are worse places I could put her. She'll be fine here, which you'll see when you do exactly as I say."

Cassandra knew it was worthwhile to comply quickly and quietly. She gave her father's hand one last squeeze, as the one comforting him this time, and stepped into the room whose door Director Roth had opened for her. "Goodbye, daddy," she said, trying earnestly to sound brave. "I love you and I'll see you again soon. I know I will." George nodded and blew her a kiss as he told her he loved her right back and was proud of her. Before Cassandra could respond further, Edward closed the door.

In almost no time, Cassandra realized how alone she was; she could no longer hear the voices from her father and Director Roth. She did her best not to cry anymore, for crying had not helped her or anyone she cared for.

What was left to do was take in the surroundings. Cassandra figured if she was to spend the night there, possibly even longer, she may as well become accustomed. The room was actually spacious, nice even. It had a bed, a connected bathroom and even windows. Considering the amenities, Cassandra wondered if other people had stayed here before and under what circumstances. Such things were okay to wonder, though Cassandra forced herself to not allow her mind to wander too much.

Laying down on the bed, Cassandra found herself falling asleep. It wasn't as if there was anything else for her to do.

***

With the death of his youngest child, George could no longer ignore everything that had been coming to a head. He had already learned that the hard way when it came to Harry's firing. Things had not necessarily improved over the past two years, but they existed at a pace where George was able to deny reality just enough. He could do that no longer, not when Amelia had been killed, Danny had been interrogated and Cassandra and Adam were both being used as bargaining chips. Of all of them, only Amelia's fate was certain, and she was dead.

If George found himself unable to cry much at the death of his daughter, it was not because of a lack of love. George believed he had most likely lost the ability to cry any more. He also had a duty to remain strong for his family, he believed. Or perhaps it was because it had yet to hit him that he would have to do something no parent should have to do, bury a child. He wondered if he would ever truly feel again. He didn't feel now, just as he hadn't for the past few years. He went through life indifferent to what happened as a means for survival.

The tears did come in small bouts as George thought more of Amelia. How she had been the only one of their planned children, coming nine months after a wedding anniversary. Her unique and remarkable talents, such as how she liked to draw pictures for her father to place in his office. It was truly these pictures which helped add a sense of home, of normalcy in such a place which otherwise felt like Hell on earth. George wished he had had more time with Amelia to appreciate her, though of course her family could not have known they would only have ten years with her. Her mother, father, brother and sister just assumed they would get to watch her grow and mature. They had been wrong. George did have to weep at the thought of not being able to watch Cassandra and Amelia become even better friends as the age gap began to matter less. He would never see anything more of Amelia.

George wondered if God was punishing him. It certainly felt like it.

***

Cassandra was awakened not long after by a knock on the door from Scott, who was coming to check on her. Cassandra told him to come in, though she wondered why he bothered knocking. It wasn't as if he needed her permission to enter. She did find it a nice gesture, though.

Cassandra tried to decide whether she should be intimidated or not. For whatever reason, despite who his uncle was and the actions he had been a part of that day, she did not need to be so afraid of him. She was nervous, though—so much so that when he came into the room, she stepped back until she hit the bed frame and could not go any further.

This was precisely what Scott didn't want. It was why he asked his uncle to be the one to check in on her, not Howard. Adam was at the hospital. Scott wasn't looking for her to help him clear his conscience, especially when it came to her little sister's death, but he *did* feel remorse over what had happened. He hoped the situation would be right for him to communicate that, to comfort her, if he could.

"I'm sorry if I startled you," he said, trying to be less intimidating. "That wasn't my intent. I just came to check on you, to see how you were doing." For some reason, Cassandra noticed, Scott seemed nervous.

She was in such shock that initially she just nodded, but then she reminded herself that she could do better than this. Even if her meekness was understandable, it would not kill her to speak to him. She said that she was fine, although she wasn't entirely sure her voice sounded very convincing. In fact, she was sure it hadn't.

Scott realized the foolishness of the question, though he had already asked it. "I'm sorry for such a dumb question. I can understand if you're not okay, especially after today."

Cassandra found herself confused now. She knew what he was referring to; that wasn't the issue. It was how polite he was, how caring and compassionate. She had not expected this from him, this touch of humanity.

Instead of asking if she was all right, which Scott could see for himself that she was not, he took a different approach. "I'm sorry, I really am. I wish there was more I could have done." It was unlikely he deserved her forgiveness, but Scott was still going to try. Not because he needed to curry favor from Cassandra Whitfield, though it would be nice to have it from such a beautiful soul as hers, but because it was the right thing to do. Cassandra didn't dare interrupt as he continued on. "I'm sorry most of all about what my uncle has done to you and your family. I get that he's not a very nice man." Indeed Scott did, which was why he hated to see his uncle terrorize anyone else.

To her surprise, Cassandra remained silent. This man's uncle was her family's enemy. *Shouldn't he be considered the enemy too?* Yet he was hardly acting like it. Perhaps he wasn't so bad at all, not like her brother claimed he was, at least.

It was in this new light that Scott came to stand closer to Cassandra. She didn't mind. In fact, she found it comforting. As she searched his face, she could see how serious he was and that kindness lived there, in his piercing blue eyes. Finally, Scott looked away after a particularly long amount of eye contact, though he was smiling, especially as Cassandra remained where she was.

Scott spoke up again, his questions becoming more thoughtful. "I know there's not much I can do. I would release you if I could, but I can't. Is there anything I can try to do for you, Cassandra?"

It didn't take her long to think of something. Scott had presumably brought Adam back with him and Howard. "What about Adam?" she asked.

Scott did not know if Cassandra had seen Adam get stabbed or if he should be the one to tell her. "He'll be okay." That wasn't a lie, as Scott believed Adam would be getting treatment. "I promise I'll send him your way."

Cassandra was as comforted as Scott hoped she would be, yet that did not stop her tears. After all, Scott himself conceded it was okay to not be okay. With how emotional she already was, Scott decided it was all for the best he didn't reveal to Cassandra about Adam what was likely to upset her.

Despite the little Scott could say or do, he still felt the need to comfort this young woman. Even though he had not fired the bullet which killed Amelia or raised his hands against Adam, he still had been enough a part of the situation that he felt sympathetic. He consequently felt determined to offer what comfort he could.

Feeling the urge to reach out to her, Scott tightly embraced her. Cassandra was shaking, she was crying so hard. Scott held her as she did so, all the while apologizing for such a situation. Surprised as she was, she was thankful for the human contact at least.

She was shivering from her tears, and though Cassandra would never think to ask, Scott felt it the least he could do to provide his suit jacket and drape it over her. Cassandra was certainly surprised, though she was also grateful. She remembered to thank him this time, as was only right.

The exchange had been an odd one. Scott and Cassandra were from families where the children were reminded on a regular basis how different and constantly competing they were, but also that socializing would be necessary on occasion for appearances' sake. There was a lot to the world her father was a part of that Cassandra did not understand. What had just transpired would not be considered by either of them to be merely socialization, and it wasn't for appearances; Scott and Cassandra were all alone in that room. Had the circumstances not been what they were, Cassandra likely would have regarded the situation and Scott very differently.

Why was he acting this way? Did he perhaps feel something for her, something beyond sympathy regarding her sister's death? Scott did, after all, find Cassandra beautiful. She was so sweet and kind. That was not why he reached out to her, though, why he felt a longing to look after her. It was because they could at least share, if nothing else, that his uncle had targeted them both. Edward seemed to think it was sufficient to keep Cassandra overnight. Scott sincerely hoped his uncle would allow him to take her home in the morning.

Whatever went into it, Cassandra seemed to benefit from the human connection. She was no longer shivering and her tears had subsided. Her breathing was returning to normal. Scott took notice and confirmed she was better, knowing not to ask if she was all right. Cassandra could say that she was at least better, though. She was even able to smile.

Before either of them could say more, they were interrupted by a loud knock at the door. It was Howard. He didn't bother entering, just called from outside.

"Scott? Are you coming out any time soon?" Howard didn't even give Scott a chance to respond. "Don't you think you've been in there long enough?"

"Yeah, just a minute."

"Well what have you been doing in there? You were supposed to check up on her, not ask her out on a date!"

Cassandra had dealt with too much already that day to be affected by such a joke. Scott, however, turned bright red.

"Jesus, Howard! I said just a minute. Christ almighty!" Cassandra started at the harshness, ever so slightly and without realizing. Scott noticed it, however, and quickly apologized, his tone much softer.

Had Howard not come by, would Scott have stayed longer? Would she have wanted him to? Regardless of the answer, which Cassandra herself didn't know, Scott would have to leave her now. She supposed their time together had been pleasant enough while it lasted.

Cassandra also assumed she would have to do without his suit jacket. She couldn't very well keep it. He insisted she did though. Scott grasped her by the shoulders and kept her from removing the jacket. The suddenness of his actions shocked them both.

She did not understand. "Why are you doing this?" Cassandra asked. "Why have you been so kind to me, Scott?"

There was another knock at the door. Howard was getting impatient. "Howard, I swear to God, if you don't give me just another moment…" He didn't finish the threat; it was not worth wasting his time. He turned himself and his attention back to Cassandra. "You are such a good person. Too good for this to have happened to you, Cassandra. You don't deserve any of this trouble. Forgive me for not being able to do more."

Then he left her. Cassandra could hear him chastising Howard, and then once more she heard nothing. Cassandra was on her own, but not completely in a sense. She had her thoughts to occupy her, trying to figure out why the last person she could have imagined had done so much for her. She could at least say she was thankful for the opportunity for she and Scott to treat each other like human beings.

***

Adam had just gotten his stitches, which George and Cassandra had yet to find out about. Howard was not apologetic about it, though he took Adam to the hospital. It wasn't anything personal, Howard assured Adam in a not-all-that-believable explanation. Adam just nodded in response.

Howard had been taken aside by Edward while Adam was getting the family and given a personal task. Were the situation to get out of hand, Howard was to keep Adam from intervening, whatever it took. A non-fatal stabbing was acceptable.

Even if Howard saw his actions as simply following a personal order, Adam did not doubt that Howard didn't mind. He may even have taken pleasure in it.

Confirming that Adam was alive and conscious was all Edward needed to have Adam brought back to headquarters for them to have their talk, joined by George, so long as he was not in too grievous a state following his daughter's death. Edward found it very suitable to his schedule, then, that George was more in shock than anything, including about Adam's condition. He would not have the opportunity to react to the stabbing, regardless.

The shock came not only from Amelia's death, but his encounter with Scott as well. As Scott came to collect George from the office where he was made to wait, Scott mentioned that he had seen Cassandra. There was no time for more words between the two other than a brief word of thanks from George. Edward was speaking and did not need his nephew getting in the way.

George remained looking lost for some time after Edward mentioned he would bring up funeral arrangements at a later time. This was not good for Edward's patience, especially when he needed to get confirmation from George that he understood what was happening. No matter, if Edward had to go back and explain things over again he supposed he could live with that. He did send Scott and his distracting presence out, however.

Edward was going to make things simple for George's sake and all their sakes. He only wished to say things once.

Adam was going to be given a promotion of sorts, just as George had been given the sham promotion to Deputy Director. Adam was no longer going to be working directly under George, as he could no longer be trusted in such a position. No, he was going to be working under Edward and his part of the department, which meant more time alongside Howard and Scott. In a matter of days, Adam went from experiencing a fulfilling dream job under his father's best friend to his boss losing his position and his family, in more ways than one. In all his time working in the department, Adam had been able to handle working for Director Roth because he rarely ever saw the man; he worked directly for Deputy Director Whitfield. That was about to change.

"I need to hear you say, George," Edward explained once he was done, "that you understand and you are conceding to Adam working directly under me now."

Another punishment openly disguised as a promotion. This wasn't just affecting George, though, but also Adam, the young man George had sworn to protect even if he failed at protecting Adam from Harry or Harry from himself. He had also assured Cassandra that he would do what he could to help Adam. He should have been honest with his daughter, who knew and loved him so well, and told her that there was very little if anything he could do.

Edward caught onto George's momentary hesitation. "I know that you want to fight me on this. The truth is you can't. I've already killed one child of yours, interrogated another, and I have your precious Cassandra in custody. I will get what I want, and what I want is Adam."

Edward gestured to Adam, who was being talked about as if he weren't sitting right there. "What's it going to be, George?"

Though he hadn't been able to fight in years, George wished he could in this moment. He wasn't able to do anything, though; he wasn't even able to try for Adam. Edward was right. Far too much was at stake.

While George took the moment to compose his thoughts, Adam spoke up. "Deputy Director Whitfield, sir," he meekly called out, only using the full title when he was in Director Roth's presence. "Please don't tell me that you're—"

Edward didn't even let him finish before he started chastising the young man. "Don't tell me, Adam, that you're going to dare speak unless directly spoken to. Right now you are here for my use and nothing more. The adults are talking and thus you *will* remain silent. Is that understood?" Adam nodded, deciding not to risk speaking again.

George wondered, for not the first time, what Adam was doing there, instead of at the hospital, if he was not allowed to speak. Edward often made such decisions that only made sense to one person, himself. Adam was, in all likelihood, being used to make the situation that much more painful for George. It was very possible he was there to guilt George, even if that would never be Adam's intention.

While George did feel conflict and guilt, looking at Adam did provide a kind of insight. Adam wanted George to give him up. He considered it his duty in helping the Whitfield family.

Speaking barely above a whisper, George told Edward he could have Adam.

This was not enough for Edward. "Speak up, now, George. I need to hear you say it."

With a deep sigh, George did as he was asked. "Fine. I consent to Adam working directly under you."

"And? You know there's more to this."

"And I promise to not interfere."

Edward was still not finished with him. "Because you'll know what could happen if you do, whatever it takes to get you to listen."

George was correct in his assumption that Edward had drawn this out to further conflict and torture him. He wished there was something he could say to lessen the pain. There was nothing, though.

"George, I do believe I've gone easy on you in some ways." Inside, Adam was screaming that killing a child could in no way be considered having 'gone easy.' He wisely remained silent, however. "Adam is not as torn up as he could be, and Cassandra is fine." Adam might have seemed all right now that he had gotten stitches, but the pain and guilt were eating him up inside.

Edward continued. "I am sorry to say that pleading and begging will do no good, unless you have something that I want. I now have Adam working for me, and you'll still be doing things here and there as well. Make no mistake, you won't be rid of this position *that* easily. If I were you, I'd have made sure to have gotten used to it by now."

George didn't think he would ever get used to such a position and now having Adam taken from him. He just nodded, though. It was a good thing Edward could already see exactly how he felt, as George had a hard time hiding it.

"But let us end on a positive note," Edward said cheerfully, as if they were about to go to a party. "Adam seems to be recuperating and Cassandra is going home tomorrow. This way you can maintain that you remained a good father, at least with this one."

That was that. Edward was done with them. He did not care what George and Adam did, so long as they did not bother him and were ready to meet with Edward at a moment's notice.

In the time that they had, George figured it was as good a time as any to talk to Adam.

As Adam remained seated and George came closer to him, he could tell how broken and beaten the poor young man was. It made him feel so guilty, all over again.

"How are you doing, Adam?" he asked, hoping it was not an inappropriate question. He doubted Adam would be entirely honest, but he still felt the need to ask.

"This really hasn't been the easiest day or well, week," Adam said. "For any of us. But I'm all right. I'll manage, Director Whitfield, I promise. Thank you, sir."

George wished Adam hadn't thanked him, though he had to appreciate it, and with Edward no longer there, he could explain why.

"I wish I had fought for you, but I didn't. I just stood by, doing nothing, while this man stole you away to make your life even more of a living Hell."

Adam said something quite poignant then. "With all due respect, sir, one could very well say that *your* position is a living Hell and has been for years now. I've always admired the way you were able to carry on. Besides, I firmly believe that you had no other choice. At least Cassandra gets to go home and Danny will be okay for now."

These points were all good ones that George could not in good conscience argue with. He still owed Adam an explanation, however.

"Be that as it may, I did have an earnest request from Cassandra. She had me promise that I would try to do what I could for you. I worry that I have now lied to my daughter in these difficult circumstances we find ourselves in. Not to mention that I deeply care for you."

Adam had a response right back. "What you could have done, sir, was nothing. You have a responsibility to your family. Even and especially in this situation Director Roth has thrust us into." While George wanted to add that he considered Adam family, he let the young man continue. "While I appreciate your concern, I would rather not have it on me that you beat yourself up over this."

George was able to concede Adam's point. To further discuss the situation would likely make the both of them feel worse. There truly was nothing George could have done. It was time for him to admit that.

During a lull in the conversation, George saw Adam wince. He wasn't even sure that he realized it. It was enough to remind George of the ordeal the young man had been through, however.

"How are you feeling, truly, Adam?" George asked. "Please know that you can tell me the truth."

"I'm managing, sir," Adam said. Though his smile was weak, it was at least there. That smile soon disappeared, however. "Actually, if I may bring up something, painful though it may be?" George nodded for him to continue. "Thank you, sir. The thing is, I saw Director Roth point the gun at your daughter. I saw him shoot her. I saw it. I wanted to do something. I felt I *had* to. I tried, sir. I really did. But Howard stopped me. He was told to do so at all costs. I couldn't get past him, not when he had that knife blocking me."

George sighed. At least Adam acknowledged he couldn't do anything. He hoped the young man would not fixate on blaming himself for such tragedies. His relief would be short-lived, however, as Adam began to choke up. George had not seen him do so yet that day.

"I am sorry, Director Whitfield, sir, truly sorry."

Seeing the anguish this young man felt made George want to cry himself. He willed himself to be strong, though.

"Please know, Adam, that I hold no ill will or place any blame on you." George would remind Adam of this as many times as he needed to. He looked him straight in the eyes as he said so.

Adam had a self-sacrificing tendency to lessen his own problems and take on those of others. George knew this, just as he could sense that the emotional guilt as well as the physical pain were taking their toll on Adam, who looked so very young to George then.

That Edward had sprung the news on George, that Adam had had to be stopped from intervening and that's how 'he got himself stabbed,' didn't help the situation.

The wound had not been as deep as it could have been though; the doctor who stitched him up said he had been lucky, Adam passed along to George. When George asked him how he was, however, Adam knew well enough to admit the truth. It still felt sore, but he had taken painkillers and they seemed to be working. They could only hope.

***

Danny was a wreck, and that was putting it mildly. He had just gotten over his paranoia and felt physically better from the interrogation days prior. Now, after feeling betrayed by his best friend, his anger came back out, and he didn't know how he could ever feel differently ever again.

Most of all, Danny felt hopeless. One sister was dead; there was nothing he could do to bring her back. While Cassandra was very much alive, he didn't know what, if anything, he could do to bring *her* back.

When Maria had come back in, Danny noticed her flustered in a way he could quite not place. He correctly assumed it had to do with Adam, though he would never be able to guess how exactly that was. There was blood on her, a lot of it, even more than he initially thought he saw.

Regardless of what he knew, or, more accurately, didn't know, Danny knew deep down it would do him no good to focus on hate or bitterness. He didn't care what would do him good, however. He wanted to be angry. It may not have been better, but it was, at least in the present moment, easier to hate than it was to forgive.

Danny asked his mother then if Adam and the rest of them had left. He was thinking not of others, but only of his own pain and sense of feeling betrayed.

Maria beat Danny to his questioning, however, when she asked where Amelia was.

"In her bedroom," Danny answered without much emotion. "I'll call the coroner soon. Did they leave? Are they gone?"

Maria could only nod her response through her tears. Danny hoped it was not about Adam. They needed to concentrate on mourning Amelia, leaving Adam out of this. He had chosen to be left out of it when he had done nothing, not even moved an inch.

It was his focus on such emotions that left Danny unable to realize his mother seemed all the more distraught about Adam, as if there were something else she was not letting on, and Danny was too blinded by bitter hate to see it.

"Adam left, but he…" Maria wanted to tell him, to make her son understand how Adam was also affected. She knew Danny was hurting too, though. Besides, she had made a promise to the young man that she would not tell her son. It was a promise she intended to keep; that was the least she could do for him in the moment.

"He what? What did he do, mom? Did he do something? So help me God, if he did…"

"No, Danny. He's done nothing! Nothing at all. Please, let's not talk of Adam anymore."

That was something Danny could agree on as he and his mother held each other close.

***

It was dark when Cassandra woke again, realizing she must have cried herself to sleep. She wasn't sure what else there was to do. Someone had been kind enough to bring her food and magazines as well as provide her with a towel, soap and a toothbrush. She ate little, however, and figured she would put off showering until the morning. She did wish for pajamas, though, hating to wear her outfit from that day, though she supposed she would survive, as she had no other alternative. Cassandra did pull Scott's suit jacket more tightly around her. She wondered—not the first time—if he knew how much comfort it brought her.

After hours of attempting to distract himself with work, Adam figured he would go check on Cassandra. He hoped to surprise her, as he didn't want her getting her hopes up of counting on seeing him. With Director Roth having no use for him for the rest of the evening and with Director Whitfield's blessing, he went.

Adam did indeed surprise her. She had been unable to make out that it was him in the darkness and dared not let the person who had entered know she was awake lest he had nefarious intentions. Cassandra supposed it wasn't the most foolproof idea, but she hoped that he would leave her be if he realized she was asleep.

Then Cassandra felt him sit down on the bed. She was about to emit a startled cry when he spoke. "Shh, Cassandra, it's me, Adam," he said comfortingly, sensing her distress.

Upon hearing his voice, Cassandra buried her face into his chest, practically sobbing as she did so. She had gone through so many emotions in so little time. Now Adam was here with her, though, her dearest Adam, who always made her feel at peace when he was around, even in moments as this.

"I am so sorry if I scared you. You've had quite the day, I know. But I'm here now, and you're going home tomorrow. All will be as well as it can be." That disclaimer was important, for no longer would Cassandra go home to

Amelia, and God only knew when her father would return to them.

The cry ended up being a good cry for Cassandra as she experienced that release. Adam wished there were more he could do for her, but for now, his presence would be enough. He hoped to always provide her such comfort, something which he saw as God's task for him with his time on earth. If there was anyone's shoulders they were glad to have to cry on, it was each other's.

When her tears subsided, Cassandra dared to ask Adam how he was. It was a question he balked at answering. He wished she never had to know about the stabbing, because he was sure she would worry herself sick. Then again, he also figured she would find out eventually, and it was likely best it be from him.

"Cassandra, I want to assure you that I will be just fine, though I do have something to tell you."

"What? What is it?" She was immediately alert.

How was he supposed to tell her? He had to just come out with it, and he did, trying to conceal his own emotions as much as possible. Adam correctly assumed that Cassandra would react, and react she did. She felt so troubled for this young man who took so much, likely too much, upon himself to help her and her family.

"Are you sure you're all right?" Cassandra asked, for not the first time.

"I am now that I'm with you," Adam answered, and he was, truly. This was not only due to finally getting himself stitched up but because Cassandra would be going home tomorrow. Such was news Adam came bearing for her.

"Cassandra," he said ever so gently, "I am happy to be able to tell you that your father has arranged for you to go home tomorrow morning. I'll even get to take you."

Cassandra was suspicious though, just as Adam had feared. "Why am I going home, though?"

"Because it's where you belong."

"That's not what I meant, Adam." Her voice had a bit of an edge to it. Adam knew what she meant, he just had foolishly hoped there would be a way to avoid such discussions.

"I've agreed to work directly under Director Roth." Adam continued on before she could react. "Cassandra, it was always most important to me that you be able to go home. Like I've said, it's where you belong, and I believe that my working for him and you returning within a reasonable timeframe are things which would have happened regardless, mutually exclusive of each other, if need be."

Adam did not always want to share all the details with Cassandra, but he never wished to lie to her. Such words were true. It was even how he justified having to work for such a man.

Cassandra asked Adam to turn on the light. When he did so, she looked deep into his eyes, studying them for a few moments. Ultimately she decided she could believe him, just as she always could. He had been realistic with her while still being a comforting presence. It was what she truly loved about him.

Though it was late, especially for how early Cassandra would be leaving tomorrow morning, she was in no rush to turn out the lights. She craved, needed these moments with Adam, especially since it felt like the world was collapsing around them.

If Adam were to ask Cassandra what sudden interest she had in studying his face, he would have received an answer about her trying to memorize it, for she knew well enough to fear it could be some time before she would see him again. Instead of asking, however, Adam simply responded with a kiss.

The two kissed as if it were the last time. Not only did they not know when they would meet again, they did not know under what circumstances. Though she would be going home in a matter of hours, Cassandra almost felt as if she did not want the night to end. She wished she could remain in this moment, forever, with her Adam.

The moment though, and the kiss, did end. As it did, with the light on, Adam noticed what he had not before. The suit jacket clutched around Cassandra. It was not his, but then again he had not been the first or the only visitor that night. He had to keep that in mind. Even more so, he couldn't fault her for it, though she was already launching into an explanation.

"I'm sorry. Scott was here earlier. I was cold and he was kind enough to give me his jacket. I shouldn't need it anymore, not when you're here."

As Cassandra began to shed the jacket, Adam stopped her. He wished she could be wearing his suit jacket. Adam wasn't even wearing one to give her, though, and the one from earlier that day had blood stains on it. No, he could not fault her for this, not even for a moment. He doubted he could fault Cassandra for anything. "I'm just glad he was there when you needed him."

He even dared an attempt at bold humor. "It would have been nice if the time between your gentlemen visitors could be shortened. I do like the look of you in the jacket. I'll give you mine, someday, I'm sure." At that, they kissed again. Cassandra was smiling. Such was a nice way for them to fall asleep together, for who knew how long it would be before they could enjoy such nights together.

***

George thought more than a few hours of sleep would be impossible. He had been right.

***

The next morning Adam was gone, just as he had told Cassandra he would be. It still felt odd to feel and find the spot beside her empty. She would have to be thankful for the time she had had with Adam and accept that today she was going home.

Seeing no better time than that moment, Cassandra made use of the towel and soap she was given and took a shower. It provided a release with her, as her tears could blend together with the water droplets, both of them flowing indistinguishable from one another as they went down the drain. It was beautiful and tragic at the same time.

Cassandra could not distract herself for long, however, as there was a knock at the door. Scott had come to collect her while she had yet to finish up. As she called out that she would just be a few minutes, Cassandra made use of the provided toiletries and put on her clothes from the day before, the suit jacket included.

Neither Scott nor Cassandra knew what to say to each other. They felt they could not address Adam or the suit jacket, and so they did not speak beyond Scott explaining he was taking Cassandra to see her father so that they could say goodbye, then he was taking her home.

As they reached the office where her father was, Cassandra wondered if he had been forced to sleep there. She was even more grateful for the accommodations she had been given.

Scott had to unlock the door to let Cassandra inside the office, though it was not a detail she could dwell for long on, not if she wanted to cherish every last moment she had left with her father. As she cautiously entered, she did not yet see him as his chair was turned away from her. Just as she began to fear what she might see, he turned towards her.

Without any hesitation, Cassandra ran towards her father and embraced him. She forgot any awkwardness, lingering questions or confusion. This was still her father before Cassandra, and she had been given a wonderful opportunity to see him before returning home where she indeed belonged. It was an opportunity which her brother and mother did not have.

George and Cassandra had a special bond with each other which made this moment all the more special and heartbreakingly difficult. Cassandra did not know if—no, she must not think that way—*when* she would see him again. She did not know when her mother and brother would; Amelia would not get to ever again, at least not in this lifetime.

Young though she was, Cassandra had been there for her father in more ways than she could know. Through all of the trials and tribulations of taking on the position of Director of Ethics, to feuding with Thomas and Gregory, to his father's death, to George's change in position, and Harry and Leah's deaths, Cassandra always had loved and revered her father as a good and capable man. Even when it felt everyone else was against him, he still had his Cassandra.

George had meant it when he said Maria was free to leave him, to take the children and go to her brother's in America. He would not hold it against her. In fact, after the recent tragedies, he was hopeful she would do such a thing to keep herself and the children safe. At least he wanted her to do so if Edward were not making such a move impossible.

As she looked up at him upon breaking the embrace, Cassandra could see that her father looked mostly the same, albeit a bit tired and drained. This was to be expected. Cassandra wondered if her father had slept at all, never mind slept in a bed as she had, a luxury she had had which she was even more grateful for now. Cassandra brushed such thoughts aside however; her father would not wish for her to dwell on such things.

Not knowing what else to say or do, Cassandra embraced her father once more. "I love you, daddy. I'll be praying for you." Since Cassandra had nothing else to say, she remained quiet as she held her father for dear life.

"Thank you, my dear," George said, his voice threatening to break.

George told his daughter that he loved her and was proud of her, something which could not be said enough. The two had been given the gift of having a moment together, however, something George felt necessary to address.

"Whatever the reason, Cassandra, you and I have been given something your mother, brother and dear sister have not. I'd like to use it, if you'll permit me, to ask you for a favor."

"Of course, anything in the world," Cassandra practically cried.

"I need you to be brave, not only for your mother and your brother, but for yourself. You owe it to yourself to take care and live your life. I know you won't forget me, but I need you to keep on living, not be held down by wondering and waiting for me to return. Is that understood?" He hoped he wasn't being too harsh with her.

"I…" She at first did not know what to say. "Yes, it is understood," Cassandra finally could answer, not without some difficulty.

"This includes going away to school. That's where you belong, anywhere but here. I will miss you, but I will be able to carry on knowing that you are in a place far better for you." Cassandra once more confirmed she understood, though now she was weeping. "I am so sorry my dear, but please, know this is how it must be."

Cassandra did not merely love her father in such a moment, she revered him. George had sacrificed much for her and her siblings. It was no longer his happiness that George had lost, but his freedom as well. Danny and George had had their differences, to be sure, but without any hesitation, Cassandra's father had made it so her brother was free from having to face immediate consequences.

All too soon there was a knock at the door. Scott had come to collect Cassandra. Though she did not wish to cause a scene and drag the unpleasantness any further, Cassandra still wished she didn't have to leave her father like this.

As Cassandra prepared to say her final goodbye, George had one last thing to say. "While I wish the situation had turned out better for your brother, mother and especially Adam, I can be at peace, at least somewhat, knowing you have one another. Please forgive me for not doing more."

"Oh, father, of course I can forgive you. Please, as I leave, know how much I love and appreciate all that you have done for us."

Cassandra could be grateful for the moment. Though it was with a heavy heart, Cassandra was ready to tell Scott to come in so he could bring her home.

Her father had comforted her and she had comforted him. It felt as if Cassandra had matured and aged years in a matter of moments.

***

Even though Director Roth had been clear that he intended to keep Cassandra at headquarters for a day or so, Danny had been determined to wait up for her. He had hoped that it was all just a bluff. The result was that Danny fell asleep at the kitchen table.

Danny woke in the morning to a car pulling up in the driveway. It was Scott and Adam bringing Cassandra home. Though Danny was disappointed his father was not there with them, no matter how unlikely that would have been, Danny was at least relieved he didn't have to deal with Howard.

The male aggression was palpable, and while Cassandra could understand it, she wished she didn't have to deal with it. Tensions were high. Tragedy was staring them straight in the face. *Why couldn't they just behave around one another?* She hoped they would not fight; there had been far too much blood already.

While Cassandra figured her brother would want her inside as quickly as possible, she was still set on saying goodbye to Scott and Adam. Both had been kind to Cassandra; one of them intrigued her immensely. As much as she understood Danny, Cassandra did not expect her brother to understand her thoughts.

Cassandra had barely gotten out of the car when Danny tersely told her to get inside.

"But I have to—"

He didn't even let her finish. "No buts. You're home, they brought you here so you can go home, so now it's time for you to get inside.

Danny did not expect her to fight back. Her words and tone surprised even Cassandra. "And I will go inside, once I've said thank you and goodbye." He responded by way of mumbling for her to make it quick; he knew it was likely he'd never hear the end of it if he didn't let her.

It was certainly an emotional departure for Cassandra to say goodbye to Adam, for just as had been the case with her father, she wasn't entirely sure when she would see him again.

They had already had their goodbyes the night before, in a way. Cassandra would have to find such a memory sufficient then. In a move to reaffirm that home was the proper place for her to be, Adam released Cassandra from the embrace, even if it was difficult to do. Danny nodded his appreciation.

Once Cassandra had said her goodbyes to Adam, Danny fully expected her to go inside. He would never have guessed she'd approach Scott. Seeing her do so just made him feel all the more enraged. Cassandra was not doing so to frustrate her brother, who she realized had been through so much himself. It just felt like the right thing to do. Cassandra wasn't sure about much that was going on, but she was sure about this.

Danny was thus in an even worse spot when Cassandra walked away from the two young men, foes of his at that moment, even as she was doing exactly as he commanded of her.

It was the suit jacket, still clutched tightly around Cassandra, which drew particular ire, especially when Cassandra was holding it close to her as she began to walk up the driveway. Without thinking twice, Danny approached his sister to take the offending garment off of her.

"Whose is this?" Danny did not appreciate the stunned silence. When he asked again, it was through gritted teeth.

Danny did not understand why Scott was stepping forward. He had assumed it was Adam's and that Adam had just been too timid to own up to it. He would have never fathomed Scott and his sister would do much interacting, never mind enough so where she would be wearing his jacket.

Scott confirmed what Danny dreaded all too much and could deny no longer. The nightmare was becoming worse. "It's mine. She can keep it, though. I don't mind."

"No, she cannot! Are you fucking kidding me right now? You may not mind, but I do. I *definitely* do."

Cassandra was saddened by her brother's harsh tone and choice of words, though there was nothing she could do. With a forlorn look on her face, and after making eye contact with Adam and Scott one last time, she headed back inside. Danny tossed the suit jacket back at Scott.

Danny was relieved to see Cassandra go, not only because she belonged inside, but because he could deal with Scott and Adam as he saw fit without her getting in the way.

"I didn't think I would have to tell you that the shit you pulled with my sister was beyond inappropriate," Danny began. "I also didn't think I would have to remind you that I want you staying far away from Cassandra. There's no reason for you to be interacting with her. For all of this shit, you can just go fuck yourself. You got that?"

Rather than argue, Scott quietly responded that he did. Feeling rather awkward, Adam looked anywhere but at them.

Turning slightly only to confirm that Cassandra was inside, Danny no longer felt any need to hold back. "I want to know what the hell has been going on. Now."

Danny expected an apology from Scott, which would have been the only fair and appropriate thing. Instead, Adam stepped forward. Danny figured that he *would* try to fix the situation.

"Danny, I understand how you're feeling right now, but Cassandra was fine. She's going to be just fine."

It had been the wrong thing to say. For while Adam had been referring to how no harm had come to Cassandra during the time she was at headquarters, the situation was already far too loaded. After their younger sister had just been killed and their father taken from them, Danny couldn't say if Cassandra, or any of them, were going to be fine. As mature as Cassandra was, she was also still impressionable and far too kind, often to a fault, for Danny have to worry about anyone such as the likes of Scott to try anything with her, no matter what it was. His approach had always been to act as if Scott didn't exist and it had been working just fine for him until Scott and Cassandra had to ruin that. So no, Danny did not think that Adam understood, not at all.

"Oh, you do, Adam?" Danny was not content just saying that much, however. He couldn't help the dripping sarcasm. "Well that makes me feel *so much* better." He knew Adam felt guilty about what had happened to Danny, George, Amelia and Cassandra. Danny still brought it up though. "My younger sister is dead. My father has been taken away. I've been interrogated and beaten, not to mention betrayed by you, my best friend. But you *understand*, so that makes it all better now, doesn't it? Doesn't it, Adam?"

Adam just hung his head. He wished he had not said a word. In fact, it likely would have been better had they dropped Cassandra off without even getting out of the car. *How foolish they had been for not doing so,* Adam thought.

As Adam was considering having them turn around and get back in the car to leave, before the situation escalated further, Scott had to distract Danny as he shook his head and sighed.

"And what is *your* problem?" Danny asked Scott.

"I think you should go easy on Adam here. I'm sorry about everything that's happened these past few days. We both are, but at least Cassandra is home, safe now."

It was bad enough for Scott to have given Cassandra his suit jacket, even saying she could keep it. Danny decided though that he didn't even want to hear Scott saying her name.

"Hey, why don't you do me, and yourself, a favor and just not talk about my sister from now on. Period."

Adam's discomfort continued to grow. They needed to leave, at that very moment, before things went too far.

It was too late.

"I really think you need to calm down, Danny." It had not been the smartest thing for Scott to say, even he knew that. Scott was beyond out of patience, though. He dismissed Adam's pleas that they just go.

Adam turned to another tactic then. "I think Scott actually does want to help here, hard as that may be to believe."

Not only was it too late to leave, but Adam had just made things worse. As Danny saw it, it was Scott and Adam acting against him.

"So you're on his side now," Danny accused.

"No, I'm not." Adam tried in vain to speak calmly to Danny. "No, I'm not," he repeated. "I can see why you would think that way, but I promise you I'm not."

Any progress was ruined by Scott jumping in. "See, it's okay now."

The next few moments were a bit of a blur. All the while the suit jacket laid crumpled in a pile. Danny got defensively angry once more. "Nobody fucking asked you," he yelled. Adam got in between the two of them to tell Scott to stay out of it, only for Scott to tell him to shut up, even shoving him. Adam shoved him right back, almost as a reflexive defense mechanism, and told him not to tell him to shut up and to calm the fuck down.

After a few punches and pushes had been traded, Danny finally found his voice enough to call "stop" and for them to get the hell out of his driveway, and to take that suit jacket with them. He expressed that he didn't give a damn what else they did to each other, he was not going to have it happen in his driveway. Danny wasn't even sure if that was the truth or not. *Did he really not care?* He didn't know. He was too uncertain about too many things at the moment. What he *was* certain though was that it was time to break up this nonsense, even if he had, admittedly, made it worse.

Without so much as a goodbye, Danny spun on his heel and went back inside. He cursed to himself for getting punched again while he was still recovering. Danny's mother and sister would not be happy.

Danny didn't think much about himself, however, his mother, or even his father or his baby sister. He thought about Cassandra. He knew she liked to do for others, but Scott didn't get to count as one of her pet projects. Danny didn't trust the man, not at all, especially with who his uncle was and what he knew Edward to be capable of. With any hope, Danny would never have to worry about such an instance between his sister and the nephew of that monster ever again.

Life Goes On

Much changed in the following months for the Whitfield family. As far as most of the rest of the world, especially Edward, was concerned, however, everything went on as usual.

Amelia's funeral was less than a week after her death. By the time Maria could bring herself to tell Thomas, it was too late for him to come, and likely not very safe. Maria had put off telling her brother out of fear he would blame George, or even her.

Per Edward's order, the cause of death was a sudden illness.

George had been told at work, and then was given the chance to relay that information to his wife over the phone. Doing so in person was out of the question. If George thought he had reason to be angry about the stated cause of his daughter's death, he needed to only wait for his wife's response.

It truly broke George's heart that he could not be there for his wife and surviving children at such a time. George wished there was nothing to grieve at all. Here they were, forced to grieve separately.

Cassandra had heard her mother on the phone with her father. She could only imagine her mother's pain in losing her daughter in one way and her husband in another, but it was her father she especially felt for.

Maria was near to hysteria. Not only had she lost her youngest child, her cause of death was hidden from the world, and then Maria couldn't even grieve alongside her husband or either of her daughter's uncles.

When George hung up the phone, he put his head in his hands and cried as he had never cried before. George not only missed Amelia, but he felt he had failed as a father and a husband.

George's position being what it was, Amelia was given a formal, well-attended funeral. Nobody would be the wiser about her true cause of death or George's imprisonment at his office. Warned about revealing this, George was able to sit with his family.

Maria cried the whole time. Danny sulked in bitter anger. Cassandra sat with Adam, the two trying to provide one another with comfort. Danny would not look at Adam, never mind speak to him.

The afternoon was the last the Whitfield family would have together for the foreseeable future. They cried and held each other and missed their daughter and sister. Their tears were simply thought to be on account of grieving a young soul's death. The truth, though, was that they were crying just as much for how things would never be the same. It was their fate as a family which truly weighed on each of them.

***

Adam was affected in his own way, for Edward had a long-term plan in mind for him. That Adam and George barely saw each other anymore was only part of it.

For the first few weeks, Adam had been left alone in his position. Foolishly, he had thought that this was the slightest bit of mercy coming from Edward, but Edward had merely been biding his time.

One afternoon, Adam was quickly collected by Howard for Edward to reveal what plans had been drawn up for him. The only indication Adam was given was Howard telling him there were going to be changes.

As he was practically thrown into a seat by Howard, Adam could see that Scott was sitting to his right. Edward gave Howard a pointed look about his rough treatment towards Adam but otherwise did not rebuke him. Scott remained silent.

Seeing no reason to delay the discussion, Edward began with a bit of good news. Adam was doing well in his new role. Adam kept it to himself that he didn't believe he had any other option but to excel.

Once he gathered that Adam was not going to respond to the compliment, Edward moved on to the business at hand. Because Edward wished to keep a better eye on him, Adam would have a curfew at which point he would report back to headquarters. Adam was to head home immediately upon being dismissed to collect what he needed. Edward wanted him at headquarters with George.

Adam was stunned, even heartbroken. He could barely hide his reaction. Just like that, though, Edward was done with him. There was no room for further discussion or explanation.

As they walked out to Howard's car, all of Adam's actions were completely automatic. It was almost as if everything were happening in slow motion.

Try as he did, Adam was having a hard time facing reality. Perhaps it was naive of him not to expect such a punishment to come, but he had not.

Arriving was inevitable. Howard looked as if he was going to get out of the car, but Scott stopped him. Adam didn't need any distractions, especially when he had ten minutes to get ready. There was no time to waste.

Adam took a deep breath as he walked inside his house. When he left that morning, he could not have imagined it would be for the last time for the foreseeable future. He had not been as neat as he normally was. It was not the first time that week Adam forgot to put his cup in the dishwasher. He set the machine going so that when he returned, there would be clean dishes.

Fortunately, he had done laundry the night before, so packing the needed clothing was an easy enough task.

There was a brief moment of panic when Adam couldn't find his suitcase, but, upon closer examination, it was discovered in the back of the closet.

Adam was normally a tedious packer, but the nature of the situation called for a more hurried pace. This time he dumped his clothing in and set to pack his toiletries.

Checking his watch, Adam saw that he still had time. He had to accept that while he hoped to be back, it was quite possible he wouldn't be. It was now or never.

Adam had been in his parents' room. He, after all, had to get his mother's locket to give to Cassandra. Adam hadn't been in there for any other reason though, and he certainly had not moved into the master bedroom; the thought hadn't even crossed his mind. If he was saying goodbye to his home, however, he might as well say goodbye to the bedroom as well. There was the dining room too, where the murder-suicide had occurred. In those years, Adam had not been back since. He had eaten all of his meals in the kitchen. Adam found that room more difficult than the bedroom, in part because of the faint blood spatter still on the wall.

Adam was just about to run his finger over the faint crimson spot when he heard Howard honk his horn. It was time to leave. Forcing himself out of his thoughts, Adam almost tripped over his suitcase.

Howard was about to beep again, when Scott elbowed him to let him know Adam had emerged. Adam put his suitcase into the popped trunk, and then they drove back to headquarters in silence. Even Howard did not speak.

Upon their return, Adam headed straight to the bathroom, where he became sick. Thankfully he had the rest of the day off.

Adam had been through difficult situations before, but never had he felt so thoroughly hopeless. In such a low ebb, Adam wondered if perhaps God had abandoned him, if He were even there to begin with. Here he was, stuck in this Hell on earth not only where he dreaded working but also would be staying.

Terrible though his thoughts were, they forced Adam to snap back to reality. He had to get over himself. It was true that it was possible he wouldn't be home again, but it also was not a foregone conclusion. Hopeless and helpless though he might feel, Adam had to carry on, to live to fight another day. Adam recognized that he did not have control over much—very little, in fact. If there was anything he had control over, though, it was holding onto hope.

Adam reminded himself that he could be thankful to be staying with Director Whitfield. Perhaps they could encourage and support one another.

Adam told himself now that from here on in, he would not let hope be regarded as a foolish notion. It might have seemed that his life had never been so difficult before, but he had made it through in the past. God would help him through all of this, Adam believed, just as He had all the times before.

***

In addition to his living situation, Adam had to get used to the nature of his position.

Edward had more plans in store for the Whitfield family. Fearing that Maria would take the children and go to her brother's, Edward sent Howard and Adam to confiscate valuables they could sell for money and to lay down some rules.

Most of the rules were part of Danny's agreement to be an informant. Unless he was doing something specified by Edward, he was to have a midnight curfew. Contact with his uncles was also forbidden. Just in case stopping a future coup was as simple as cutting off communication, Edward was sure as hell going to take advantage.

Edward did not send his nephew because he didn't have time for Scott's moral conflicts. He sent Adam as a teachable moment. Howard was sent with him to make sure things got done. Edward also suspected that, like himself, Howard was not afraid to be cruel when the situation dictated and could benefit.

Adam was informed by Howard striding over to his desk, expecting him to drop everything and come with Howard at that very moment. They would be taking Howard's car, as Howard was not about to have Adam racing over there to beat him and warn the family. It wasn't as if the Whitfields had *no* warning. They had been told that there would be follow-up visits of sorts.

Howard, always one to have something to say, couldn't even do Adam the favor of a silent car ride. He did not spare Adam from his opinion. For as far as Howard was concerned, the Whitfield family deserved what was coming to them. When Adam boldly asked if that included gunning down a ten-year-old child, Howard just shot him a dirty look.

Such a remark did not stop Howard in his tracks, as it might a more prudent person, however. "You're lucky, you know that?"

"Oh, how is that? Please, tell me," Adam asked.

Howard wore that smirk which often adorned his face. Adam found it just awful. "I don't know how you fail to realize that you could have been killed for your involvement and your death ruled a suicide. Had I stabbed you slightly to the right or left, or twisted the knife at all, you might not be here. I'm sure you and I both know Director Roth could have found creative ways to further torture you as well." Adam didn't say, though he did think, that he *had* been tortured. It was just more in emotional ways than physical.

"Whatever, Howard." Adam had nothing more to say. He didn't wish for Howard to best him, but the truth was that bringing up Director Roth was a sore subject for Adam. He believed that Director Roth's actions were still, even now, tied to trying to punish Harry, after the man was already dead and buried.

Though Howard had managed to shut his mouth for a few minutes at a time, Adam was no more relieved. The silence engulfing the car as they pulled up the driveway freed up Adam's mind to recall the last time he had been there with Howard.

Maria's car was not in the driveway. Adam hoped it meant she would be spared. Adam cursed himself for not being able to text Danny and Cassandra, but Howard wouldn't even let him have his phone out.

Howard not only forbade Adam from sending notice about their arrival, he pushed past Adam to be the one to ring the doorbell. Howard was the one conducting most of the business. Adam was there to watch and learn.

Before Adam could get an answer from Howard as to what, exactly, they were there to do, Danny came to the door. Howard barged right in, beckoning for Adam to follow. Danny's face was difficult for Adam to read. Adam hoped Danny could understand the seriousness of the situation. It was entirely possible their lives depended on Danny and Cassandra cooperating.

Adam felt relieved that they at least made it to the parlor without incident. He could see Cassandra sitting on the couch in expectation, quite anxious. Before Adam could even think to go over to her, Howard ordered Danny to sit down next to her, and for Adam to stand off to the side.

This visit was about reminders. For Director Roth had made it clear last time that his father's arrest did not mean that Danny was completely off the hook. Adam, just as Danny and Cassandra, waited with bated breath for what was to come next. Fortunately, there was no indication Danny was to be arrested. He was safe for another day.

That did not mean that anyone would be getting too comfortable. There were rules, ones Adam was hearing for the first time.

Such rules were particularly aimed at Danny. In addition to a midnight curfew, Danny's time working at the bookstore was coming to an end. The Whitfields' savings were not only being taken from them, but so was their ability to make as much money as possible. They would instead be given an allowance by the Department of Security and Action.

With attitude in his voice, Howard mentioned that they had all suspected what a hub for black market activities the bookstore would be. Adam didn't dare admit that Howard had a point.

Howard also had to take Danny's gun away. Though he knew it was futile, Danny still questioned it.

"I'm not even a felon. Despite all of those charges the department may have against me, I haven't actually been found guilty of anything."

Howard not so sympathetically waved the notion off. "Well, that may very well change soon. This is a precaution. And regardless, I'm still here to take it." Howard released him to go get it. Adam could hear Danny muttering under his breath, and didn't blame him for it. If Howard heard Danny, he didn't act.

Cassandra was quietly crying, doing her best to compose herself. Adam wanted to go over to her, so badly, but he didn't want to take the slightest risk making anything worse for them. Danny was back with his gun in a moment's time.

Danny had never had to use his gun before, though that didn't mean it wasn't his right to own one in case the need to protect himself or his family arose. He had had it since before Harry killed Leah and himself, though he thought of getting rid of it shortly thereafter, to be more sensitive to Adam. While Adam appreciated the sentiment, he saw no reason for it.

Harry was the one who pulled the trigger of his own gun. Nobody else. Harry had had a choice in how to use his gun, issued to him by work and never taken back. Everyone else had that choice too. Adam knew Danny would never make the same decision his father had made. Adam impressed Danny then when he explained his reasoning.

Adam snapped back to reality when it came to more rules. Though many were aimed at Danny, not all of them were. Cassandra would not be attending university after all in the next few months. She realized then that that was why she had yet to receive her orientation packet in the mail. Adam's heart broke for Cassandra then. Danny began to protest on behalf of his shocked sister, though Howard held up his hand to stop him. It was not his call, but Director Roth's, who had conferred with the university that it was best not to invite such a scandal by permitting Cassandra to attend.

The family would also be having their mail, email, and phone calls monitored by the department. They could consider themselves lucky that they were even being told, however. Their mail was being monitored in part because, unless Danny informed on them, they were not to have contact from Gregory or Thomas. All mail from the United States was to be flagged. Any hope for assistance from Maria's brother was gone.

While Howard might have finished explaining the new rules, the purpose of his and Adam's presence was not complete. The valuables still had to be taken.

While Howard was searching the rooms, Adam could at least go comfort Cassandra. The poor thing had so much to overcome, including now being told she wouldn't be attending university.

Adam had felt invisible and useless up until that moment. Even if there were nothing he could do about it, Adam still apologized over and over as he held her up against his chest, letting her cry there. They could faintly hear Howard rifling through their items upstairs in between Cassandra's tears. It just made her cry harder then. When Adam made eye contact with Danny he wasn't met with a comforting glance, but it at least wasn't an angry one either. It was a pained one.

The minutes went by unbearably. When Adam checked his watch, though, once Howard was back, he could see he hadn't been gone all that long. Sure enough, Howard had not come downstairs empty-handed. He had taken one of their duffels to fill with mostly books and documents. Adam wondered if he'd be able to find out what he took back at headquarters.

Once he was finished, Howard wanted to leave, seeing no problem in interrupting the moment between Adam and Cassandra. Hurried goodbyes would have to do. Then Howard stopped and told Adam to sit right back down. He was looking at Danny's watch.

"What is it?" Adam wondered if Danny was really that naive, or if he was just hoping that playing dumb could get him somewhere.

"The watch."

"What about it?" Adam didn't see how Danny could not know.

"I want it."

Justifying his actions that it could very well be worse if Danny were the one to jump in, Adam risked making a remark, reminding Howard that they weren't here for the watch. Besides, Howard himself wanted to leave. Howard responded with a non-answer, telling Adam it was none of his concern. "Your watch," Howard repeated to Danny, ignoring Adam and sounding very impatient.

Grumbling unintelligibly, Danny forked it over. He had resisted long enough and now saw himself as having no other choice. At least Danny could say he tried.

Now that Howard had the watch, Adam just really wanted to get the hell out of there, especially if he couldn't be of any more help. Howard was looking at Cassandra, though, at her locket, to be precise. Adam knew he was thinking of taking it, but just as Danny had been naive about the watch, so Adam was going to be about this. Cassandra had worn it since the evening Adam put it on her, only taking it off to shower and sleep.

Unlike Danny, who deep down knew better, Cassandra didn't quite piece it together. The thought was too horrible. She started tearing up all over again once Howard let her know he was going to need the locket as well. Danny tried to intercede, but Howard was in no mood.

"Help her take it off." He beckoned to her brother before stopping him, having gotten another idea. The others dared to hope that Howard was having a change of heart.

"You gave it to her, didn't you, Adam?"

"Yeah, I did. As a birthday present. It was my mother's." Adam didn't bother hiding that he was trying to guilt Howard. "So what?"

"So you should do it, then." What he said next showed his intentions were anything but noble. "I'm sure it won't be the only thing you've taken off of her."

Cassandra gasped and the situation nearly escalated as Danny dared Howard to disrespect his sister like that again. Howard pointed out it didn't matter, since they all knew there was nothing Danny could do without making "the situation a whole lot fucking worse." Howard told Adam once more take it off her.

Adam hated the idea of all this, of Howard having something that was his mother's, of what it would do to Cassandra. Deep down, Adam knew it would be best if he was the one to take it off. He maintained this even as his fingers trembled.

Once it was done, Adam apologized for what he had to do. He kissed Cassandra on the forehead and wiped away her tears before handing the locket over to Howard. Adam even dared risk calling him out for the asshole that he was.

Nobody had been injured or killed, thankfully, though Adam still hated himself for what he had to do in the name of his job. The scene at the house was also not likely to provide Adam any favors with Danny. Howard's sharing that he thought Adam did good in there just made Adam feel worse. He risked telling Howard to "just shut the hell up." Adam was pleasantly surprised when Howard didn't react further at all. The car ride back to work was silent.

Scott was waiting in their office to meet them upon their return. Adam's anger along with Howard's fairly cavalier attitude warranted an explanation.

"What the hell happened?" Scott asked.

Adam wasn't entirely sure who Scott was asking. Adam let it be known he wasn't going to stick around to answer. "Ask your best friend," Adam shot back as he strode off, not making eye contact and not issuing any apologies as he bumped into Scott on his way out of the office.

***

Without Adam around as much as he was used to, Danny found himself not only bitter and angry, but lonely. That did not mean Danny was ready to become friends again and let bygones be bygones. Far from it. Danny was still his stubborn self.

That loneliness was all but guaranteed to continue with Danny being forced to quit his job at the bookstore, or so he thought.

It was during his last few weeks working when he saw her come in. He would find out on one of his last few days that her name was Samantha James.

She was unlike any other young woman he had ever seen. Danny knew very little about her, except that she bought a children's book at around the same time each day. She barely spoke to Danny, though she was by no means rude. It was not merely that this young woman was shy and quiet; Danny suspected something else afoot. He was committed to providing her with the best customer service, which included a smile and offer to help her with anything, even if each time she politely declined him.

It was after Samantha had already been in for a few times that Danny gathered the courage to approach her while she was shopping.

When he went to go look for her on one particular day, though, she was not in the children's section, like she normally was. Danny found this odd. *Had she perhaps slipped out, without Danny noticing?* The children's section was sizable, but it was not big enough for Samantha to go undetected by Danny.

Danny was about to figure she had left, or, that she hadn't even come in today, and was rather just a figment of his imagination. Then he heard it. She was crying. Danny followed the sound.

He found her crouched over a stack of books, gently weeping as she flipped through one of them. Though she was crying, she treated the reading material with utmost care, ensuring not to get any of the books wet. Danny didn't care in the slightest, he just wanted to make sure she was all right, especially when he saw she was reading books on leukemia.

Samantha had still not noticed him, and Danny didn't know what to say. Asking if she needed his help sounded too informal. It would be silly to ask if she was all right, when she clearly wasn't. Danny decided not to ask her anything at all then.

"Excuse me." Slightly startled, this beautiful and tragically sad young woman looked up at him. "I'm Danny, hi, I work here. I just wanted to let you know I'm here if you need me, in looking for books, but also for other things. If you just need someone to talk to. I'm here for whatever you need, though I don't mean to bother you. If you prefer, I can just leave you alone." Danny was rambling, he thought to himself. Hopefully he could still quit bothering her before he really dug himself a hole.

Samantha thought for a moment, conflicted, put the book down, and then burst into tears. Danny, springing into action, held her. He was relieved when she did not pull away.

"I'm sorry. I'm so sorry. Thank you for all your help, today and these past few days. *I'm* fine. My nephew isn't, though. He's at the hospital with leukemia. I've been bringing him books but today I decided to read up on the disease, and well, it seems that must have done more harm than good. He's doing pretty poorly right now, and he's only seven years old. I come here and buy him a book because I don't know what else to do. I'm not very useful at being good company with how anxious I am." It seemed this young woman had a penchant for rambling herself. Danny no longer felt so self-conscious then. "I'm sorry. I was ranting there, wasn't I?"

Perhaps she was, but Danny didn't see any harm in it, especially when he himself was prone to it. "No, you're fine," he said, not quite believable. Judging from the look on her face she didn't quite believe him, but at least she wasn't crying anymore. "Okay, maybe a little bit, but I don't mind."

Samantha laughed to herself and shook her head and then actually thanked Danny.

"For what, for being a bad liar?"

She went quiet for a moment. "For helping me be able to laugh." Danny smiled at her, and was rewarded with her telling him her name. "I'm sorry for not sharing it sooner," she added, though Danny could hardly fault her for this, or anything.

Moments ago these two young souls each had their reasons to grieve and lament. Now they were laughing with one another. "It's quite all right, Samantha, though I'm happy to know your name now."

"You're Danny Whitfield, aren't you?" Samantha said, putting together why he looked so familiar.

"Yup, that I am." Danny didn't know what he felt, perhaps some kind of embarrassment in a way?

"I ask because I was thinking about your sister, Amelia. She was sick, wasn't she?"

Danny didn't know what to say. They were told Amelia's public cause of death was illness, but had not been given further instruction for moments such as this. He had to say something though; he couldn't be rude. While Danny hated to lie to Samantha, he reminded himself to tell her the truth could put his family, and potentially her, in danger.

"Yeah," he said, swallowing nervously. "She was. Not leukemia, though." Danny hoped he didn't sound insensitive. "It's been tough dealing with her death, you know?"

Samantha, as it turned out, did know. She cautiously put her hand on Danny's, her touch so gentle and sweet. She explained to him that she lost her younger sister in a car accident when she was eight and her sister was five.

For the good part of an hour, Danny and Samantha got to know one another before it was time for Samantha to head to the hospital. When Samantha asked Danny if she would see him again next time, there was a moment of quietness. How to answer her? He had to tell her some version of the truth, for if she looked for him there, Samantha would not find Danny. Such was also an opportunity for Danny to get her phone number, which she was all too happy to provide. Danny found himself excited, giddy almost, in a way he had not felt in some time.

Before she left, Danny thought to mention to Samantha that he'd be praying for her nephew, whose name was Jake. She was genuinely touched and grateful, and mentioned that she would be praying for his family as well.

Danny was so excited about this new friendship and the prospect of having a date that he almost texted Adam, momentarily forgetting they were not speaking. Not wishing to get their hopes up or stir gossip, Danny kept his meeting Samantha from his mother and sister as well. It was Danny's way to shield them from his personal life, including and especially after these past few months. This was the case despite how Maria and Cassandra had urged him to be able to open up to them.

After a few days of texting, Danny decided to finally ask Samantha out. That she didn't respond made Danny all the more relieved that he hadn't told anyone about her.

When Danny did receive a response, it was several days later, in the form of a tearful phone call from Samantha. She apologized profusely and for not letting him know right away, but also what she was about to say. She couldn't see him, no matter how much she wanted to, she just couldn't.

It was her family. Well, more accurately, it was Danny and his family. Samantha's sister didn't want them to date on account of the problems plaguing the Whitfields. They had had enough concerns with Jake; they didn't need to be a part of any drama.

Danny's heart sank, yet he knew he shouldn't be so surprised. He also couldn't be angry with Samantha, not when she already felt so guilty. She had tried to reason with her sister, she explained, but to no avail. Samantha tried to tell Danny that her sister was a good person, except for now, and that they normally were not so judgmental, and that she especially was not. The hardest part for Danny to have to hear, however, was Samantha confiding in him how much she really did like him. He liked her too, but it must not have been meant to be. They hung up not long after.

The two young people both felt tortured in their own way, so sure that they were about to become friends and perhaps even lovers through shared tragedy. Their families had to tear them apart before they even really had a chance.

Both had been lonely for far too long. Danny was still not speaking to Adam, and Samantha had just moved in with her sister and brother-in-law to help with Jake. She did not have any friends in the city. It wasn't that Samantha was so much looking for a romantic partner as it was that she saw herself as having met Danny at the right time.

Danny almost got back in touch with Adam—almost. When his mother and sister asked him what was wrong over meals he almost told them—almost. Danny couldn't bring himself to dump this pain on others, especially when it would likely seem trivial compared to what else was happening. It didn't occur to Danny, to his detriment, that his mother and sister longed to be there for him in any way they could.

After the days had gone by and Danny was starting to give up hope, he got a text message, out of the blue, during dinner, from Samantha. She asked if she could call. Danny wondered why she was bothering to ask, though he could hardly be happier. He figured she had likely felt bad for how they had last left things, which endeared her to him even more. Perhaps Danny was foolish for getting his hopes up all over again, but he could not help it.

Danny's excitement was getting the better of him, and he asked if he could excuse himself, with a promise he would help clean up after his phone call. It was a young woman, Danny finally admitted to them, whose name was Samantha. Upon being told to go, Danny left a very surprised mother and sister behind downstairs in the kitchen. The dishes could wait, they both decided, for this news was far too interesting, and would hopefully be welcoming.

Upon hearing her voice over the phone, Danny could tell that Samantha had been crying. Before he could even ask, she explained to Danny that Jake had died. They had had the funeral that morning. Though she missed him terribly, now that her nephew had left them, Samantha realized that there was no reason to fear what would come of her being with Danny. She had waited a few days and then Samantha told her sister and brother-in-law that she was taking that date, even if it meant she had to find a new place to live. Luckily, it had not come to that.

During the time she had taken to think about her nephew, and her sister, and what was best for them, Samantha had been unable to justify not giving Danny a chance. She hoped he wouldn't fault her for it, because she really wanted to give this a go.

Danny could not fault her in the slightest. So much had happened. His watch and Cassandra's locket had been taken away. One sister had been killed and another traumatized. His father had been taken from them. Danny himself had been beaten and interrogated. It actually all went back to when George was forced into his position, Danny figured. For the first time in a long time, he had something to actually look forward to.

***

Now that Danny was occupying his time with someone who was, quite possibly, his soulmate, the void left from Adam was not so noticeable. That didn't mean he was free of Adam, however.

While Danny had thought, many times, of trying to make peace with Adam, the time spent apart between them made the animosity all the more worse. It was not a pleasant feeling; rather it was a plague. It became easier not to love Adam, but to hate him. Even Danny himself could not say why.

In the first few weeks following Amelia's death and George's imprisonment, Adam stayed away from Danny. He and Cassandra saw each other while Danny was at work or out. Now that Danny's job had come to an end, however, he was going to be spending time with his former best friend. Danny knew better than to ask his mother and sister to not have Adam over, though he told himself he would not have to welcome him.

Adam was still on Danny's mind. One of the last conversations between Danny and his father was George asking his son to consider forgiving Adam. It would help everyone, Danny included. Though Danny told his father he would think about it, the truth was he felt no closer to letting his pent-up resentment go. He was far too stubborn for his own good.

Time did not help Danny get over anything, though it did lead into a routine. Part of that routine included getting used to not having any news about when George would be coming home. It also involved Adam coming over. To Danny it felt as if that was every waking moment. Danny wondered which would come first, him growing tired of Adam, or his mother and sister growing tired of Danny.

The weather for that particular day was certainly matching Danny's mood. It was raining on and off for most of the day and quite hard at times.

It happened to be raining particularly hard when Danny heard the doorbell ring. It was surely Adam. Worse, Danny was left to answer it, as his mother and sister were both busy in the kitchen. Danny, very briefly, thought of not answering, though he reasoned quickly enough that such a move was cruel and would go unforgiven by his mother and sister.

The best, or, in this case—only—option was for Danny to open the door straightaway and hurry Adam inside away from the rain, which was hard enough to make someone sick. Instead, upon opening the door, Danny just stared at Adam who stared right back.

Adam patiently waited and then, after a few moments, he politely greeted Danny. He didn't ask to be let inside yet, despite how drenched he was. Adam just said hello. It worked. Danny eventually grew tired of their standoff and beckoned him inside. Adam didn't need to be told twice.

The amount of time it took did not go unnoticed. "I don't know what you boys were doing out there, or if I even want to know," Maria said pointedly. "I hope you were not waiting out there too long, Adam," she continued. "I will not stand for you getting any sicker."

Adam had indeed been feeling unwell for weeks now. In addition to all of the stress of the situation, he was not eating or sleeping properly, even with all the times he came over for dinner. With no discernible illness, Adam attributed it to nerves. Danny had had no idea. He failed to see what was right in front of him. Now that he looked at Adam, though, he could believe it.

Though Danny had been able to get it together enough to let Adam inside, dinner felt awkward from the start. Something about Adam's presence just made things worse for Danny.

The evening went by around him. It was as if he wasn't even there, especially as everyone else was enjoying themselves. Adam and Cassandra were particularly enamored with each other, lost in their own world, as they sat next to one another.

It wasn't for lack of trying that Danny's mood remained despondent. Trying to feed off of the positive energy around him didn't get Danny very far, however. He began to feel ignored, and worse, forgotten.

Danny would show him, though. He did it by slamming his fork down on the table. It made a louder noise than he anticipated, but Danny would not apologize for that, especially when it accomplished what Danny had set out to do.

Maria looked alarmed as she asked Danny what was wrong. He felt bad at first but then reasoned she should feel this way. *How could they all be acting this way? How could they all stand it? Were they not ashamed of themselves?*

"What's wrong, mom, is that I seem to be the only one affected by anything. I don't understand it, not at all."

Danny wasn't necessarily wrong, Maria reasoned. She didn't know what to say to him. His sister wasn't saying anything. After a moment Cassandra covered her face with her hands. That Adam stayed out of it both calmed and infuriated Danny.

Validation would likely be a good place to start, Maria reasoned. "I am sure that this must be a difficult time for you, Danny."

It only helped so much. It was a difficult time, yes. It shouldn't be about that though.

"That's not it, though, mom. Why am I the only one having a difficult time?"

Maria didn't know how to explain it to him. Adam tried to involve himself in the conversation, hoping it would not bring more harm than help. "Danny, if I may…?"

"No, Adam, you may not." Danny enunciated his words for effect.

Cassandra detached herself from Adam and looked as if she wanted to say something. Adam tried to quiet and calm her, but she would not have it. "Oh, would you leave him alone," she directed at Danny. "After what he's been through, after what we've *all* been through, I wish you would have some more empathy."

"Cassandra," Adam whispered.

"No, Adam. Please, let me speak."

Danny did not provide his sister with the respect of a response. Instead, he decided he was done with the conversation, and done with Adam. It was completely irrational, but Danny had not been feeling very rational lately. His anger had been getting worse, despite him wanting to change that.

"It's time for Adam to go."

Maria had a distraught look on her voice as she tried to assure them that was not necessary. Cassandra also spoke up to voice her disagreement. Adam respected Danny's wishes, though, and stood up to leave. He left a letter on the counter. Maria understood what it entailed. It brought a rush of emotions to her in what was already a tense situation.

Danny, unfortunately, was not in any kind of a position where he could feel like he won. Adam getting up to go didn't have the desired effect. In fact, Danny worried he was starting to see it as Adam acting like he was better than him. Perhaps it was because, deep down, Danny *did* consider Adam to be the better man in this.

In what amounted to a split-second decision, Danny got up and pushed Adam. Not anticipating it, Adam fell right into the nearby countertop.

Danny had had no idea about the knifing. Not a clue. Maria had kept her promise. His sister and mother looked on much more horrified than Danny expected for such a simple push. Then, Adam lifted up his shirt. He was checking to see what Maria and Cassandra feared, how his stitches were.

Danny had not wanted to hurt Adam. He had just wanted him to leave. Now Adam would not be leaving, not any time soon at least.

They could breathe a sigh of relief, at least all of them except for Danny.

Stitches? When the hell did Adam get stitches, Danny wondered.

"Adam, dear," Maria asked, trying to remain calm. "Are you sure that you're all right?"

Though Adam was fine, for now, Danny could see that his stomach must have at one point been quite a mess. "Is anyone going to clue me in here?" he practically demanded.

As Maria looked to her son, Adam figured they had hidden this from Danny long enough. He would tell him. Adam owed him that much now.

"Danny, it turns out that when your sister was… when Amelia was shot, I had been blocked by Howard. That's why I couldn't reach out. I was… I had been stabbed. Howard had a knife and he stuck it right into me."

Cassandra, whom Danny had almost forgotten was there, buried her head into her hands.

"Why wasn't I told of this?" Danny questioned, his tone once more stern. He was not ready to be sympathetic, not until he made sense of this.

Maria looked as if she was about to answer, but Adam stepped in once more. "Because I asked your mom. I begged her, in fact, to not tell you."

"Why…" Danny began, no longer sure of how he was feeling. "Why didn't you want me to know?"

"Because I was trying to protect you. I know you had been conflicted about us as it was; you didn't need to be saddled with this."

Danny curtly nodded. He was becoming less and less sure. "Why did Howard stab you?"

Adam sighed. "Because Director Roth had told him earlier that morning to make sure I didn't intervene too much, at whatever the cost. So he took that upon himself to use such force." Adam found himself with more to say, especially since nobody was stopping him. "I tried. I swear to you, Danny, I wanted to be there for you guys, even if there was nothing I could do. I tried so hard. I couldn't, though. I couldn't push past him. Not a day goes by when I don't regret that situation. Not because I was stabbed, but because in the end it looked like I did nothing. I'm sorry, I'm sincerely sorry, for even just it appearing that way."

Nobody said anything for quite some time. They didn't know what to say. Amelia had been senselessly killed, they could all agree there. There was now also a consensus, when Danny knew better, that with what he now knew about Adam, he could no longer cling to hate.

It was as if Adam had read his mind. "I know you probably hated me. You had reason to. Even if you didn't know if you wanted to feel that way, at least you could say you knew how you felt."

Danny nodded. There were still questions he wanted answered though. Danny assumed Cassandra knew, with she and Adam both at headquarters. What about his mother, though?

Maria swallowed nervously before answering her son. Even though Danny seemed to have calmed down, she could sense he still felt pained.

"After you brought Amelia inside I went up to him. I remember noticing all the blood there was. There was so much of it."

Danny recalled seeing the increased amount of blood on his mother. It made sense now.

Danny had to pay attention once more when Adam wished to speak up. "I didn't even want your mother or sister to find out. Once they did, well, then there was nothing I could do about it."

"You're right about that, dear," Maria said. "I must say, now that we all know, it's not the worst thing in the world."

"I can agree there, Mrs. Whitfield," Adam conceded. "Which is why I think I should fill you in a bit more."

"Oh, Adam," Cassandra, who had been relatively silent, pleaded. "It's what I think it is, isn't it?"

Adam sighed. He hated how he had to give her any more reason to feel distress, when she already had so much to mourn. Part of what made Cassandra a true beauty to him was how she was such a wise, mature, feeling soul. "It is, and more. As upsetting as this situation is, I think you all should know."

Adam came over to clasp Cassandra's hand in his own. Even Danny could accept that Adam wasn't going anywhere just yet.

So Adam told them. He told them how he had been taken to the hospital to be stitched up, how during the meeting with Director Whitfield and Director Roth it was announced that he would be moving to a different position, alongside Scott and Howard, to work directly under this man who had not only taken so much from them and still continued to exercise such force. Lest Danny, or really, any of them, feared Director Whitfield had not done enough, Adam could not emphasize enough that their father and husband truly had had no choice; Cassandra's fate depended on George acceding to it, something which brought him no pleasure. George even fought it until Adam was the one to persuade him to accept Director Roth's demands. Adam would do anything for the Whitfield family, and he hoped that that much was clear and would always remain so.

Danny was almost amazed at the clarity which he now had by letting go of his hate. It was as if an enormous weight had been lifted from his eyes. For this was the

Adam he knew and considered his best friend, who Adam had always been, one willing to lay down his life for his friends. Danny did not know if a more godly man existed. Danny was sorry and deeply regretted how he had acted towards Adam for far too many weeks now, especially when he took it, even when he was enduring so much else. Danny would apologize to him, once Adam was done speaking. Because Adam was such a good and charitable person, Danny didn't have to feel guilty, though. He could instead concentrate on the relief he felt.

As he had promised, there was still more that Adam had to say. He seemed even more conflicted about it, which did not go unnoticed by Cassandra, who, although Adam noted her distress, still asked to hear him out. There was a sincerity to his voice as Adam mentioned that he could not bear to keep secrets any longer.

Taking a deep breath, Adam acknowledged that he had been coming to their home every night for the past few weeks. It was not Danny's imagination then. It was Adam's house. While he assured them that his house was still standing, Adam couldn't help wondering if it even made a difference. As part of his work requirements, Adam was due back at headquarters for the evening and had not been allowed home in weeks.

"So, I'm here every night because I don't really have anywhere else to go," Adam said.

"This is such bullshit," Danny interjected. "I'm so sorry, Adam." Now seemed as good a time as any to apologize. All eyes were on him. "I'm so sorry for what this man has done to you, and how, I, in my own way, contributed to making this worse. I hope you can forgive me."

Adam nodded. Then, he got up and embraced his friend. "It's okay," he whispered. It helped that Adam was a kind and merciful soul. He had a feeling he would always be able to forgive his best friend, though. Danny had been through so much on his own that Adam really couldn't blame him. That their friendship survived this was a true testament. Edward Roth had taken so much from Adam. This friendship was not one of them.

That night, Adam stayed for as long as he could before having to return to headquarters. Danny told Adam about ideas for a potential new job, and even about Samantha, something he was beyond happy to finally share. It was almost as if things were back to normal.

***

When Adam left the Whitfields' that night, the rain had held off just until he had gotten out of his car and ran back to headquarters. He was soaked, even with his raincoat on, but he didn't care. One of the things which could not be dampened was his present mood.

Unbeknownst to Adam, George was worried. While Adam did not have to be back until two o'clock in the morning, George wasn't sure if Adam had ever stayed out that late. It was because George saw him as having no reason to, what with the sad reality that Adam and his son were no longer friends.

While George would not say that he had given up hope, he wasn't sure how much longer it was practical to hold on, especially when it felt like that hope was hanging by a thread.

That Adam returned soaking wet but smiling mightily was certainly a distraction from George's thoughts.

It was Adam who spoke up, as George was not entirely in the mood. His tone was as bright and as cheerful as ever; it may have been weeks since George heard him this happy. "Hello, Director Whitfield."

"Hello, Adam. I see that you're quite happy about something? Dare I ask in hopes it could improve both of our moods?"

Adam debated how much to tell Director Whitfield about the incident. "I… yes. I almost had an issue with my stitches but that's not what's important, sir."

George did see it as important. "Did it happen here, Adam?" George prayed to himself that Adam had not gotten into another altercation with Scott, or Howard.

"No, sir, it happened… it actually happened at your house." As Adam predicted, George was quite distressed. "Sir, if I may explain, please?" George nodded. "All right, thank you. Danny did push me, but it was an accident. And he didn't know, at least not until tonight, that I had gotten stitches." George hoped Adam was right, and that he was not merely defending Danny.

"Once he saw my side," Adam continued, "I couldn't keep from him that I had been stabbed. We got to talking, and I told your family about my position and having a curfew. While it did involve some painful truths, it does mean something else, sir."

"What is that, Adam?"

"It means Danny and I are friends again. I forgave him. He was so happy and relieved and thankful, sir, as if he could ever think that I wouldn't forgive him, as if there were any way I couldn't." George could rest assured that his hope had not been for naught. Adam continued. "I hope that you don't mind me mentioning such things, Director Whitfield, sir, about my working and living situation. I thought that it could, well, help them to understand more, Danny especially."

The poor young man had been so excited, as he should have been, and was now dejected. "No, Adam, I do not mind in the slightest. Forgive me for reacting in such a way. I'm just, well, emotional about the situation."

Fortunately that smile from Adam was quickly back, and George was able to return it.

Adam then went to retrieve a letter from his jacket pocket, which he apologized for being so wet. For a moment he seemed distressed once more at the possibility that the writing was wet enough to be illegible. George just laughed, though, that the weather could not be helped and emphasized that he was beyond grateful for any efforts Adam had gone through to make the situation that much easier on George's family.

Still, in some ways George worried that Adam would go too far and could get into trouble for it. George prayed that it would never come to that. He thought of bringing it up to ask Adam that he not endanger himself but decided against it. Adam asked George if he was sure that he was all right. Not knowing what more to say, George simply replied that he was. He found it fitting to turn out the light, especially with the late hour.

Adam did end up speaking then, though. "I'm sorry, sir. I hope you do not find me rude." George told him that he had not, not at all. "I just don't know what more to say, other than I am happy to pass these letters along."

George thought that surely he must find something to say in response. Perhaps he could just emphasize how grateful he was in hopes that Adam would understand that he did not need to go through such dangerous lengths to do more.

"You know Maria and I could not be more grateful, Adam."

George could sense Adam's internal conflict. "I only wish there was more I could do, sir," Adam said.

How George knew it. "You have been a tremendous comfort, a wonderful man, and a gentleman to my daughter. You, my son, have done plenty." As George said these words, an idea came to him.

"Actually, Adam, I think that there is something you could do for me, and my family."

Even in the dark, George could see Adam sitting up as he said, "yes, sir."

"The suddenness of which I am mentioning this may come as a shock, Adam, I'll warn you now."

"Okay, sir?" He seemed hesitant, though George hoped his hesitation would turn to excitement when he heard his request.

"I cannot know when either of us are to be released, I'm sorry to say. I hope and believe, though, that you will be released before me. Truth be told, it may be some time if ever. Now I know that is a horrible thought, but it may very well become reality. That being said, I would be much more at ease to know that you and Cassandra were to be married upon your release."

Adam did not immediately answer. George was not so surprised, for it was sudden. Adam was shocked and happy all at once. Here was something he had been dreaming of for some time now. To be sure, it wasn't that Adam had planned rushing to ask George for his daughter's hand in marriage. She had only recently come of age. Their circumstances had changed things, to be sure, however. Adam also knew where his dear friend was coming from with such a request.

While it was somewhat of a surprise for George to spring the idea on Adam at that very moment, the overall idea was not entirely shocking. George thought to himself how it felt as if they had been planning for Cassandra and Adam to be married from the time Cassandra was born. What started off as an inter-family joke, however, turned into something more once Adam and Cassandra developed genuine feelings for each other. George also had no doubt that had circumstances been different, he and Adam would still be having a similar conversation. It was just a matter of having it years before either of them would have anticipated.

Adam called George out of his thoughts soon enough. "You're serious, sir? Even if you cannot be there?"

"Yes, Adam, even if I cannot be there. Though I would love nothing more than to give my daughter away at your wedding, it would still give me great comfort to know that she would have you as her husband."

George could hear in Adam's voice that he was getting emotional now. "Well, thank you, sir. I would be honored to have your blessing, sir, assuming Cassandra will want to marry me."

George couldn't help but chuckle a bit. "Oh, I have no doubt that she will, Adam."

Along with the excitement and emotion, though, George still felt a sense of urgency. "Adam, will you promise me this? If I find it appropriate for you to ask Cassandra at an earlier time, I'll let you know. Otherwise, if you could do this one thing for me, if you could promise to ask her, as soon as you're released, on that very day, then I'll be able to sleep easier at night."

"Yes, sir, I'll promise you that." Adam had himself together enough for George to trust.

"Thank you, Adam. From the bottom of my heart, thank you."

So much had happened in a matter of months. And yet, *life goes on,* George thought to himself. For both better and worse. For the first time, in a long time, since he had been assigned his position, in fact, George felt himself looking forward to and having hope for these plans for the future.

George and Adam stayed up late into the evening, into the early morning hours even, planning how the proposal, the engagement, the wedding would take place. Adam became despondent occasionally at George's fate being so uncertain, but George felt it necessary to prepare and remind Adam of this, especially so he could help Cassandra come to terms. In that case, Adam was all too happy to take on such a responsibility. He saw it as his duty and his honor, as Cassandra's future husband.

Sleep did eventually come though, and Adam slept the best he had in some time. He dreamed that night of the life he would have with Cassandra, of not just their wedding but of their marriage, the children they would have together, the trips they would take and how their lives would eventually go back to normal, something Adam was sure would happen. It was good that he was able to enjoy these dreams for as long as he could and that Adam could sleep late since the next day was Saturday. It was good because little did Adam and George know, that's all they were and would ever be for Adam, dreams. They were the best kind of dreams anyone could ever hope to have.

End Book One

Discussion Questions

Do you see Cassandra's birthday as a focal point for the novel? What do you think will happen at other birthdays?

What do you think Danny's options are now? Do you think he can find saving power in Samantha or that he needs something more?

Do you consider it to be a happy ending? Why or why not?

How does this speak to the power and also burden of family? Do you think George has done right and best that he could for his family? Have his efforts been worthwhile?

How do you perceive Scott? Can we definitively say if he's a good or a bad guy?

Who do you think is the most complex character? In what way?

How are George and Edward different? What about George and Gregory?

About Rebecca Rose

Rebecca Rose is a native of Long Island and currently lives in the Washington, D.C. area with her husband and their two daughters. She is a graduate of Fordham University and of Regent University Robertson School of Government. Rebecca is a fan of politics, movies, and the Washington Nationals. She has written extensively as a journalist and is excited to release her debut novel with the Love, Politics, and Survival series.

Social Media

Twitter: https://twitter.com/RebeccaRoseGold
@RebeccaRoseGold

Facebook: https://www.facebook.com/RebeccaRosePress2/
@RebeccaRosePress2

Acknowledgements

This book has gone through so many drafts and revisions, about fourteen years' worth, which is half my lifetime. My parents, Traci and Ken, have always been supportive of my writing, and I likewise appreciate the enthusiasm from my brother and sister, Gabriel and Eliza.

College was quite the time for writing, and Caitlin and Sebby especially were incredibly supportive. Words cannot explain my gratitude, and I hope you know how much you mean to me.

I'd also like to give a special thanks to Ryan and Aileen, who not only encouraged me to go for my dream, but to

split this story into series. I'm so glad I listened. The same goes for Syliva, that wonderful woman who not only sold me a wedding dress but gave me much needed tough love and constructive criticism!

My friends, Courtney and Karen, and Olivia, you three are such great cheerleaders! As is Nicole, who has cheered me on throughout this book publishing process.

Last but not least, there are two people I've saved. Paige, you have provided such invaluable support and encouragement which means the world. I don't think this book series would be where it is without you. And then there's my rock, my love, my partner, Adam. Thank you for being the supportive man, husband, and father that you are.

I'd also like to express my gratitude to the Lord who has blessed me with so many things, including my talents and passion as a writer. May I always remember that through Christ, I can do all things!